The Haunted Dusk Stories

The Haunted Dusk Stories

One Novelette & Twelve Short Stories,
of the Ghostly & Peculiar Including 'The
Little Room,' 'The Sequel to the Little
Room', 'A Faded Scapular', 'Perdita' &
'His Apparition'

Edited by Henry Mills Alden

LEONAUR

The Haunted Dusk Stories
One Novelette & Twelve Short Stories, of the Ghostly & Peculiar Including 'The Little Room,' 'The Sequel to the Little Room', 'A Faded Scapular', 'Perdita' & 'His Apparition'
Edited by Henry Mills Alden

FIRST EDITION

Leonaur is an imprint of Oakpast Ltd

ISBN: 978-1-915234-32-2 (hardcover)
ISBN: 978-1-915234-33-9 (softcover)

http://www.leonaur.com

Contents

The Christmas Child

By Georg Schock

The moonlight was so bright across the clock that it showed the time, and its tick was solemn, as though the minutes were marching slowly by. There was no other sound in the room except the breathing of Conrad, who lay in shadow, sleeping heavily, his head a black patch among the pillows. Mary's hair looked like gold in the pale light which reflected in her open eyes. She had been lying so, listening to the tick and watching the hands, for hours.

When they marked eleven, she began to stir; her feet made no more sound than shadows; the cold air struck her body like a strange element. Conrad did not move as she went into the kitchen and softly closed the door. She groped her way to the chair where she had left her clothes and put them on, wrapped herself in a shawl, and slipped out.

There was no snow, but a keen cold as befitted the night of the 24th of December, and between two fields the ice on the Northkill glittered. The air was so clear that far away appeared the great black barrier of the mountains. Across the sky, as across deep water, was a radiance of light, serene and chill—of clouds like foam, of throbbing stars, of the moon glorious in her aura. In the towns at that hour the people were ready to begin the coming day with prayer and the sound of bells: here sky and earth themselves honoured the event with light and silence in a majestic expectation.

As she made her way over the frozen grass she looked as detached from the world's affairs as some shrouded lady at her nightly journey along a haunted path. The great Swiss barn was dead silent; its red front, painted with moons and stars, looked patriarchal; it had its own pastoral and dignified associations. She hesitated at the middle door, then she lifted the wooden bar and pushed it back cautiously. The darkness seemed to come out to meet her, and when she had shut herself in, she was engulfed as though the ready earth had covered her a few nights too soon.

The straw rustled when she stepped on it, and she was afraid to risk a movement, so she crouched and made herself small. The air was thick and pungent, freezing draughts played upon her through the cracks of the door, and her foot tingled, but she did not move. After a while she saw two luminous disks which halted, glared, and approached, and she patted the furry body until it curled up on her skirt and lay there purring. She felt it grow tense at a tiny squeak and scuttle, but she kept still.

More than half an hour had gone when something happened. A horse stamped, a cock set up a sudden chatter, the cat leaped to a manger, and a cow scrambled to her feet. The darkness was full of movement—wings fluttered, timbers shook under kicking hoofs and rubbing hides, tossed heads jarred the rings that held them fast. Then from the corner in which stood the splendid yoke of black oxen, the pride of the farm, there came a long, deep sound, as of something primeval mourning.

Two minutes after, Conrad was roused by a noise in the kitchen. The house door stood wide, showing a great rectangle of moonlight, there was a rush of cold air, and his bare foot struck Mary, doubled up where she had fallen. He shouted, and an old woman ran in with her grey hair flying.

"Conrad!" she exclaimed, almost in a scream.

"I don't know," he answered. He had his wife in his arms and held her out like a child showing a broken toy.

The old woman bethought herself first. "Take her in and lay her on the bed," she ordered. While she worked, he began to hurry on his clothes, moving as though he were stupid; then he came up to the bed.

"Aunt Hannah, what has she?" he begged. She gave him a look, and he suddenly burst into a great storm of tears.

"Hurry!" she said. "Take Dolly and a whip and go to Bernville first. If the doctor isn't home, go along to Mount Pleasant; but bring a doctor. *Ach!*" she seized his hand in her excitement.

Mary's eyes were opening—blue, wide, and terrified. "Don't take Dolly," she said, quite loud. "Dolly knows too much." Then her eyes closed again.

Conrad went into the kitchen, still sobbing, and the old woman followed.

"I must take Dolly," he whispered. "Aunt Hannah, for God's sake, what has she?"

"I don't know what she means about Dolly. Maybe I can find out till you get back. She'll soon come to. You better be careful going out of the barnyard. It might worry her if she hears the hoofs."

The young man checked his crying. "I take her through the fields," he said, and went out softly.

In the light of the candle which contended with the moonbeams Hannah's wrinkled face looked witchlike as she bent over the bed. Presently Mary started and her eyes searched the room with a terrified stare; she seemed to be all at once in the midst of some dreadful happening.

"Aunt Hannah," she exclaimed, "don't let them come for me!"

The old woman bent over her. "How do you feel?" she asked, in her soft and friendly Dutch.

"Don't let them come!"

"Nobody comes, Mary. It is all right, only you are not so good. After while somebody is coming. Then you are glad!"

"Keep them out! I don't want to go!"

"You don't go off; you stay right here with me and Conrad."

"They said—"

"Who?"

"The oxen."

Hannah's hand shook, but she still spoke reassuringly. "Were you in the barn, Mary?"

"Yes. You know how it is said that on Christmas eve, twelve o'clock, the animals talk. I thought so much about it, and I made up my mind to go and hear what they had to say. I was in the middle stable that's empty, and I waited, and all of a sudden—" She stopped, trembling.

"Just don't think about it," Hannah urged, but she went on:

"All of a sudden—Dolly stamped—and they all woke up—the cows and the sheep, and the cat was scared and the big rooster cackled—and then the oxen—*Ach*, Aunt Hannah! One of them said, 'They will carry out the mistress in the morning.'"

"You don't go, for all," the old woman soothed her. "Think of who is coming, Mary. That's a better thing to think about. It's so lucky to have it on Christmas day. She will have good fortune then, and see more than others."

The pinched face grew bright. The trembling soul was not to go out alone before, becoming a part of the great current of maternity, it had had the best of what is here.

9

"I take such good care of her. I look after her all the time," said Mary.

★★★★★★★★

The sun was gone, but the west was still as pink as coral and the twilight gave a wonderful velvety look to the meadows. In the rye-fields the stalks, heavy-headed already, dipped in the wind which blew the last apple-blossoms about like snow. A row of sturdy trees grew along Conrad Rhein's front fence, and there was a large orchard in the rear. The log house was just the colour of a nest among the pale foliage.

The place was so quiet that the irritable note of a couple of chimney-swallows, swooping about in pursuit of an invisible purpose, sounded loud. Hannah Rhein looked up from the small stocking she was knitting to watch them. Her secular occupation was contradicted by her black silk "Sunday dress," and there was a holiday appearance about the little girl who sat very still, looking as though stillness were habitual with her.

"You better run out to the gate. Maybe you can see them," Hannah said. The child went, and stood looking down the road so long that she rolled up her knitting and followed. "There they are!" she exclaimed. "Father and Aunt Calista. Don't forget to give her a kiss when she gets out."

Conrad Rhein's austere face expressed no pleasure as he stepped from the carriage and helped his companion, but she was not to be depressed by a brother-in-law's gravity. Calista Yohe, moving lightly in her pink delaine dress, resembled the prickly roses coming into bloom beside the gate, which would flourish and fade imperturbably in accordance with their own times and seasons. At present she looked as though the fading were remote. She shook hands joyfully and seized the carpet-bag which Hannah had taken.

"I guess I don't let you carry that," she said. "It's heavy."

The little girl put up her face, and Calista kissed her without speaking to her, and went on talking:

"You are right, Dolly is hot. We drove good and hard. Conrad didn't want to do it to give her the whip, but I don't like to ride slow. Let's sit on the porch awhile."

The child placed her bench near the old woman's chair, but she watched the young one admiringly. Calista did not notice her.

"How are the folks?" Hannah asked.

"They are good."

10

"Had they a big wedding?"

"I guess! It was teams on both sides of the road all the way down to where you turn, and they had three tables. She wore such a nice dress, too; such a silk it was, with little flowers in."

"How did it go while you were there?"

"Oh, all right; she's a nice girl and he and I could always get along; but it wasn't like my home. If a man gets married once, he doesn't want his sister afterwards," Calista said, cheerfully.

"Well, you stay here now. We are glad to have you. Conrad he is quiet and I am getting along, so it's not such a lively place, but I guess you can make out."

"Well, I think!" said Calista, "I like to work. Is Conrad always so crabbed? He hardly talked anything all the way over."

"He hasn't much to say, but he is easy to get along with. He doesn't look much to anything but the farm."

"Doesn't he go out in company?" Calista asked, eagerly.

"Once in a while, but not often. He doesn't look for that anymore." Hannah sighed and stroked the child's head, which rested against her knee, and the movement caught Calista's eye.

"She favours Mary," she said. "All that light hair and her white skin. That's a pretty dress she has on." She stooped and examined the blue merino. "Did you work that sack?"

"No, I had it worked. I think she looks nice. Conrad bought her those blue beads for a present. She was so glad."

"Does she always wear white stockings?"

"When she is dressed. Conrad, he wants it all of the best."

"Does he think so much of her?"

"He doesn't make much with her; he is not one to show if he thinks much; but would be strange if he didn't. And as well off as he is, and no one to spend it on!"

Calista looked out through the orchard and across the fields of rye and wheat over which the spring night was falling. "He has a fine place for sure," she said. "He takes long in the barn."

"I guess he went off," said Hannah, peacefully.

"I didn't see him leave."

"It maybe he went to Albrecht's."

"Who are they? Young people?"

"Yes. John Albrecht he is about Conrad's age, and his wife was such a friend to Mary. They have two little ones come over sometimes to play around."

11

"Is that all in the family?"

"His mother; she lives with her, a woman so crippled up she can't walk."

Calista looked as satisfied as a strategist who finds himself in control of a desired situation: its difficulties made her spirits rise. Her eyes wandered about and fixed upon the child again. "She gets sleepy early for such a big girl," she said. "Wasn't she five on Christmas?"

"Yes. She wanted to see you, so I let her stay up tonight; and anyhow I didn't want to be sitting upstairs when you got here."

"Do you sit with her evenings?"

"Till she goes to sleep. If you leave her in the dark, she is so scared I pity her, and I don't want her to get excited. I have no trouble with her other times. She listens to me, and she is real smart to help; she can pick strawberries and pull weeds, and she always enjoys to go along for eggs. She is like her father, she hasn't much to say. She will run around in the orchard and play with her doll-baby the whole day, and she is pretending all the time."

The little girl opened her eyes, very blue with sleep. With her rosy colour and the white and blue of her little garments she looked like a cherub smiling out of the canvas of a German painter—the soft companion of an older and more pensive grace. Hannah watched her tenderly.

"Now come, Mary, we go to bed," she said.

"I guess I'd make such a fuss with that child and sit with her nights!" Calista thought, her prominent hazel eyes following in rather a catlike fashion. They followed in the same way more than once during the next few weeks. She would brush the little girl's hair when Hannah was busy, or call her to a meal, but at other times she passed her by. At first Mary was inclined to pursue the pretty stranger, and on the second evening she ran up to her to show the results of the egg-hunting, but she never did it again.

She was the only one whom Calista failed to please. The neighbours who came to visit soon returned, and on Saturday night there were three carriages at the gate and three young men in the parlour. Conrad did not pay much attention to her, but one day he told her that one of her admirers was "not such a man that you ought to go riding with," and she said: "All right. It was two asked me to go tonight. I take the other one." She went through the work singing, and Hannah sat on the porch more than usual, and began to wonder how she had gotten on so long alone.

Calista had been there only a few weeks when Hannah said at supper one evening: "I guess I go to see your Aunt Sarah, Conrad. It's six years since I went. I couldn't leave the work before, but now Calista gets along so good I can go a little."

"Just do it," said Calista, heartily. "Mary and I can keep house."

The child smiled and made a timid movement.

"All right," Conrad said. "I take you to the stage any time."

Mary cried when Hannah went, and the old woman was distressed. "I feel bad to leave her," she said. "I would take her along if I had time to get her ready."

"*Ach*, go on!" Calista said, laughing. "There is Conrad now with the team. Mary will have good times. She can stem the cherries this morning." She picked up the little girl and held her out to kiss her aunt. "Don't you worry," she called, as the carriage started.

She came out on the back porch presently with a large basket of ox-hearts.

"Now let's see how smart you can be," she said. "Sit down on the step and I put the basket beside you. Pick them clean." Mary looked rather frightened at the size of the task, but she set to work. She stemmed and stemmed until her hands were sticky and her fingers ached. A thick yellow sunbeam came crawling to her feet; the flies buzzed, diving through the air as though it were heavy; the cat beside her slept and woke. It seemed to the child that she had always been in that spot and that there would never be anything but a hot morning and piles of shining cherries. She was looking toward the orchard where her swing hung empty when Calista hurried by the door. "Have you done them all?" she called. "Not? Well, then you finish them quick."

The cherries lasted until dinner-time, and when that was over Mary climbed on her father's bed and slept all afternoon. When she came out the first thing, she saw was the egg-basket piled full. "If you want to go along for eggs you ought to be here when I am ready," said Calista.

The little creature made no noise, but her father looked at her hard as he sat down to supper. "What's the matter?" he asked.

She did not answer, and Calista said, "Oh—!" with the peculiar German inflection of contemptuous patience. Conrad said no more.

After supper Mary wandered out, and her aunt had to call her several times. "Where were you?" she asked.

"Down there." The child pointed to the orchard. "A lady was

there."

Calista went to the edge of the porch and shaded her eyes. "I don't see her," she said. "Who was she?"

"I don't know."

"Did you never see her before?"

"No, ma'am."

"What did she look like?"

Mary thought hard, with the puzzled face of one who lacks words and comparisons to convey an image that is clear enough. Calista walked a little way into the orchard, then she looked up and down the road.

"Wasn't it Mrs. Albrecht?" she asked. "Well, I guess it makes nothing. Come, you must go to bed. I stay with you." With a mocking expression she held out her hand as to a very small child, and the little girl walked into the house without a word, not noticing the hand.

When she was asleep Calista came back to the porch with some sewing. Conrad appeared from the barn, stood about for a moment, and strolled toward the orchard; then he walked in the garden for a while; finally, he sat on the step with his back to her, saying nothing and looking at the sky. She preserved the silence of a bird-tamer.

"It's a nice evening," he said at last.

"Yes."

"Good weather for hay."

"Yes, fine."

"One field is about ready to cut. You better tell Aunt Hannah to come home. It's too much work for you, with the men to cook for."

"Just you let her stay and enjoy herself. I get along all right."

After a pause she asked, "Did you see someone in the orchard just now?"

"No."

"Mary, she ran down after supper, and she said a strange lady was there. I wondered who it was."

"I didn't see her," he said, dully, as though he spoke from the midst of some absorbing thought; then he got up and walked away. "You better go in and light the lamp if you want to sew," he said, roughly.

Calista took her things and went at once, looking as though she were so well satisfied that she could afford to be amused.

Though in the next two weeks she had plenty of company Conrad never joined them: he spent the evenings with John Albrecht, drove to Bernville, or went to bed early. He worked much harder than usual,

14

and his cheeks grew thin under his stubble of black beard. Calista did not trouble him with conversation.

"Don't you feel good?" she once asked, and when he gave a surly answer she said, carelessly, "You better get something from the doctor," and began to sing immediately afterwards. But she knew how he looked even when her back was turned, and she often stared at Mary in a meditative way as though the child were the doubtful quantity in an important calculation.

She was watching her so one day, when little John Albrecht and his sister had come over and the three were very busy on the grass near the kitchen window with two dolls and the old tiger-cat. In the afternoon silence their little voices sounded clear and sweet. The cat escaped to a cherry-tree and they chased him gayly, but he went to sleep in an insulting way in spite of the lilac switch that John flourished.

"Look out!" Mary called.

John looked around and said, "For what?" and she went over to him.

There was a conversation which Calista could not hear; Mary pointed several times to a spot in the sunny grass; then he went running down the road and Katie followed, looking as though she would cry when she had time, and leaving her doll behind her.

Calista went out. "What did you say to John to make them run off?" she asked.

"I told him to look out, he would hit the lady with the switch."

"What lady?"

"She was there."

"Where is she now?"

"I don't know."

"Can't you see her?"

"No, ma'am."

Calista looked all about. Not a soul was in sight on the road; in the orchard and the fields nothing moved but the wind; the yard was empty except for the cat slipping round the corner with his mottled coat shining. "Now listen," she said, not unkindly. "I saw you out of the window, and there was no lady here. Why do you tell a story like that?"

The child looked at her in a preoccupied way and did not answer.

"I can't have you say things that are not so, Mary. If you do it again, I have to whip you. Now pick up your doll-baby and come in."

She spoke of it to Conrad that evening, but he did not pay much attention.

"I don't know if there is something wrong with Mary or, if she does see someone, who it is," she said. "Do you know if there are gipsies around?" He scarcely answered, and in a few minutes, she heard him drive down the road. She smiled to herself as she hurried through her work. Then she put Mary to bed, though it was much earlier than usual, and began to dress, while the little girl lay watching from among the pillows.

Calista enjoyed the water like a sleek creature of two elements; her white skirts crackled and flared; her hair hid her waist. When she had finished her green dimity looked like foliage around a flower, and her hazel eyes turned green to match it.

"I'm going on the front porch," she said. "You go to sleep like a good girl."

She had sat with Mary in the evening as long as she could do so without inconvenience. Now she saw no reason for continuing it. She had not imagination enough to know what she was inflicting. Mary gazed after her as a shipwrecked woman might watch a plank drifting out of reach, but she said nothing; she shut her eyes and lay still for many minutes. She was a timid child but not cowardly, and such tangible things as a cross dog, a tramp, and a blacksnake in the orchard she had faced bravely, but her terror of the dark was indefinite and unendurable.

She opened her eyes, shut them, and opened them again, looking for something dreadful. The furniture was shapeless, the bedclothes dimly white, and each time she looked it was darker. She did not know what she expected, and to see nothing was almost worse. A carriage going down the road comforted her as long as she could hear it, but it left a thicker silence. She pressed her lids together, breathing quickly,—to move was like inviting something to spring on her,—then she slid out of bed and ran down the stairs, gave a frightened glance at the front door behind which sat her aunt, who would send her up again, and slipped across the back porch into the orchard.

Calista heard nothing. In the hot June evening she was fresh and cool enough to be akin to the rejoicing fields, a nymph of beech or willow. Now and then she looked down the road and saw no one, but she did not seem disappointed. It was quite dark and the fireflies were trailing up and down when wheels stopped at the gate, and she drew back behind a lilac-bush that screened the porch, and sat still.

Conrad, striding up the path, started when he saw her. "Oh, it's you!" he said, coldly. She gave a short answer, and he stood frowning at nothing and looking very tall and black. "Want to take a little ride?" he asked.

"No, I guess not."

"You stay at home too much," he said, presently. "You haven't been off the place since Aunt Hannah left."

"I don't care to go. I can't leave Mary here all alone. It wouldn't be safe."

She stayed silently in her corner as though waiting for him to leave—a white shadow beside the black mass of the lilac-bush. Dolly at the gate tossed her head until the reins scraped on the gate-post. Down in the orchard a whippoorwill cried.

He was like a horse that takes the bit and the driver was his own will—his own self. She made no resistance when he threw himself down beside her: she was pliant, her cheek cool, she even looked at him haughtily. He did not know that she slipped out of his arms just before he would have released her, nor that she was all one flame of triumphant happiness. She seemed as untouched as the starlight.

"Calista," he stammered, "I hope you overlook it."

"What about my sister Mary?" she asked, dryly. "I thought you didn't look to anyone else."

"I didn't. I tell you the truth. I was unwilling. I fought it off all I could, but now I give in. I can do no more."

"So, you think you like me as well as you like her?"

"Calista, I would ask you if Mary stood here and heard us."

The woman seemed to bloom like an opening rose. She looked at him, but it was as though she saw some vision of success that she was just about to grasp. "I am satisfied," she said.

There was a sound on the walk, and they lifted their heads; then they were scarcely conscious of each other's presence. Up from the gate, her nightdress hanging about her feet, her hair pale in the dim light, came the little girl. She climbed the steps and passed fearlessly into the dark house, smiling at the two with the radiant content of happy childhood, soothed and petted—her small right hand held up as if in the clasp of another hand.

★★★★★★★★

Calista would have chosen to clean the whole house or do a harvest-time baking rather than write one letter, so she asked most of the guests verbally and put off the others as long as she could. Conrad had taken Hannah to Bernville to have a new silk dress fitted and buy coloured sugar for the wedding-cakes when she began the invitations. By three o'clock they were finished, and she counted them and laid them beside the inkstand. Then she washed her hands, spread a sheet on the floor, and got out a pile of soft white stuff, all puffs and lace and ruffles—the work of weeks.

She sewed happily, looking out now and then at the trees, which tossed like green waves under the roaring August rain. Sometimes a gust drove a shower down the chimney and made the logs hiss. The room was warm and still; in the interval of work it seemed to have paused and be sleeping. The tiger-cat, with his paws folded under him, lay beside the hearth, and Mary on her little bench nursed her doll peacefully. Calista began to sing a German hymn; the words were awful, but their very solemnity made her happier by contrast:

Wer weiss wie nahe mir mein Ende!
Hin geht die Zeit, her kommt der Tod.

"Look here, Mary," she said. "Isn't this pretty?" The child came, and Calista held up the soft stuff around her; it made the little face look beautifully pink and white. She touched it lightly, smiling, then she wandered over to the window with her doll and looked out into the rain.

"*Es kann vor Nacht leicht anders werden,*
Als es am frühen Morgen war,"

Calista sang.

Five minutes later she asked, good-naturedly, "What are you looking at?" Mary did not answer. "Didn't you hear what I said? What's going on out there?" Calista repeated.

"You said I shouldn't say it," the child whispered.

"Say what?"

"When I see the lady."

"Where do you see her?"

"Coming out of the orchard."

Certain old stories returning to Calista's mind made her look at Mary for a minute as though the child had manifested strange powers. She went to the window and her thimble clicked on the sill as she leaned forward; then she touched her cheek. "Do you feel good?" she asked.

"Yes, ma'am."

She looked out again. "I want you to know for sure that no one is there," she said, earnestly. "Now tell me: do you see a lady?"

"Yes, ma'am. She is coming up here."

Calista was very sober. "If your Aunt Hannah doesn't teach you not to tell stories, then I must," she said. "I can't have you like this. Soon I can't believe you anything. Come here." Mary came as if pulled. "Now mind, I do this so that you don't say what isn't so again." She gave the child two good slaps on the mouth with her strong hand.

The inherited spirit of resistance to coercion, that had made pioneers and martyrs of Mary Rhein's ancestors, was let loose too soon: it made an imp of her. She darted silently like an insect from under Calista's hand, seized the inkstand, and threw it with all her might at the beautiful white gown. The ink poured out, dripping from fold to fold, and the stand thudded on the sheet and scattered the last drops. Mary gave one look and ran across the porch and out to the road in the rain.

Calista sat still for a moment, then she got up weakly. "Doesn't look much like a wedding-dress now," she murmured. "It's no use doing anything to it. It's done for." She wiped the inkstand on a stained flounce before setting it on the table. "*Now*," she said, as though some one were present who would disapprove, "I give it to her good. I better fetch her in and have it done before they get back."

The sky was low but the rain was gentle when she started down the road, and her shawl made a bright spot between the fields, green as chromos. Mary had gone toward the creek, and she followed as far as the bridge; then, as there was no one in sight, she turned upstream. It was deep just there and very full, carrying leaves and twigs so that it was like a little flood, and the water caught the dipping branches of the willows and swept them along. The shellbarks looked forlorn in the rain, and the ground was so soft that it gave under her feet. Her skirts and shoes were heavy with wet before she saw Mary.

The child looked as though she were being crowded out of life. She was crying, with small weak sounds like a wretched little animal, her hair was dark with water, and the rain drove across her face. At the sight of Calista, she began to run slowly with much stumbling; her crying mixed with the sound of the stream. Calista followed as fast as she could.

A little way up the creek was a log bridge without a rail. Conrad had put it up for his own convenience, and Calista never tried to cross it.

"*Ach!*" she thought, "I don't hope she runs out there!" Then she began to call, but Mary did not look back. She fell over a root, picked herself up, and went on, with her knees shaking.

Suddenly she began to cry very loud, as a child does when it sees comfort, and went on much faster, making for the bridge. As she ran along the log her arms were out to meet someone.

Calista stared for a couple of seconds, then she raced like a savage down to the first bend, her red shawl flying behind her.

It lay in a pool on the kitchen floor when Conrad and Hannah came in; it was the first thing they saw, and their voices stopped as though a hand had been laid upon their mouths. Mary was lying on the settle and Calista was doubled up against it with her face hidden.

"What's wrong?" Conrad asked. She said nothing, and when he tried to lift her, she writhed away from him. Hannah ran to Mary. The blankets were warm, but the small creature was quite cold.

"Now it is time you say what has happened," she said, and Conrad stood silently by.

Calista sat up, looking deadly sick. The story came out in fragments, and at the end she bowed her head, shivering and staring at nothing.

"Did she say this before?" Hannah asked.

Calista told wearily, and the old woman listened, a spectator of strange things to which she alone had the clue.

"Is that all?"

"*Ach*, yes! I can't remember any more. Now do what you want to do."

Hannah spoke like a judge sentencing a criminal: "So you thought she told lies and you whipped her—that little thing! Now I tell you something, Calista Yohe. That night she was born I said to Mary—your sister Mary!—that once she came on Christmas she would be lucky and see more than we see, and Mary was glad, and the last thing she said was: 'I look after her. I take care of her.' And they say one that dies and leaves something unfinished must come back to finish it up. I guess Mary knew when to come.

"And you are glad. I don't say you just wished this to her, but you thought would be fine not to have her around once you got married to Conrad. She was lucky not to be here till you got a good hold of her.

"You might have thought whether I would let her with you that didn't want her, to be in the way. But I am old. It is a good thing Mary fetched her. Now I see to her myself. Don't you dare touch her."

Conrad had been perfectly still, with the face of a man in a night-

20

mare, but now he went to the shaking woman and lifted her in his arms. Hannah looked at them for a moment. Then she set a great kettle of water to heat, took up the child and went out, leaving them alone together, and they heard her footsteps in the room above as she went back and forth, getting what she needed.

The White Sleep of Auber Hurn

By Richard Rice

The thing happened in America; that is one reason for believing it. Another land would absorb it, or at least give a background to shadow over its likelihood, the scenery and atmosphere to lend an evanescent credibility, changing it in time to a mere legend, a tale told out of the hazy distance. But in America it obtrudes; it stares eternally on in all its stark unforgetfulness, absorbing its background, constantly rescuing itself from legend by turning guesswork and theory into facts, till it appears bare, irremediable, and complete,—witnessed at high noon, and in New Jersey of all places, flat, unillusive, and American.

The thing was as clear a fact in its unsubtle, shadowless mystery as was he—that is, as was the shell and husk of him lying there in the next room after I had watched the life and the person drawn out, leaving only mere barren lees to show what had gone. Hours it lay there to prove the thing, to settle it in my mind, to let me believe eternally in it. Then we buried it deep under the big pile of scree on my hill. As I write I can see the white stones from the window.

It is not all guesswork to begin with; indeed, it is not guesswork at any moment if the end is always in view, and we had to begin with the end. I tell you it was as plain as daylight. People saw him, heard him talk; saw him get off the train at Newark to mail my letter—this one—addressed to my engineers in Trenton; heard him say, "Promised Crenshaw to post this before reaching the city; guess this is my last chance to keep it." It is a little thing that counts; you can't get by that; it alone is final; but there were a dozen more. Ezekiel saw him on the platform hunting for the right box for west-bound mail, and saw him post the letter after considerable trouble. When I heard that, I yielded to the incredulous so far as to telephone to Trenton, asking if the firm had received it. I did that, though I held the letter in my hand at the time, and knew it had never left this house.

23

Ezekiel was sure that he mailed the letter, that it went from his hand into the box. He was watching carefully because just then the train began to move; but Auber, leisurely ignoring this, appeared to be comparing his watch with the station clock, and finally looked up at the moving train as if in disapproval. Ezekiel lost sight of him in the crowd, and then, at the same moment, he was taking his seat opposite again.

Ezekiel said, "I thought you were going to miss the train, characteristically, for the sake of setting your watch." And Auber replied, rather queerly: "Great God! It's impossible now; I can see that." Ezekiel did not know what he meant, but remembered it afterward when we were talking the whole thing over in this room.

Besides Ezekiel, there were four men who saw him after the train left Newark; and the porter remembered holding the vestibule door and trap-platform open for someone as the train pulled out.

Then there is my coachman who drove him to the train, here in Barrelton, who had his tip of a silver dollar from him. Put it in his pocket—and then—lost it, of course. You see, there's the most conclusive link in the chain. If William had produced his dollar, or my engineer had received that letter, the whole thing would fall through—jugglery and imposition, mere ordinary faking. The hypnotic theory might still hold, but it must stretch fifty miles to an improbable source in a man who is, at the time, dying strangely on my bed.

Of course, there is no use asking if anyone on the train touched him—not only saw and heard him, but shook hands with him, let us say. It is the same story as William's, or not so good. Ezekiel is sure that he shook hands when Auber first boarded the train; Judson is sure that he did so when he stepped across the aisle to ask about me. Yet, I tell you that would have made no difference; let him have been as impalpable as the very air of the car, those men would have felt the flesh, just as William felt his silver dollar. "Fulfilment of sure expectation on the ground of countless identical experiences," your psychologist would explain. Illusion and fact were indistinguishable; and though I happened to watch the facts, and the others the illusion, their testimony is as good as mine.

There is the testimony of four men that, when the smash came, they saw him thrown from his seat, head first, into the window-jamb, and lie for a moment half through the shattered pane. Just before this, he had taken out his watch. Its familiar picture-face, and also its enamelled hands exactly together at twelve o'clock, had caught Ezekiel's eye. He said that Auber looked at the watch, and then leaned forward as if to call attention to the view from the window. It was then that the smash came. When Ezekiel and some others, who were only thrown to the floor, looked up again, Auber was gone.

You see, the time is identical; we calculated it exactly, for the train left Newark on time and takes just six minutes to reach the bridge; that is, at exactly noon. When I noticed the hour here, it was, perhaps, a few minutes later, and that is not a difference in timepieces, for it was by his own watch on the bedside table. No one saw him on the train or on the bridge after that. It seems conclusive, just that alone. They finally decided that he must have fallen from the window and somehow rolled from the sleepers into the river.

Actually no one else in the Pullman was badly hurt. The men picked themselves up and rushed to the doors of the car, or climbed out of the windows. Ezekiel put his head through the shattered pane which Auber had struck. Men were running toward the car ahead, from which screams came. In the excitement of rescuing those from the telescoped coach, Auber was forgotten; but when it was all over, Ezekiel and Judson looked everywhere for him, till they assured themselves that he was not on the bridge.

At all events, that is how he came to be reported among "The Missing—known by friends to have been on the train—Auber Hurn, the artist."

During that night, when Ezekiel and Judson had come down in response to my telegrams, we sat here, talking endlessly, guessing, relating, slowly developing the theory of the thing, delving into our minds for memories of him, gradually getting below the facts, gradually working back to them, examining the connections, completing the chain. The main fact, the culmination, had to be the soulless shell of him, lying there in the next room. Our theory began far away from that, in what he used to call "white sleep," and more especially in a curious occasional association between the dreams of this sleep and the landscape pictures that he painted. What impressed you most as he recounted one of those half-conscious dream concoctions, that he named "white-sleep fancies," was the remarkable scenery, the setting of the dream.

This was in character with his pictures, for about them both you felt that peculiarly pervasive "sense of place," for which his landscape is of course famous, and which in these dreams was emphasised through a subtle ominousness of atmosphere. You perceived what the place stood for, its sensational elements, and you began vaguely to imagine the kind of event for which it would form a suitable background. In his pictures the element was a sort of dream-infusion, as though in each scene the secret goddess, the Naiad of the spot, must have stood close to him as he painted, and thrilled him to understanding at her impalpable touch. Whatever the exact nature of these creative intuitions, there was between his art and his dreams a lurking connection, out of which, as we believed, finally grew his strange faculty for seeing beyond the scene, an intuition for certain events associated with what we called "an ominous locality."

This faculty began to distinguish itself from mere psychical fancy through a curious contact of one of Auber's dreams with his actual experience.

The dream, which came at irregular intervals during a number of years, began with a sense of colour, a glare to dazzle the eyes, till, as Auber insisted, he awaked and saw the sunset glow over a stretch of forest. He was on a hillside field, spotted with daisies and clumps of tall grass. On one side a stone wall, half hidden by the grass and by a sumac hedge in full bloom, curved over the sky-line. All this was exactly expressible by a gesture, and when he reached the bottom of the field he looked back for a long time, and made the gesture appreciatively. It was at this point that he always recognised the recurring dream; but he could never remember how it was going to end.

Then he entered the wood on a grassy path, and for a long time the tall tasselled grasses brushed through his fingers as he walked. Suddenly it grew dark, and feeling that "it would be folly to continue," he tried hard to remember the point of the dream. Just as he seemed to recollect it, the sound of running water came to him, as from a ravine, and he knew that "he could not escape." The low sound of running water—the little lonely gurgle of a deep-wood brook, all but lost in the loam and brush of the silent forest—why should he feel an incomprehensible distaste for the place? He tried feverishly to recollect the outcome of the dream, but all memory of it had fled. Nor could he bring himself to continue on the path; when he tried to take another step, his leg dangled uselessly in front, his foot beating flimsily on the ground till he brought it back beside the other. The longer he listened to the sound of the running water, the stronger grew his aversion for the place. This continued indefinitely, till he awoke.

You perceived the vague sense of "ominous locality" developed out of the simplest details. There is a recognisable introduction, the field, the stone wall, the grass striking his fingers; but there is no ending, nothing happens; the dream-spell at last dissolves, and the sleeper wakes. His aversion to the sound of the brook can, therefore, come from no conscious knowledge of a portending catastrophe in the dream. It was always Auber's fancy that the dream would really end in a catastrophe, which, though the mind proper continue in ignorance, casts its ominous shadow through the subconsciousness upon the surroundings of the event.

It was also a fanciful idea of his that dreams in general imply a subconscious state coexisting constantly with the actual realm of thought, but penetrated by our consciousness only when the will is least active, or during sleep. With ordinary mortals, sleep and consciousness are so nearly incompatible that the notion of actual mental achievement during sleep is unthought of. Dreams are allowed to run an absurd riot through the brain, disturbing physical rest. The remedy for this universal ailment and waste of time was to be found in "white sleep," a bit of Indian mysticism, purporting to accomplish a partial detachment of mind and body, so that the will, which is always the expression of the link between these two, is, for the time, dissolved. The body rests, but the unfettered mind enters upon a "will-less state of pure seeing," where dreams no longer remain the meaningless fantasies of blind sleep, but become luminous with idea and sequence. With the body thus left behind, the intellect rises to the zenith of perception, where the blue veil of earthly knowledge is pierced and transcended.

How often had we heard Auber talk in his fantastically learned fashion, with an amused seriousness lighting up his face. At what point he began to see something more than amusement in his dreams and theories, I never knew; but the serious beginning of the thing took shape in an incident which not even the most fervent theorist could have created for the sake of a theory.

It was up among the little knobby hills to the north of my farm. We were as usual sketching, and Auber had been going on all the afternoon about the mournful scenery, talking of nothing but browns, and greys, and "mountain melancholy." He had a way of stringing out a ceaseless jargon while he worked—an irritating trick caught in the Paris studios. At the end of the afternoon, he held up a remarkable sketch, suggesting the colour scheme for a picture in the atmosphere of oncoming dusk—a bit of path over the hill toward the sun.

"You have struck it most certainly," I said. "Be wary of finishing that; it is strangely suggestive as it is."

He nodded; and then, as we packed up, he said, "Do you know, I have felt vaguely intimate with this spot, as if I had been here before, as if I were painting a reminiscence." I remarked tritely on the commonness of this feeling.

At the bottom of a hillside meadow I was hunting for the entrance of a path into a patch of woods. Auber, instead of helping me, kept gazing back at the fading light while he made random observations on the nature of the skyline—one of his cant hobbies. "See how crudely the character of everything is defined up there against the sky," I heard him say, while I continued to search for the path. "Now even a sheep or a cow, or an inanimate thing, like that stone wall, for instance—see how its character as a wall comes out as it sweeps over the top." At this moment, a little drop of surprise in his voice made me look around. He was walking backwards, one arm extended toward the hill in a descriptive gesture. "Why, it is the dream!" he murmured in hushed excitement. "Ah, of course! I might have known it. Now, I'll turn to find the path."

"I wish you would," I said.

He started abruptly. Then he came slowly, and touched me in a queer evasive way on my shoulder. Finally, he drew a long breath, and gripped me by the arm. "Don't you recognise it? It's the dream! See! The stone wall—the field—the sumac! Now that's the first sumac—"

"Oh, come along!" I said; "there are twenty such fields. That is curious, though: you made the gesture. Do you recognise it all exactly?"

"It's it! the whole thing—and now, you see, I'm turning to find the path."

I admitted that it was curious, and said that it would be interesting to see how it all turned out.

For a long time, Auber followed in silence, which I tried to relieve by bantering comments. I was some distance ahead, when I heard him say, "The grass is brushing through my hands."

"Why not?" I laughed, but it rang false, for I recollected the detail. It was childishly simple; perhaps that was why the thing bothered me. I noticed that in the growing darkness the forest took on a peculiar look. It had been partly burnt over, leaving the ground black, and some of the trees gaunt, upbristling, and sentinel-like. The place, even in broad daylight, would have had a night-struck appearance. At this hour, when the sudden forest darkness had just fallen, there was a sense of unusual gloom, easily connecting itself with strange forebodings.

Perhaps it had been five minutes, when Auber said, "I am conscious that I cannot take my hands out of the grass."

As I said, it was a simple thing. With an odd impulse, I groped back toward him till I found his wrists, and then shook them violently above his head. We stood there for several moments performing this absurd pantomime in the darkness. His arms, with the sleeves rolled up, felt heavy with flesh in my grip. I seemed to be handling things of dead, cold flesh.

Then Auber said, "I can still feel my hands down in the grass."

I drew back in a strange horror; but, at the same moment, we both stood stock-still to listen: from some distance to the right came the trickling sound of water. It was barely perceptible, and we listened hard, indefinitely, while the silence congealed in our ears, and the darkness condensed about our eyes, filling up space, and stopping thought save just for the sound of the brook. It seemed a sort of growing immobility, eternal, like after death.

At last Auber spoke, laying a hand on my shoulder: "It is over; let us go ahead."

After a while we talked about it. There was little to "go" on. You see, nothing happens, and, as Auber expressed it, "the psychological data are ineffective for lack of an event." But though the whole thing remained then a purely psychical experience, and did not "break through," yet it had something of the fulness of fate. Auber, as usual, had a theory: in the dream some manifestation was undoubtedly striving to break through, but he had been unable to facilitate the process. The present experience, he decided, was immature, a mere coincidence. The outcome might yet, however, be foreseen through the dream, if the creative perception of "white sleep" could be attained.

That is the affair which started the whole thing. Auber must have taken the suggestion it contained much more seriously than any of us for several years imagined; nor did we connect the long contemplativeness of the man with any definite purpose. The thing was too vague and illusive to become a purpose at all.

Before long there were half a dozen instances, some trivial, or seemingly coincidental, but all forming our theory. There is one Ezekiel recounted, as we sat here talking that night. It was just a matter of old Horace MacNair's coming in on them once during a thunderstorm. The family were sitting in the big hall; the ladies with their feet up on chairs to insulate them from the lightning; young Vincent Ezekiel teasing them by putting his on the mantelpiece. At one point in the storm came a terrible crash, and Auber jumped up, starting toward

29

the door. Then he came back and sat down quietly. They laughed, and asked if he had been struck.

"No," he said, quite seriously, "not by the lightning, but by a curious idea that I saw Horace MacNair opening the door. I suppose I must have dreamed it; I was nearly asleep."

The Ezekiels looked at one another in surprise, and Mrs. Ezekiel said: "There is something curious in that, for the last time Horace was here, just before he died, he came in the midst of a thunderstorm as we were sitting here, much as we are now. And, why! I remember that he had come over because he expected to see you, but you had not arrived."

"That's so," put in young Vincent, "because he said that if you had been here, you wouldn't have been too afraid of the lightning to stand up and shake hands. And by Jove! I had my feet on the mantelpiece! I remember that, because when he saw me he laughed, and lined his up beside mine."

"He was wearing a grey raincoat, and high overshoes that you made fun of," added Auber, shortly, and then kept an embarrassed silence.

That was true, Ezekiel said; and Auber had not seen the man in five years.

There were many cases which we strung that night on the threads of our theory, all working toward its completion; and yet we neared the end with misgiving and doubt, for we had the necessity of believing, if we would keep ourselves still sane. All of us had noticed that so far as there was an element of terror in the strange incidents, it lay in the fact of a subtle undercurrent of connections, as if Fate were dimly pointing all the while toward the invisible culmination. Suddenly there would be a new manifestation of Auber's faculty, and a new instance would be added, illusive, baffling, and yet forming each time new threads in the vague warp and woof of something that we called our theory. "There it is again," we would say to ourselves, as we sent the ghostly shuttle flying in our psychological loom.

This undercurrent appeared to touch the incident of Horace Mac-Nair, for it seemed that the old artist had walked over to the Ezekiels that night on purpose to talk with Auber about making a series of pictures of the salt marshes along the Passaic River. Old Horace was dead of his heart before Auber arrived, but the suggestion was repeated by Ezekiel; and Auber, taking it as something like a dying request from his old master, besides appreciating its value, set to work at once.

The long reaches of the Passaic tidal lagoon, with their mists and blowing swamp-grass, are crossed by the trestles of all the railways which enter New York from the south. It was old Horace MacNair's idea that this place, more travelled, more unnoticed, and yet more picturesque, perhaps, than any spot near the metropolis, might be the making of Auber's reputation. The varied, moody tones of the marshland, forever blending in a pervasive atmosphere of desolate beauty, suited Auber's peculiar style. Here he would paint what passed in the popular eye for the dullest commonplace, and would interpret, at the same time, both this landscape and his little-understood art.

While he worked I frequently visited Auber on his yawl *Houri*, which was canvassed over for an outdoor studio, and anchored at the point from which he wished to paint. One day we were tied up to a pile by the Central Railroad trestle. It was just the heat of the day, and Auber, stretched out on a deck chair, was taking a sort of siesta. His eyes were closed, and he had let his cigar go out. Whether it was due to the light through the coloured awning, I was not sure, but I was suddenly attracted by a dull vacancy that seemed to be forming in his countenance. It stole upon the features as if they were being slowly sprinkled with fine dust, blotting their expression into a flat lifelessness. Then the rush of a train passing over the bridge disturbed him. With a fleeting look of pain, he sat up, glanced first furtively at me, and then stared hard around.

"Was there a train?" he asked, at length.

"Yes—an express."

"It did not stop here on the bridge for anything?"

"No, of course not."

"Of course not," he agreed, absently. "How long ago?"

"Perhaps two minutes," I said.

He examined his watch. After a while he got up, seeming to pull himself together with an effort, and began scraping nervously on his picture. I noticed that the palette-knife trembled in his hand.

"What is the matter?" I asked, finally.

"I feel very much upset," he replied, and sank weakly on the hatch. "I was on that train and—"

I had to jump below to the ice-chest; Auber seemed to have fainted. Jerry, the skipper, and I applied cold water for five minutes, and then Auber revived and asked for whiskey.

"I was on the train," he began again, persistently. "Several people, whom I knew, must have been in the chair-car with me, because I seemed to be taking part in a conversation. Was there a Pullman on the train?" he asked, abruptly.

"Yes," I said; "at the end."

The answer seemed to reassure him unhappily. "I was on the train," he continued, "but I could not think where I had come from. There were vague recollections of a walk, then of a long drive in the dark. Now I was on the train, and yet I was somehow not there even now." I poured out more whiskey, but he pushed it aside absently. "I was not there, nor was I here; for when I moved, something seemed to be folded about me, like bedclothes. It was all a kind of duplication, and I could be on the train or in the other place at will. That is why it seemed confused and unreal. We were talking about some matter of business. I held a list of figures that I referred to now and then.

Once I leaned forward to look out of the window; it was just here. I was pointing, and saying to someone, 'There is my last salt marsh!' when a great shock stopped the words, and sent me against something in front. For a moment I was conscious that you were leaning over me. Then I had a strange feeling of becoming gradually detached, as if from my very self. A weight and a feeling of bedclothes slipped from me; there was alternate glaring light and enveloping darkness. Finally, the light prevailed, and I found myself looking up into this hideous awning."

"Well," I said, "that is a very queer dream!"

"Yes; it was white sleep," he replied, slowly; "but something was added this time." He put his hand on my arm appealingly. "I knew it would come; I have had the beginnings of that dream before." He spoke as if from a tragic winding-sheet, a veil spun in the warp of his own fancy and also in the very woof of Fate; and out of this veil, through which none of us ever saw, he was stretching his hand to ask of me—what?

I did what I could. Auber consented to come at once to my farm till rest should partly restore him. We reached here that night. It was just two weeks ago; in thought, it is, for me, a lifetime. It was a time of suspense and waiting when diversion seemed almost irreverent, but at last it was forced upon us by that ever-moving providence which stood back of the whole affair. My dam broke at the upper farm. Chance? Nothing of the sort! I went up to see how it had happened, and found some rotten joists and rust-eaten girders. They are in the course of events. Auber went with me while I should see things set to rights.

It was a simple incident, but somehow, I suspected it of finality even as we started out of the yard on the long drive. I was suspicious of that knobby hill region, which was connected with the incipient indications of the whole affair. On arriving in the late afternoon, however, nothing could be more natural than that Auber, having inspected the dam, should stroll on to the pasture, where he once sketched the path that runs down to his dream-meadow.

I went back to the farmhouse, and wrote to my engineers a detail of the breach in the dam, then sat down on the porch to enjoy a smoke. The day was warm and dreamy; the sun, filtering through the September haze, rested on the eyelids like a caressing hand. I was soon half asleep, peering lazily at the view which zigzags down between the knobby hills to the more cultivated farmlands that we had left hours behind us, when the telephone rang. I got up and answered it:

"William?—at the farm? Oh yes—a message, a telegram—for Mr. Hurn, you say? Is it important?—Well, go ahead—What! Must take 11.10 express—crisis on Wall Street?—meet on train—Who?—Ezekiel."

It had come, then! Chance? No. A railroad merger; stockholders interested. At first, I said: "I won't tell him." Then I thought: "After this supposed Sentence is delayed and delayed till he no longer looks on the world as his prison cell, and the whole matter evaporates in a psychological mist, he will say: 'Our superstitions, my dear friend, and your loving care, cost me just twenty thousand dollars that trip. My picture of the twilight path, which you would have interrupted, won't replace a hundredth part of that.'"

I wandered down to the broken dam; there beside the breach, with the river sucking darkly through, Josiah Peacock stood, contemplating the scene with his practical eye against tomorrow's labour. Suddenly I found myself mentioning the telegram. He said, "Then you'll have to drive back tonight." I felt alarmed; surely this was none of my doing. Presently I was taking the short cut through the woods. The red glow of sunset was fading behind me, and darkness already gathered among the trees. Aware of a vague anxiety that impelled me forward, an odd notion that I might be late for something, I began to hurry along, the gaunt tree trunks watching like sentinels as I passed. Was I looking for Auber Hurn? It was strangely reminiscent, not a real experience. "This is absurd," I said to myself at length, and straightened my foot to stop. Instead, I unexpectedly leaped over a fallen log, and continued with nervous strides, while I flung back a sneaking glance of embarrassment.

On the turns of the path darkness closed in rapidly; the outlines of objects loomed uncertainly distant through the forest. Gradually I became aware that at the end of a dim *vista* down which I was hurrying, something white had formed itself in the path. I stopped to look, but could make out nothing clearly. It remained dimly ahead, and I approached, a few steps at a time, peering through the obscure grey shadows, striving to concentrate my vision. At last I recognised that it was Auber Hurn in his shirt-sleeves, standing still in the middle of the path. Apparently, he, too, was trying to see who was coming.

"Auber!" I called. I was not sure that he replied.

When I was very close, I began at once, as if involuntarily: "Auber, you see, I came to meet you. There is a message from Ezekiel—a Wall Street panic, or something. He wants you to meet him on the 11.10 tomor—It will be necess—Auber?" Had I been talking to the air? I looked about me. "Auber!—Auber Hurn!" I called. There was no one there; but in the hush of listening there came, as if wandering to me through the forest, the little lost gurgle of a distant brook.

For a moment I stood fascinated by a reminiscence—and then, a sudden fear swelling in my throat, I ran. Back on the path I fled, my legs seeming to go of themselves, hurling my body violently along; my feet pounding behind, as if in pursuit, whirling around the turns, then down the last straight aisle, past the sentinel trees, out into the light.

When I reached the farmyard, a fresh team was being hitched to our carriage.

"What! Has Mr. Hurn come back?" I asked, shakily.

"No," said Josiah, "but I thought maybe you'd want things ready. Didn't you find him?"

"Why—no," I replied, and then repeated firmly, "No, I did not."

I sat down, exhausted, on the porch, and waited. At the end of ten minutes Auber Hurn entered the gate, crossed to the buggy, and got in. Josiah, from between the horses where he was buckling a knee-guard, looked up in surprise. "You got that message, Mr. Hurn?"

"Yes," said Auber, speaking very distinctly. "Mr. Crenshaw just gave it to me."

Josiah turned to me. "I thought you said—" he began.

"I was mistaken—I mean, I misunderstood you," I interposed.

Josiah stared, and then finished the harnessing. "Your coats are here under the seat," he remarked. I took my place mechanically. Mrs. Josiah came with some milk and sandwiches. I finished mine hurriedly, and took the reins.

Auber sank back into his corner without a word, leaving me to feel only a sense of desperate confused isolation, of lonely helplessness.

At length Auber said, in a voice that startled me, a low, contented voice: "You were on the path? You went to find me yourself?"

"Yes," I answered; and then, after a long time, "And you were not there—yourself?"

"No, I was not there." He leaned back against the cushions, and I thought he smiled. "I was in that hill meadow. I went to sleep there for a short time."

It was two o'clock when we drove into the yard. William was waiting to take the horses.

As we went into the house, William asked if he should have the trap for the 11.10 express. I could not answer, and Auber said, looking at me in the light of the open door, "Yes, certainly."

I can see him now in the cheerless white hallway, his tall figure exaggerated in a long driving-cloak, his high features sharpened in the light of the lantern.

In taking off my coat I felt, in the pocket, the letter I had written to my engineer in Trenton. I laid it on the hall table. "You might post that tomorrow before you get to New York," I said, casually.

Then I lighted him to his room, and we said "goodnight."

Undressing mechanically, I went to bed, and after a long time I slept, exhausted.

A rumbling noise; then, after it had ceased, the realisation that a carriage had driven out of the yard—that was what woke me up. The clock on my bureau said half past ten. For a moment I forgot what that meant; and then sliding out of bed, I tiptoed quickly down the hall. Putting my ear to Auber's door, I listened—till I had made sure. From within came the dull breathing of a sleeper. Throwing on a few clothes, I went downstairs. The waitress was dusting in the hall.

"Where has the carriage gone?" I asked her.

"Why, sir," she said, "William is taking Mr. Hurn to the station."

After a while I had the courage to say cautiously, "I thought Mr. Hurn was still asleep; I did not hear him come down."

"He came down ten minutes ago," she replied, "and in a great hurry, with no time for breakfast."

"You saw him?" I cross-examined.

"Yes. The carriage was waiting, and he seemed in a great hurry, though he did run back to take a letter from the table there."

I was standing between the table and the maid.

"Well, of course you're right," I said, carelessly, and at that moment I put my hand on the letter. I turned my back and put it in my pocket.

I went hurriedly to the barn. The runabout trap and the mare were out. Then I finished dressing, and had breakfast. Soon after, William drove into the yard, and I called from the library window—"Where have you been?"

"Just to the station, sir."

"What for? Has my freight arrived?"

"Mr. Hurn, for the 11.10,"—he explained respectfully.

"Ah, yes!" I cried, in an over-voice; "I keep forgetting that I have just waked up. You saw him off? Ah—did he leave any message for me? I overslept, and did not see him this morning."

"No, sir; I had no message," he replied. "But he's a liberal man, Mr. Hurn, sir." He grinned and slapped his pocket; then, with a look of doubt, he straightened out one leg to allow his hand inside; the look grew more doubting; he stood up and searched systematically, under the seat, everywhere.

"Guess it rolled out," I said, very much interested. "What was it?"

"A silver dollar," he answered, mournfully.

"Oh, well, I'll make that up," I called, and shut the window.

I took out my watch and made a calculation; Auber's train was probably at Newark. I could stand it no longer, and I went toward his room, stamping on the bare floor, whistling nervously, and rattling the rickety balustrade. I banged open the door and began to shout: "Auber! you've missed your——"

He did not move. He was lying on his back, with his arms extended evenly outside the bedclothes, which were tucked close around his breast. He lay as if in state, with that dull dusty pallor on his face, and that eyeless vacancy of an effigy on a marble tomb—a voidness of expression, with masklike indications of duration and immobility. On the reading-table, at his bedside, I noticed his watch lying face up. It was two or three minutes of the noon hour.

Sitting down on the bed, I touched Auber on the shoulder. He did not move. An intuition, growing till it all but became an idea, and then remaining short of expressibility, unable to perceive even its own indefiniteness—a film for impressions where there is no light—such was the vagueness of my guess concerning the metamorphosis that was taking place.

Yet I began to understand that Auber Hurn, the real man, was not there, not on the bed, not in my house at all. It was as if the Person were being gradually deducted, leaving only the prime flesh to vouch for the man's existence. Even as I sat in wonder, with my eyes upon him, the life tinge faded utterly from his skin. There was a fleeting shadow as if of pain. His breast sank in a long outbreathing, and then, after seconds and minutes, it did not rise again. I listened. The room seemed to be listening with me. The silence became stricken with awe, with the interminable and unanswering awe—the muteness of death.

We believed in the thing. Ezekiel and Judson came down in response to my telegrams, and we sat here talking it all over, hours through the night. It was inevitable to believe in it. We took his body up in the darkness, and buried it in the scree on my hill; then we came back to Auber's room, and faced each other by the empty bed.

"This is not for the practical world, or for the law," I said. "No coroner on earth could return a verdict here."

"We could never see the thing clearly again if the practical world got hold of it," said Judson. "Look; you have to believe so much!" He had picked up Auber's purse from the table, where it had lain beside his watch. He opened it over the bed. A roll of bills fell out—and one silver dollar.

"That belongs to William, before the law," said Ezekiel.

In Tenebras (A Parable)

By Howard Pyle

One morning, after I had dressed myself and had left my room, I came upon an entry which I had never before noticed, even in this my own house. At the further end a door stood ajar, and wondering what was in the room beyond, I traversed the long passageway and looked within. There I saw a man sitting, with an open book lying upon his knees, who, as I laid one hand upon the door and opened it a little wider, beckoned to me to come and read what was written therein.

A secret fear stirred and rustled in my heart, but I did not dare to disobey. So, coming forward (gathering away my clothes lest they should touch his clothes), I leaned forward and read these words:—

"WHAT SHALL A MAN DO THAT HE MAY GAIN THE KINGDOM OF HEAVEN?"

I did not need a moment to seek for an answer to the question. "That," said I, "is not difficult to tell, for it has been answered again and again. He who would gain the kingdom of heaven must resist and subdue the lusts of his heart; he must do good works to his neighbours; he must fear his God. What more is there that man can do?"

Then the leaf was turned, and I read the Parable.

1

The town of East Haven is the full equation of the American ideal worked out to a complete and finished result. Therein is to be found all that is best of New England intellectuality—well taught, well trained; all that is best of solidly established New England prosperity; all that is best of New England progressive radicalism, tempered, toned, and governed by all that is best of New England conservatism, warmed to life by all that is best and broadest of New England Christian liberalism. It is the sum total of nineteenth-century American *cultus*, and in it is embodied all that for which we of these days of New World life are striving so hard. Its municipal government is a perfect model of a municipal government; its officials are elected from the most worthy of its prosperous middle class by voters every one of whom can not only read the Constitution, but could, if it were required, analyse its laws and by-laws. Its taxes are fairly and justly assessed, and are spent with a well-considered and munificent liberality. Its public works are the very best that can be compassed, both from an artistic and practical stand-point. It has a free library, not cumbersomely large, but almost perfect of its kind; and, finally, it is the boast of the community that there is not a single poor man living within its municipal limits.

Its leisure class is well read and widely speculative, and its busy class, instead of being jealous of what the other has attained, receives gladly all the good that it has to impart.

All this ripeness of prosperity is not a matter of quick growth of a recent date; neither is its wealth inherited and held by a few lucky families. It was fairly earned in the heyday of New England commercial activity that obtained some twenty-five or thirty years ago, at which time it was the boast of East Haven people that East Haven sailing-vessels covered the seas from India to India. Now that busy harvest-time is passed and gone, and East Haven rests with opulent ease, subsisting upon the well-earned fruits of good work well done.

With all this fulness of completion one might think that East Haven had attained the perfection of its ideal. But no. Still in one respect it is like the rest of the world; still, like the rest of the world, it is attainted by one great nameless sin, of which it, in part and parcel, is somehow guilty, and from the contamination of which even it, with all its perfection of law and government, is not free. Its boast that there are no poor within its limits is true only in a certain particular sense. There are, indeed, no poor resident, tax-paying, voting citizens, but during certain seasons of the year there are, or were, plenty of tramps, and they were not accounted when that boast was made.

East Haven has clad herself in comely enough fashion with all those fine garments of enlightened self-government, but underneath those garments are, or were, the same vermin that infested the garments of so many communities less clean—parasites that suck existence from God's gifts to decent people. Indeed, that human vermin at one time infested East Haven even more than the other and neighbouring towns; perhaps just because its clothing of civilization was more soft and warm than theirs; perhaps (and upon the face this latter is the more likely explanation of the two) because, in a very exaltation of enlightenment, there were no laws against vagrancy. Anyhow, however one might account for their presence, there the tramps were.

One saw the shabby, homeless waifs everywhere—in the highways, in the byways. You saw them slouching past the shady little common, with its smooth greensward, where well-dressed young ladies and gentlemen played at lawn-tennis; you saw them standing knocking at the doors of the fine old houses in Bay Street to beg for food to eat; you saw them in the early morning on the steps of the old North Church, combing their shaggy hair and beards with their fingers, after their night's sleep on the old colonial gravestones under the rustling elms; everywhere you saw them—heavy, sullen-browed, brutish—a living reproach to the well-ordered, God-fearing community of something cruelly wrong, something bitterly unjust, of which they, as well as the rest of the world, were guilty, and of which God alone knew the remedy.

No town in the State suffered so much from their infestation, and it was a common saying in the town of Norwark—a prosperous manufacturing community adjoining East Haven—that Dives lived in East Haven, and that Lazarus was his most frequent visitor.

The East Haven people always felt the sting of the suggested sneer; but what could they do? The poor were at their doors; they knew no immediate remedy for that poverty; and they were too compassionate and too enlightened to send the tramps away hungry and forlorn.

So, Lazarus continued to come, and Dives continued to feed him at the gate, until, by-and-by, a strange and unexpected remedy for the trouble was discovered, and East Haven at last overcame its dirty son of Anak.

2

Perhaps if all the votes of those ultra-intelligent electors had been polled as to which one man in all the town had done most to insure its position in the van of American progress; as to who best represented the community in the matter of liberal intelligence and ripe culture; as to who was most to be honoured for steadfast rectitude and immaculate purity of life; as to who was its highest type of enlightened Christianity—an overwhelming if not unanimous vote would have been cast for Colonel Edward Singelsby.

He was born of one of the oldest and best New England families; he had graduated with the highest honours from Harvard, and finished his education at Göttingen. At the outbreak of the rebellion he had left a lucrative law practice and a probable judgeship to fight at the head of a volunteer regiment throughout the whole war, which he did with signal credit to himself, the community, and the nation at large. He was a broad and profound speculative thinker, and the papers which he occasionally wrote, and which appeared now and then in the more prominent magazines, never failed to attract general and wide-spread attention. His intelligence, clear-cut and vividly operating, instead of leading him into the quicksands of scepticism, had never left the hard rock of earnest religious belief inherited from ten generations of Puritan ancestors. Nevertheless, though his feet never strayed from that rock, his was too active and living a soul to rest content with the arid face of a by-gone orthodoxy; God's rain of truth had fallen upon him and it, and he had hewn and delved until the face of his rock blossomed a very Eden of exalted Christianity. To sum up briefly and in full, he was a Christian gentleman of the highest and most perfect type.

Besides his close and profound studies in municipal government, from which largely had sprung such a flawless and perfect type as that of East Haven, he was also interested in public charities, and the existence of many of the beneficial organisations throughout the State had been largely due to his persistent and untiring efforts. The municipal reforms, as has been suggested, worked beautifully, perfectly, without the grating of a wheel or the creaking of a joint; but the public charities—somehow they did not work so well; they never did just what was intended, or achieved just what was expected; their mechanism appeared to be perfect, but, as is so universally the case with public charities, they somehow lacked a soul.

It was in connection with the matter of public charities that the tramp question arose. Colonel Singelsby grappled with it, as he had grappled with so many matters of the kind. The solution was the crowning work of his life, and the result was in a way as successful as it was paradoxical and unexpected.

Connected with the East Haven Public Library was the lecture-room, where an association, calling itself the East Haven Lyceum, and comprising in its number some of the most advanced thinkers of the town, met on Thursdays from November to May to discuss and digest matters social and intellectual. More than one good thing that had afterward taken definite shape had originated in the discussions of the Lyceum, and one winter, under Colonel Singelsby's lead, the tramp question was taken up and dissected.

He had, Colonel Singelsby said, studied that complex question very earnestly and for some time, and to his mind it had resolved itself to this: not how to suppress vagrancy, but how to make of the vagrant an honest and useful citizen. Repressive laws were easily passed, but it appeared to him that the only result achieved by them was to drive the tramp into other sections where no such laws existed, and which sections they only infested to a greater degree and in larger numbers.

Nor in these days of light was it, in his opinion, a sufficient answer to that objection that it was the fault of those other communities that they did not also pass repressive laws. The fact remained that they had not passed them, and that the tramps did infest their precincts, and such being the case, it was as clear as day (for that which injures some, injures all) that the wrong of vagrancy was not corrected by merely driving tramps over the limits of one town into those of another. Moreover, there was a deeper and more interior reason against the passage of such repressive laws; to his thinking it behoved society, if it would root out this evil, to seek first the radix from which it drew existence; it behoved them first to very thoroughly diagnose the disease before attempting a hasty cure. "So, let us now," said he, "set about searching for this radix, and then so drive the spade of reform as to remove it forever."

The discussion that followed opened a wide field for investigation, and the conclusion finally reached during the winter was not unlike that so logically deduced by Mr. Henry George at a later date. The East Haven Lyceum, however, either did not think of or did not care to advocate such a radical remedy as Mr. George proposed. They saw clearly enough that, apart from the unequal distribution of wealth, which may perhaps have been the prime cause of the trouble, idleness and thriftlessness are acquired habits, just as industry and thrift are acquired habits, and it seemed to them better to cure the ill habit rather than to upset society and then to rebuild it again for the sake of benefiting the ill-conditioned few.

So, the result of the winter's talk was the founding of the East Haven Refuge, of which much has since been written and said.

Those interested in such matters may perhaps remember the article upon the Refuge published in one of the prominent magazines. A full description of it was given in that paper. The building stood upon Bay Street overlooking the harbour; it was one of the most beautiful situations in the town; without, the building was architecturally plain, but in perfect taste; within, it was furnished with every comfort and convenience—a dormitory immaculately clean; a dining-room, large and airy, where plain substantial food, cooked in the best possible manner, was served to the inmates. There were three bathrooms supplied with hot and cold water, and there was a reading and a smoking-room provided not only with all the current periodicals, but with chess, checkers, and backgammon-boards.

At the same time that the Refuge was being founded and built, certain municipal laws were enacted, according to which a tramp appearing within the town limits was conveyed (with as little appearance of constraint as possible) to the Refuge. There for four weeks he was well fed, well clothed, well cared for. In return he was expected to work for eight hours every day upon some piece of public improvement: the repaving of Main Street with asphaltum blocks was selected by the authorities as the initial work. At the end of four weeks the tramp was dismissed from the Refuge clad in a neat, substantial, well-made suit of clothes, and with money in his pocket to convey him to some place where he might, if he chose, procure permanent work.

The Refuge was finished by the last of March, and Colonel Singelsby was unanimously chosen by the board as superintendent, a position he accepted very reluctantly. He felt that in so accepting he shouldered the whole responsibility of the experiment that was being undertaken, yet he could not but acknowledge that it was right for him to shoulder that burden, who had been foremost both in formulating and advocating the scheme, as well as most instrumental in carrying it to a practical conclusion. So, as was said, he accepted, though very reluctantly.

The world at large was much disposed to laugh at and to ridicule all the preparation that Dives of East Haven made to entertain his Lazarus. Nevertheless, there were a few who believed very sincerely in the efficacy of the scheme. But both those who believed and those who scoffed agreed in general upon one point—that it was altogether probable that East Haven would soon be overrun with such a wilderness of tramps that fifty Refuges would not be able to supply them with refuge.

But who shall undertake to solve that inscrutable paradox, human life—its loves, its hates?

The Refuge was opened upon the 1st of April; by the 29th there were thirty-two tramps lodged in its sheltering arms, all working their eight hours a day upon the repaving of Main Street. That same day—the 29th—five were dismissed from within its walls. Colonel

Singelsby, as superintendent, had a little office on the ground-floor of the main building, opening out upon the street. At one o'clock, and just after the Refuge dinner had been served, he stood beside his table with five sealed envelopes spread out side by side upon it. Presently the five outgoing guests slouched one by one into the room. Each was shaven and shorn; each wore clean linen; each was clad in a neat, plain, grey suit of tweed; each bore stamped upon his face a dogged, obstinate, stolid, low-browed shame.

The colonel gave each the money enclosed in the envelope, thanked each for his service, inquired with pleasant friendliness as to his future movements and plans, invited each to come again to the Refuge if he chanced to be in those parts, shook each by a heavy, reluctant hand, and bade each a goodbye. Then the five slouched out and away, leaving the town by back streets and byways; each with his hat pulled down over his brows; each ten thousand times more humiliated, ten thousand times more debased in his cleanliness, in his good clothes, and with money in his pocket, than he had been in his dirt, his tatters, his poverty.

They never came back to East Haven again.

The capacity of the Refuge was 50. In May there were 47 inmates, and Colonel Singelsby began to apprehend the predicted overflow. The overflow never came. In June there were 45 inmates; in July there were 27; in August there were 28; in September, 10; in October, 2; in November, 1; in December there were none. The fall was very cold and wet, and maybe that had something to do with the sudden falling off of guests, for the tramp is not fond of cold weather. But even granting that bad weather had something to do with the matter, the Refuge was nevertheless a phenomenal, an extraordinary success—but upon very different lines than Colonel Singelsby had anticipated; for even in this the first season of the institution the tramps began to shun East Haven even more sedulously than they had before cultivated its hospitality. Even West Hampstead, where vagrancy was punished only less severely than petty larceny, was not so shunned as East Haven with the horrid comforts of its Refuge.

3

As was said, the records of the Refuge showed that one inmate still lingered in the sheltering arms of that institution during a part of the month of November. That one was Sandy Graff.

Sandy Graff did not strictly belong to the great peregrinating leisure class for whose benefit the Refuge had been more especially founded and built. Those were strangers to the town, and came and went apparently without cause for coming and going. Little or nothing was known of such—of their name, of their life, of whence they came or whither their footsteps led. But with Sandy Graff it was different; he belonged identically to the place, and all the town knew him, the sinister tragedy of his history, and all the why and wherefore that led to his becoming the poor miserable drunken outcast—the town "bummer"—that he was.

There is something bitterly enough pathetic in the profound abasement of the common tramp—frouzy, unkempt, dirty, forlorn; without ambition further than to fill his belly with the cold leavings from decent folks' tables; without other pride than to clothe his dirty body with the cast-off rags and tatters of respectability; without further motive of life than to roam hither and yon—idle, useless, homeless, aimless. In all this there is indeed enough of the pathetic, but Sandy Graff in his utter and complete abasement was even more deeply, tragically sunken than they.

For them there was still some sheltering aegis of secrecy to conceal some substratum in the uttermost depths of personal depravity; but for Sandy—all the world knew the story of his life, his struggle, his fall; all the world could see upon his blotched and bloated face the outer sign of his inner lusts; and what deeper humiliation can there be than for all one's world to know how brutish and obscene one may be in the bottom of one's heart? What deeper shame may any man suffer than to have his neighbours read upon his blasted front the stamp and seal of all, all his heart's lust, set there not only as a warning and a lesson, not only a visible proof how deep below the level of savagery it is possible for a God-enlightened man to sink, but also for self-gratulation of those righteous ones that they are not fallen from God's grace as that man has fallen?

One time East Haven had been Sandy Graff's home, and it was now the centre of his wanderings, which never extended further than the immediately neighbouring towns. At times he would disappear from East Haven for weeks, maybe months; then suddenly he would appear again, pottering aimlessly, harmlessly, around the streets or byways; wretched, foul, boozed, and sodden with vile rum, which he had procured no one knew how or where. Maybe at such times of reappearance he would be seen hanging around some store or street corner, maundering with someone who had known him in the days of his prosperity, or maybe he would be found loitering around the kitchen or outhouse of some pitying Bay-Streeter, who also had known him in the days of his dignity and cleanliness, waiting with helpless patience for scraps of cold victuals or the dregs of the coffee-pot, for no one drove him away or treated him with unkindness.

Sandy Graff's father had been a cobbler in Upper Main Street, and he himself had in time followed the same trade in the same little, old-fashioned, dingy, shingled, hip-roofed house. In time he had married a good, sound-hearted, respectable farmer's daughter from a neck of land across the bay, known as Pig Island, and had settled down to what promised to be a decent, prosperous life.

So far as anyone could see, looking from the outside, his life offered all that a reasonable man could ask for; but suddenly, within a year after he was married, his feet slipped from the beaten level pathway of respectability. He began taking to drink.

Why it was that the foul fiend should have leaped astride of his neck, no man can exactly tell. More than likely it was inheritance, for his grandfather, who had been a ship-captain—some said a slave-trader—had died of *mania a potu*, and it is one of those inscrutable rulings of Divine Providence that the innocent ones of the third and fourth generation shall suffer because of the sins of their forebears, who have raised more than one devil to grapple with them, their children, and children's children. Anyhow, Sandy fell from grace, and within three years' time had become a confirmed drunkard.

Fortunately, no children were born to the couple. But it was one of the most sad, pitiful sights in the world to see Sandy's patient, sad-eyed wife leading him home from the tavern, tottering, reeling, helpless, sodden. Pitiful indeed! Pitiful even from the outside; but if one could only have looked through that outer husk of visible life, and have beheld the inner workings of that lost soul—the struggles, the wrestling with the foul grinning devil that sat astride of him—how much more would that have been pitiful!

And then, if one could have seen and have realised as the roots from which arose those inner workings, the hopes, the longings for a better life that filled his heart during the intervals of sobriety, if one could have sensed but one pang of that hell-thirst that foreran the mortal struggle that followed, as that again foreran the inevitable fall into his kennel of lust, and then, last and greatest, if those righteous neighbours of his who never sinned and never fell could only have seen the wakening, the bitter agony of remorse, the groaning horror of self-abasement that ended the debauchery—Ah! that, indeed, was something to pity beyond man's power of pitying.

If Sandy's wife had only berated and abused him, if she had even cried or made a sign of her heart-break, maybe his pangs of remorse might not have been so deadly bitter and cruel; but her steadfast and unrelaxing patience—it was that that damned him more than all else to his hell of remorse.

At last came the end. One day Sandy went to New Harbor City to buy leather for cobbling, and there his devil, for no apparent reason at all, leaped upon him and flung him. For a week he saw or knew nothing but a whirling vision of the world seen through rum-crazy eyes; then at last he awoke to find himself hatless, coatless, filthy, unshaved, blear-eyed, palsied. Not a cent of money was left, and so that day and night, in spite of the deadly nausea that beset him and the trembling weakness that hung like a leaden weight upon every limb, he walked all the thirty-eight miles home again to East Haven. He reached there about five o'clock, and in the still grey of the early dawning.

Only a few people were stirring in the streets, and as he slunk along close to the houses, those whom he met turned and looked after him. No one spoke to him or stopped him, as might possibly have been done had he come home at a later hour. Every shred and filament of his poor remorseful heart and soul longed for home and the comfort that his wife alone could give him, and yet at the last corner he stopped for a quaking moment or so in the face of the terror of her unreproachful patience. Then he turned the corner—

Not a sign of his house was to be seen—nothing but an empty, gaping blackness where it had stood before. *It had been burned to the ground!*

Why is it that God's curse rests very often and most heavily upon the misfortunate? Why is it that He should crush the reeds that are bruised beneath His heel? Why is it that He should seem so often to choose the broken heart to grind to powder?

Sandy's wife had been burned to death in the fire!

From that moment Sandy Graff was lost, utterly and entirely lost. God, for His terrible purposes, had taken away the one last thread that bound the drowning soul to anything of decency and cleanliness. Now his devil and he no longer struggled together; they walked hand in hand. He was without love, without hope, without one iota that might bring a flicker of light into the midnight gloom of his despairing soul.

After the first dreadful blast of his sorrow and despair had burned itself out, he disappeared, no one knew whither. A little over a month passed, and then he suddenly appeared again, drunken, maudlin, tearful. Again, he disappeared, again he reappeared, a little deeper sunken, a little more abased, and henceforth that was his life. He became a part of the town, and everybody, from the oldest to the youngest, knew him and his story. He injured no one, he offended no one, and he never failed, somehow or somewhere, to find food to eat, lodging for his head, and clothing to cover his nakedness. He had been among the very first to enter the Refuge, and now, in November, he was the last one left within its walls. He was the only one of the guests who returned, and perhaps he would not have done so had not his aching restlessness driven him back to suffer an echo of agony in the place where his damnation had been inflicted upon him.

Between Colonel Singelsby upon the one side, the wise, the pure, the honoured servant of God, and Sandy Graff upon the other side, the vile, the filthy, the ugly, the debased, there yawned a gulf as immeasurably wide and deep as that which gaps between heaven and hell.

4

The winter of the year that saw the opening of the East Haven Refuge was one of the most severe that New England had known for generations. It was early in January that there came the great snowstorm that spread its two or three feet of white covering all the way from Maine to Virginia, and East Haven, looking directly in the teeth of the blast that came swirling and raging across the open harbour, felt the full force of the icy tempest. The streets of the town lay a silent desert of drifting whiteness, for no one who could help it was abroad from home that bitter morning.

The hail and snow spat venomously against the windows of Dr. Hunt's office in one of those fine old houses on Bay Street overlooking the harbour. The wind roared sonorously through the naked, tortured branches of the great elm-trees, and the snow piled sharp and smooth in fence corners and around north gables of the house.

Dr. Hunt shuddered as he looked out of the window, for while all his neighbours sat snug and warm around their hearths, he had to face the raging of the icy blast upon the dull routine of his business of mercy—the dull routine of bread-getting by comforting the afflictions of others. Then the sleigh drew up to the gate, the driver already powdered with the gathering whiteness, and Dr. Hunt struggled into his overcoat, tied the ribbons of his fur cap under his chin, and drew on his beaver gloves. Then, with one final shudder, he opened his office door, and stepped out into the drift upon the step.

Instantly he started back with a cry: he had trodden upon a man covered and hidden by the snow.

It was Sandy Graff. How long he had been lying there, no one might tell; a few moments more, and the last flicker of life would have twinkled mercifully out. The doctor had him out of the snow in a moment, and in the next had satisfied himself that Sandy was not dead.

Even as he leaned over the still white figure, feeling the slow faint beating of the failing heart, the doctor was considering whether he should take Sandy into the house or not. The decision was almost instantaneous: it would be most inconvenient, and the Refuge was only a stone's-throw away. So, the doctor did not even disturb the household with the news of what had happened. He and the driver wrapped the unconscious figure in a buffalo-robe and laid it in the sleigh.

As the doctor was about to step into the sleigh, someone suddenly laid a heavy hand upon his shoulder. He turned sharply, for he had not heard the approaching footsteps, muffled by the thick snow, and he had been too engrossed with attention to Sandy Graff to notice anything else.

It was young Harold Singelsby; his face was very white and drawn, and in the absorption of his own suppressed agitation he did not even look at Sandy. "Doctor," said he, in a hoarse, constrained voice, "for God's sake, come home with me as quickly as you can: father's very sick!"

★★★★★★★★

I had often wondered how it is with a man when he closes his life to this world. Looking upon the struggling efforts of a dying man to retain his hold upon his body, I had often wondered whether his sliding to unconsciousness was like the dissolving of the mind to sleep in this life. That death was not like sleep was at such times patent enough—it was patent enough that it was the antithesis of sleep. Sleep is peaceful; death is convulsed—sleep is rest; death is separation.

That which I here following read in the book as it lay open upon the man's knees seemed in a way dark, broken, indistinct with a certain grim obscurity; yet if I read truly therein I distinguished this great difference between death and sleep: Sleep is the cessation of consciousness from an interior life to exterior thought; death is the cessation of con-sciousness from the exterior mind to an interior life.

****

When Sandy Graff opened his eyes once more, it was to find him-self again within the sheltering arms of the Refuge. That awakening was almost to a full and clear consciousness. It was with no confusion of thought and but little confusion of sight, except for a white mist that seemed to blur the things he saw.

He knew, instantly and vividly, where he was. Instantly and vividly everything found its fit place in his mind—the long rows of cots; the bald, garishly white walls, cold and unbeautiful in their immaculate cleanliness; the range of curtainless windows looking out upon the chill, thin grey of the winter day. He was not surprised to find himself in the Refuge; it did not seem strange to him, and he did not wonder. He dimly remembered stumbling through the snowdrifts and then falling asleep, overpowered by an irresistible and leaden drowsiness. But just where it was he fell, he could not recall.

He saw with dim sight that three or four people were gathered about his bed. Two of them were rubbing his legs and feet, but he could not feel them. It was this senselessness of feeling that first brought the jarring of the truth to him. The house-steward stood nearby, and Sandy turned his face weakly toward him. "Mr. Jackson," said he, faintly, "I think I'm going to die."

****

He turned his face again (now toward the opened window), and was staring unwinkingly at a white square of light, and it seemed to him to grow darker and darker. At first, he thought that it was the gathering of night, but faint and flickering as were his senses, there was something beneath his outer self that dreaded it—that dreaded be-yond measure the coming of that darkness. After one or two efforts, in which his stiff tongue refused to form the words he desired to speak, he said, at last, "I can't see; it's—getting—dark."

****

He was dimly, darkly conscious of hurry and bustle around him, of voices calling to send for the doctor, of hurrying hither and thither, but it all seemed faint and distant. Everything was now dark to his sight, and it was as though all this concerned another; but as outer things slipped further and further from him, the more that inner life struggled, tenaciously, dumbly, hopelessly, to retain its grip upon the outer world. Sometimes, now and then, to this inner consciousness, it seemed almost as though it were rising again out of the gathering blackness. But it was only the recurrent vibrations of ebbing powers, for still again, and even before it knew it, that life found itself quickly deeper and more hopelessly in the tremendous shadow into which it was being inexorably engulfed.

He himself knew nothing now of those who stood about the bed, awestruck and silent, looking down upon him; he himself sensed nothing of the harsh convulsive breathing, and of all the other grim outer signs of the struggle. But still, deep within, that combat of resistance to death waged as desperately, as vividly, as ever.

★★★★★★★★

A door opened, and at the sudden noise the dissolving life recrystallized for one brief instant, and in that instant the dying man knew that Dr. Hunt was standing beside his bed, and heard him say, in a slow, solemn voice, sounding muffled and hollow, as though from far away and through an empty space, "Colonel Singelsby has just died."

Then the cord, momentarily drawn tense, was relaxed with a snap, and the last smoky spark was quenched in blackness.

Dr. Hunt's fingers were resting lightly upon the wrist. As the last deep quivering breath expired with a quavering sigh, he laid the limp hand back upon the bed, and then, before he arose, gently closed the stiff eyelids over the staring glassy eyes, and set the gaping jaws back again into a more seemly repose.

5

So, all this first part of the Parable had, as I read it, a reflected image of what was real and actual; of what belonged to the world of men as I knew that world. The people of whom it spoke moved and lived, maybe not altogether as real men of flesh and blood move and live, but nevertheless with a certain life of their own—images of what was real. All these things, I say (excepting perhaps the last), were clear and plain enough after a certain fashion, but that which followed showed those two of whom the story was written—the good man and the wicked man—stripped of all their outer husk of fleshly reality, and walking and talking not as men of flesh and blood, but as men in the spirit.

So, though I knew that which I was reading might indeed be as true, and perhaps truer, than that other which I had read, and though I knew that to such a state I myself must come, and that as these two suffered, I myself must some time suffer in the same kind, if not in the same degree, nevertheless it was all strangely unreal, and being set apart from that which I knew, was like life as seen in a dream.

Yet let it not be thought that this Parable is all a vague dream, for there are things which are more real than reality, and being so, must be couched in different words from such as describe the things that one's bodily eyes behold of the grim reality of this world. Such things, being so told, may seem as strange and as unsubstantial as that which is unreal, instead of like that which is real.

So that which is now to be read must be read as the other has been read—not as a likeness of life in its inner being, but as an image of that life.

★★★★★★★★

Sandy Graff awoke, and opened his eyes. At first, he thought that he was still within the dormitory of the Refuge, for there before him he saw cold, bare white walls immaculately clean. Upon either hand was the row of beds, each with its spotless coverlet, and in front was the long line of curtainless windows looking out upon the bright daylight.

But as his waking senses gathered to a more orderly clearness, he saw very soon that the place in which he was was very different from the Refuge. Even newly awakened, and with his brain clouded and obscured by the fumes of sleep, he distinguished at once that the strange, clear, lucid brilliancy of the light which came in through the row of windows was very different from any light that his eyes had ever before seen. Then, as his mind opened wider and fuller and clearer, and as one by one the objects which surrounded him began to take their proper place in his awakened life, he saw that there were many people around, and that most of the beds were occupied, and in every case by a man.

The room in which he lay was somewhat longer than the dormitory of the Refuge, and was connected at the further end with what appeared to be a sort of waiting-room beyond. In and out of the connecting doorway people were coming and going. Some of these seemed to be friends of those who were lying in the beds, being in every case led to some particular bedside, the occupant of which had newly awakened; others, who seemed to be attendants of the place, moved constantly hither and thither, busying themselves around other of the beds, where lay such as seemed to need attention.

Sandy looked slowly around him from left to right. Some of the occupants of the beds—and one of these lay in the cot next to him— were not yet awake, and he saw, with a sort of awe, that each of these lay strangely like a dead man—still, motionless, the face covered with

53

a linen napkin. Two of the attendants seemed to have these sleepers especially in their charge, moving continually hither and thither, to the bedside first of one and then another, evidently to see if there were yet any signs of waking. As Sandy continued watching them, he saw them at last softly and carefully lift a napkin from one of the faces, whereupon the man immediately awoke and sat up.

This occurred in a bed not very far from where he himself lay, and he watched all that passed with a keen and thrilling interest. The man had hardly awakened when word was passed down the length of the room to the antechamber beyond. Apparently, some friends of the sleeper were waiting for this word to be brought to them, for there entered directly two women and a man from the further doorway. The three came straight to the bed in which the man lay, and with great noise of rejoicing seemed to welcome the newcomer. They helped him to arise, handed him his clothes piece by piece from the chair at the bedside, and the man began dressing himself.

It was not until then, and until his ear caught some stray words of those that were spoken, that Sandy began to really realise where he was and what had happened to him. Then suddenly a great and awful light broke upon him—he had died and had come to life again—his living senses had solved the greatest of all mysteries—the final mystery; the mystery of eternity.

It happens nearly always, it is said, that the first awakening thought of those who die is of the tremendous happening that has come upon them. So, it was with Sandy. For a while he lay quite still, with his hands folded, and a strange awful brooding, almost as though of fear, breathlessly wrapping his heart roundabout. But it was not for a long time that he lay thus, for suddenly, like a second flash of lightning in the gathering darkness of a cloud, the thought shot through him that no friends had come to meet and to greet him as they had come to meet and greet these others. Why had his wife not come to him? He turned his head; the chair beside him was empty; he was without even clothes to wear.

For a while he lay with closed eyes like one stunned. Then a sudden voice broke upon his ear, and he opened his eyes again and looked up. A tall man with calm face—almost a stern face—stood beside the bed looking down at him.

Somehow Sandy knew that he had no business in the bed now that he was awake, and, with a half-muttered apology, he made a motion as if to arise, then, remembering that there were no clothes for him to wear, he sank back again upon the pillow.

"Come," said the man, giving his cane a rap upon the floor, "you must get up; you have already been here longer than the law allows."

Sandy had been too long accustomed to self-abasement in the world he had left to question the authority of the man who spoke to him. "I can't help lying here, sir," said he, helplessly. "I've no clothes to wear." Then he added: "Maybe if you let my wife come to me, she'd bring me something to wear. I hear say, sir, that I've died, and that this is heaven. I don't know why she hasn't come to me. Everybody else here seems to have somebody to meet him but me."

"This is not heaven," said the man.

A long silence followed. "It's not hell, is it?" said Sandy, at last.

The man apparently did not choose to answer the question. "Come," said he, "you waste time in talk. Get up. Wrap the sheet around you, and come with me."

"Where are you going to take me?" said Sandy.

"No matter," said the other. "Do as I tell you." His voice was calm, dispassionate; there was nothing of anger in it, but there was that which said he must be obeyed.

Sandy drew the sheet upon which he lay about him, and then shuddering, half with nervous dread and half with cold, arose from the warm bed in which he lay.

The other turned, and without saying a word led the way down the length of the room, Sandy following close behind. The noise of talking ceased as they passed by the various beds, and all turned and looked after the two, some smiling, some laughing outright. Sandy, as he marched down the length of the room, heard the rustling laugh and felt an echo of the same dull humiliation he had felt when he had marched with the other guests of the East Haven Refuge to their daily task of paving Main Street. There as now the people laughed, and there in the same manner as they did now; and as he had there slouched in the body, so now he slouched heavily in the spirit after his conductor.

Opposite the end of the room where there was the door through which the friends and visitors came and went was another door, low and narrow. Sandy's guide led the way directly to it, lifted the latch, and opened it. It led to a long entry beyond, gloomy and dark. This passageway was dully lighted by a small square window, glazed with clouded glass, at the further end of the narrow hall, upon which front-ed a row of closed doors. The place was very damp and chill; a cold draught of air blew through the length of it, and Sandy, as the other closed the door through which they had just entered, and so shut out the noise beyond, heard distinctly the sound of running water. Without turning to the left or to the right, Sandy's guide led the way down the hall, stopping at last when he had reached a door near the further end. He drew a bunch of keys from his pocket, chose one from among them, fitted it into the lock, and turned it.

"Go in there," said he, "and wash yourself clean, and then you shall have clothes to wear."

Sandy entered, and the door was closed behind him. The place in which he found himself was very cold, and the floor beneath his feet was wet and slimy. His teeth chattered and his limbs shuddered as he stood looking around him. The noise of flowing water sounded loud and clear through the silence; it was running from a leaden pipe into a wooden tank, mildewed and green with mould, that stood in the middle of the room. The stone-walls around, once painted white, were now also stained and splotched with great blotches of green and russet dampness. The only light that lit the place came in through a small, narrow, slatted window close to the ceiling, and opposite the doorway which he had entered. It was all gloomy, ugly, repellent.

There were some letters painted in red at the head of the wooden tank. He came forward and read them, not without some difficulty, for they were nearly erased.

This is the water of death!

Sandy started back so suddenly that he nearly fell upon the slippery floor. A keen pang of sudden terror shot through him; then a thought that some grotesque mockery was being played upon him. A second thought blew the first away like a breath of smoke, for it told him that there could be no mockery in the place to which he had come. His waking and all that had happened to him had much of nightmare grotesquery about it, but there was no grotesquery or no appearance of jesting about that man who had guided him to the place in which he now found himself. There was a calm, impassive, unemotional sternness about all that he said and did—official, automatonlike—that precluded the possibility of any jest or meaningless form. This must indeed be the *water of death*, and his soul told him that it was meant for him.

He turned dully, and walked with stumbling steps to the door. He felt blindly for a moment for the latch, then his hand touched it, and he raised it with a click. The sharp sound jarred through the silence, and Sandy did not open the door. He stood for a little while staring stupidly down upon the floor with his palm still upon the latch. Was the man who had brought him there waiting outside? Behind him lay the *water of death*, but he dared not open the door and chance the facing of that man. The sheet had fallen away from him, and now he stood entirely naked. He let the latch fall back to its place—carefully, lest it should again make a noise, and that man should hear it. Then he gathered the now damp and dirty sheet about him, and crouched down upon the cold floor close to the crack of the door.

There he sat for a while, every now and then shuddering convulsively with cold and terror, then by-and-by he began to cry.

There is something abjectly, almost brutally, pathetic in the ugly squalor of a man's tears. Sandy Graff crying, and now and then wiping his eyes with the damp and dirty sheet, was almost a more ugly sight than he had been in the maudlin bathos of his former drunkenness.

So, he sat for a long time, until finally his crying ended, only for a sudden sob now and then, and he only crouched, wondering dully. At last he slowly arose, gathering the sheet still closer around him, and creeping step by step to the tank, looked down into its depth. The water was as clear as crystal; he dipped his hand into it—it was as cold as ice. Then he dropped aside the sheet, and stood as naked as the day he was born. He stepped into the water.

★★★★★★★★

A deathly faintness fell upon him, and he clutched at the edge of the tank; but even as he clutched his sight failed, and he felt himself sinking down into the depths.

"Help!" he cried, hoarsely; and then the water closed blackly over his head.

★★★★★★★★

He felt himself suddenly snatched out from the tank, warm towels were wrapped about him, his limbs were rubbed with soft linen, and at last he opened his eyes. He still heard the sound of running water, but now the place in which he was was no longer dark and gloomy. Someone had flung open the slatted window, and a great beam of warm, serene sunlight streamed in, and lay in a dazzling white square upon the wet floor. Two men were busied about him. They had wrapped his body in a soft warm blanket, and were wiping dry his damp, chilled, benumbed hands and feet.

"What does this mean?" said Sandy, faintly. "Was I not then to die, after all? Was not that the *water of death*?"

57

"*The water of death?*" said they. "You did not read the words aright; that was *the water of life.*" They helped him dress himself in his clothes— clothes not unlike those which the East Haven Refuge had given its outgoing guests, only, somehow, these did not make him feel humili- ated and abased as those had made him feel. Then they led him out of that place. They traversed the same long passageway through which he had come before, and so came to the bedroom which he had left. The tenants were all gone now, and the attendants were busied spreading the various beds with clean linen sheets and coverlets, as though for fresh arrivals.

No one seemed to pay any attention to him. His conductors led the way to the anteroom which Sandy had seen beyond.

A woman was sitting patiently looking out of the window. She turned her head as they entered, and Sandy, when he saw her face, stood suddenly still, as though turned to stone. *It was his wife!*

6

With Colonel Singelsby was no such nightmare awakening as with Sandy Graff; with him, were no such ugly visions and experiences; with him was no squalor and discomfort. Yet he also opened his eyes upon a room so like that upon which they had closed that at first, he thought that he was still in the world. There was the same soft bed, the same warmth of ease and comfort, the same style of old-fashioned furniture. There were the curtained windows, the pictures upon the wall, the bright warm fire burning in the grate.

At first, he saw all these things drowsily, as one does upon newly awakening. With him, as with Sandy, it was only when his conscious life had opened wide and clear enough to observe and to recognise who they were that were gathered around him that with a keen, al- most agonizing thrill he realised where he was and what had befallen him. Upon one side of his bed stood his son Hubert; upon the other side stood his brother James. The one had died ten, the other nine- teen years before. Of all those who had gone from the world which he himself had just left, these stood the nearest to him, and now, in his resurrection, his opening eyes first saw these two. They and other relatives and friends helped him to arise and dress, as Sandy had seen the poor wretches in the place in which he had awakened raised from their beds and dressed by their friends.

****

All Colonel Singelsby's teachings had told him that this was not so different from the world he had left behind. Nevertheless, although he was prepared somewhat for it, it was wonderful to him how alike the one was to the other. The city, the streets, the people coming and going, the stores, the parks, the great houses—all were just as they were in the world of men. He had no difficulty in finding his way about the streets. There, in comfortable houses of a better class, were many of his friends; others were not to be found; some, he was told, had ascended higher; others, he was also told, had descended lower.

Among other places, Colonel Singelsby found himself during the afternoon in the house of one with whom he had been upon friendly, almost intimate terms in times past in the world. Colonel Singelsby remembered hearing that the good man had died a few months before he himself had left the world. He wondered what had become of him, and then in a little while he found himself in his old friend's house. It had been many years since he had seen him. He remembered him as a benign, venerable old gentleman, and he had been somewhat surprised to find that he was still living in the town, instead of having ascended to a higher state.

The old gentleman still looked outwardly venerable, still outwardly benign, but now there was under his outer seeming a somewhat of restless querulousness, a something of uneasy discontent, that Colonel Singelsby did not remember to have seen there before. They talked together about many things, chiefly of those in the present state of existence in which they found themselves. It was all very new and vivid upon Colonel Singelsby's mind, but the reverend gentleman seemed constantly to forget that he was in another world than that which he had left behind. It seemed to be always with an effort that he brought himself to talk of the world in which he lived as the world of spirits.

The visit was somehow unpleasant to Colonel Singelsby. He was impressed with a certain air of intolerance exhibited by the other. His mind seemed to dwell more upon the falsity of the old things than upon the truth of the new, and he seemed to take a certain delight in showing how and in what everybody but those of his own creed erred and fell short of the Divine intent, and not the least disagreeable part of the talk to Colonel Singelsby was that the other's words seemed to find a sort of echo in his own mind.

At last he proposed a walk, and the other, taking his hat and stick, accompanied him for a little distance upon the way. The talk still clung much to the same stem to which it had adhered all along.

"It is a very strange thing," said the reverend gentleman, "but a great many people who have come to this town since I came hither have left it again to ascend, as I have been told, to a higher state. I think there must have been some mistake, for I cannot see how it is possible—and in fact our teachings distinctly tell us that it is impossible—for one to ascend to a higher state without having accepted the new truths of the new order of things."

Colonel Singelsby did not make answer. He was not only growing tired of the subject itself, but of his old friend as well.

They were at that moment crossing an angle of a small park shaded by thin, spindly trees. As the colonel looked up, he saw three men and a woman approaching along the same path and under the flickering shadows. Two of the men walked a little in advance, the other walked with the woman. There was something familiar about two of the group, and Colonel Singelsby pointed at them with his finger.

"Who are they?" said he. "I am sure there is somebody I know."

The other adjusted his glasses and looked. "I do not know," said he, "except that one of the men is a newcomer. We somehow grow to know who are new-comers by the time we have lived here a little while."

"Dear me!" cried Colonel Singelsby, stopping abruptly, "I know that man. I did not know that he had come here too. I wonder where they are going?"

"I think," said the reverend gentleman, dryly—"I think that this is one of those cases of which I just spoke to you. I judge from the general appearance of the party that they are about to ascend, as they call it here, to a higher state."

"That is impossible!" said Colonel Singelsby. "That man is a poor wretched creature whom I have helped with charity again and again, it cannot be that he is to go to a higher state, for he is not fit for it. If he is to be taken anywhere, it must be to punishment."

The other shrugged his shoulders and said nothing, he had seen such cases too often during his sojourn to be deceived.

The little party had now come close to the two, and Colonel Singelsby stepped forward with all his old-time frank kindness of manner. "Why, Sandy," said he, "I did not know that you also had come here."

"Yes, sir," said Sandy; "I died the same night you did."

"Dear me!" said the colonel, "that is very singular, very singular indeed! Where are you going now, Sandy?"

"I don't know," said Sandy; "these gentlemen here are taking me somewhere, I don't know where. This is my wife," said he. "Don't you remember her, sir?"

"Oh yes," said the colonel, with his most pleasant air, "I remember her very well, but of course I am not so much surprised to see her here as I am to see you. But have you no idea where you are going?" he continued.

"No," said Sandy; "but perhaps these gentlemen can tell you." And he looked inquiringly at his escort, who stood calmly listening to what was said.

★★★★★★★★

So far, the Parable, as I had read it, progressed onward with some coherence and concatenation, a coherence and concatenation growing perhaps more disjointed as it advanced. Now it began to be broken with interjectory sentences, and just here was one, the tenor of which I could not altogether understand, but have since comprehended more or less clearly. I cannot give its exact words, but only its general form.

"O wretched man," it said, "how pitiful are thy vain efforts and strivings to keep back by thine own strength that fiery flood of hell which grows and increases to overwhelm thy soul! If the inflowing of good which Jehovah vouchsafes is infinite, only less infinite is the outflowing of that which thou callest evil and wickedness. How, then, canst thou hope to stand against it and to conquer? How canst thou hope to keep back that raging torrent of fire and of flame with the crumbling unbaked bricks of thine own soul's making?

Poor fool! Thou mayst endeavour, thou mayst strive, thou mayst build thy wall of defence higher and higher, fearing God, and living a life of virtue, but by-and-by thou wilt reach the end, and then wilt find thou canst build no higher! Then how vain shall have been thy life of resistance! First that flood shall trickle over the edge of thy defence; then it shall run a stream the breadth of a man's hand; then it shall gush forth a torrent; then, bursting over and through and around, it shall sweep away all that thou hast so laboriously built up, and shall rush, howling, roaring, raging, and burning through thy soul with ten thousand times the fury and violence that it would have done if thou hadst not striven to keep it back, if thou hadst not resisted and fought against it. For bear this in mind: Christ said he came not to call the good to repentance, but the evil, and if thou art full of thine own, how then canst thou hope to receive of a God that asketh not for sacrifice, but for love?"

Hence again the story resumed.

★★★★★★★★

Colonel Singelsby had not before noticed the two men who were

61

with Sandy, now he observed them more closely. They were tall, middle-aged men, with serious, placid, unemotional faces. Each carried a long white staff, the end of which rested upon the ground. There was about them something somehow different from anything Colonel Singelsby had ever seen before. They were most quiet, courteous men, but there was that in their personal appearance that was singularly unpleasant to Colonel Singelsby. Why, he could not tell, for they were evidently gentlemen, and, from their bearing, men of influence. He turned to Sandy again.

"How has it been with you since you have been here?" said he.

"It has been very hard with me," said Sandy, patiently; "very hard indeed; but I hope and believe now that the worst is over, and that by-and-by I shall be happy, and not have any more trouble."

"I trust so, indeed," said the colonel; "but do not hope for too much, Sandy. Even the best men coming to this world are not likely to be rid of their troubles at once, and it is not to be hoped for that you, after your ill-spent life, should find your lot easier than theirs."

"I know, sir," said Sandy, "and I am very sorry."

There was a meek acceptance of the colonel's *dictum* that grated somehow unpleasantly upon the colonel's ears. He would rather that Sandy had made some protest against that *dictum*. He approached half a step and looked more keenly at the other, and then for the first time he saw that some great, some radical, some tremendous change had happened. The man before him was no doubt Sandy Graff, but all that was low-browed, evil, foul, was gone, as though it had been washed away, and in its place was a translucent, patient meekness, almost like— There was something so terribly vital in that change that Colonel Singelsby shuddered before it. He looked and looked, and then he passed the back of his hand across his eyes. "All this is very unreal," said he, turning to his friend the minister. "It is like a dream. I begin to feel as though nothing was real. Surely it is not possible that magic changes can go on, and yet I cannot understand all these things in the least."

For answer, the reverend gentleman shrugged his shoulders almost sourly.

"Gentlemen," said Colonel Singelsby, turning abruptly upon Sandy's escort, "let me ask you is this a certain man whom I used to know as Sandy Graff?"

One of the men nodded his head.

"And will you tell me," said he, "another thing? Will you kindly tell me where you are taking him?"

"We are about to take him," said the man, looking steadily at the colonel as he answered—"we are about to take him to the outskirts of the First Kingdom."

At the answer Colonel Singelsby actually fell back a pace in his amazement. It was almost as though a blow had fallen upon him. "The outskirts of the First Kingdom?" said he. "Did I understand you? The outskirts of the First Kingdom? Surely there is some mistake here! It is not possible that this man, who died only yesterday, filthy and polluted with iniquity, stinking in the nostrils of God with ten thousand indulged and gratified lusts—it is not possible that you intend taking him to that land, passing by me, who all my life have lived to my best endeavours in love to God and my neighbour?"

It was the voice of his minister that broke the answer. "Yes, they do," said he, sharply; "that is just what they do mean. They do mean to take him, and they do mean to leave us, for such is the law in this dreadful place. We, the children of light, are nothing, and they, the fuel of hell, are everything. Have I not been telling you so?"

Colonel Singelsby had almost forgotten the presence of his acquaintance. He felt very angry at his interference, and somehow, he could no longer govern his anger as he used to do. He turned upon him and fixed him with a frown, and then he observed for the first time that a little crowd had begun gathering, and now stood looking on, some curious and unsmiling, some grinning. The colonel drew himself to his height, and looked haughtily about him.

They who grinned began laughing. And now, at last, it was come Colonel Singelsby's turn to feel as Sandy Graff had felt—as though all that was happening to him was happening in some hideous nightmare dream. As in a dream, the balancing weights of reasoning and morality began to melt before the heat of that which burned within; as in a dream, the uncurbed inner motives began to strive furiously. Then a sudden fierce anger, quite like the savage irrational anger of an ugly dream, flamed up quickly and fiercely.

He opened his lips as though to vent his rage, but for an instant his tottering reason regained a momentary poise. Checking himself with an effort ten thousand times greater than that he would have used in his former state and in the world, he bowed his head upon his breast and stood for a little while with fingers interlocked, clinching his trembling hands together. So, he stood for a while, brooding, until at last Sandy and his escort made a motion as if to pass by. Then he spoke again.

"Stop a bit!" said he, looking up—"stop a bit!" His voice was hoarse and constrained, and he looked neither to the right nor to the left, but straight at that one of the men to whom he had spoken before. "Sir," said he, and then clearing his husky voice—"sir," again, "I have learned a lesson—the greatest lesson of my life! I have looked into my heart, and I have seen—I have seen myself—God help me, gentlemen!—I—maybe I am no better than this man."

The crowd, which had been increasing, as crowds do, began to jeer at the words, for, like most crowds, it was of a nether sort, and enjoyed the unusual sight of the gentleman and the aristocrat abasing and humiliating himself before the reformed drunkard.

At the sound of that ugly jeering laugh Colonel Singelsby quivered as though under the cut of a lancet, but he never removed his eyes from the man to whom he spoke. For a moment or two he bit his nether lip in his effort for self-control, and then repeated, in a louder and perhaps harsher voice, "I am no better than this man!" He paused for a moment, and the crowd ceased its jeering to hear what he had to say. "I ask only this," he said, "that you will take me where you are taking him, and that I may enjoy such happiness as he is about to enjoy."

Instantly a great roar of laughter went up from the crowd, which had now gathered to some twenty or thirty souls. The man to whom Colonel Singelsby had spoken shook his head calmly and impassively.

"It cannot be," said he.

Colonel Singelsby turned white to the very lips, his eyes blazed, and his breath came thick and heavily. His nostrils twitched spasmodically, but still, with a supreme effort—a struggle so terrible that few men happily may ever know it or experience it—he once more controlled the words that sprang to his lips and struggled for utterance. He swallowed and swallowed convulsively.

"Sir," said he at last, in a voice so hoarse, so horribly constrained, that it seemed almost to rend him as it forced utterance—"sir, surely I am mistaken in what I understand; it is little I ask you, and surely not unjust. Yesterday this man was a vile, debauched drunkard; surely that does not make him fitter for heaven! Yesterday I was a God-fearing, law-abiding man, surely that does not make me unfit! I am not unfit, am I?"

"You are not yet fit for heaven," answered the man, with impassive calmness. And again, for the third time, the crowd roared with evil laughter.

Within Colonel Singelsby's soul that fiery flood was now lashing dreadfully close to the summit of its barriers. His face was as livid as death, and his hands were clinched till the nails cut into his palm. "Let me understand for once and for all, for I confess I cannot understand all this. You say he is to go, and that I am not to go! Is it, then, God's will and God's justice that because this man for twenty years has led a life of besotted sin and indulgence, and because I for sixty years have feared God and loved my neighbour, that he is to be chosen and I am to be left?"

The man did not reply in words, but in the steady look of his unwinking eyes the other read his answer.

"Then," gasped Colonel Singelsby, and as he spoke he shook his clinched and trembling fist against the still, blue sky overhead—"then, if that be God's justice, may it be damned, for I want none of it."

Then came the end, swiftly, completely. For the fourth time the crowd laughed, and at the sound those floodgates so laboriously built up during a lifetime of abstinence were suddenly burst asunder and fell crashing, and a burning flood of hell's own rage and madness rushed roaring and thundering into his depicted, empty soul, flaming, blazing, consuming like straws every precept of righteousness, every fear of God, and Colonel Edward Singelsby, the one-time Christian gentleman, the one-time upright son of grace, the one-time man of law and God, was transformed instantly and terribly into—what? Was it a livid devil from hell? He cursed the jeering crowd, and at the sound of his own curses a blindness fell upon him, and he neither knew what he said nor what he did.

His good old friend, who had accompanied him so far and until now had stood by him, suddenly turned, and maybe fearing lest some thunderbolt of vengeance should fall upon them from heaven and consume them all, he elbowed himself out of the crowd and hurried away. As for the wretched madman, in his raging fury, it was not the men who had forbidden him heaven whom he strove to rend and tear limb from limb, but poor, innocent, harmless Sandy Graff. The crowd swayed and jostled this way and that, and as madness begets madness, the curses that fell from one pair of lips found an echo in curses that leaped from others. Sandy shrunk back appalled before the hell-blast that breathed upon him, and he felt his wife clutch him closer.

Only two of those that were there stood unmoved; they were the two men who acted as Sandy's escort. As the tide of madness seemed to swell higher, they calmly stepped forward and crossed their staves before their charge. There was something in their action full of significance for those who knew. Instantly the crowd melted away like snow under a blast of fire. Had there not been two men present more merciful than the rest, it is hard to say what terrible thing might not have happened to Colonel Edward Singelsby—deaf and dumb and blind to everything but his own rage. These two clutched him by the arms and dragged him back.

"God, man!" they cried, "what are you doing? Do you not see they are angels?"

They dragged him back to a bench that stood near, and there held him, whilst he still beat the air with his fist and cried out hoarse curses, and even as they so held him, two other men came—two men dark, silent, sinister—and led him away.

Then the other and his wife and his two escorts passed by and out of the gate of the town, and away towards the mountain that stood still and blue in the distance.

★★★★★★★★

So far, I read, and then I could bear to read no more, but placed my hand upon the open page of the book. "What is this dreadful thing?" I cried. "Is, then, a man punished for truth and justice and virtue and righteousness? Is it, then, true that the evil are rewarded, and that the good are punished so dreadfully?"

Then the man who held the book spoke again. "Take away thy hand and read," said he.

Then I took away my hand, and read as he bade me, and found these words:

"How can God fill with His own that which is already filled by man? First it must be emptied before it may be filled with the true good of righteousness and truth, of humility and love, of peace and joy. O thou foolish one who judgest but from the appearance of things, how long will it be before thou canst understand that while some may be baptised with water to cleanliness and repentance, others are baptized with living fire to everlasting life, and that they alone are the children of God?"

Then again I read these words:

"Woe to thee, thou who deniest the laws of God and man! Woe to thee, thou who walkest in the darkness of the shadow of sin and evil! But ten thousand times woe to thee, thou who pilest Pelion of self-good upon Ossa of self-truth, not that thou mayst scale therefrom the gate of Heaven, but that thou mayst hide thyself beneath from the eye of the Living God! By-and-by His Day shall come! His Terrible Lightning shall flash from the East to the West! His Dreadful Flaming

Thunder-bolt shall fall, riving thy secret fastnesses to atoms, and leaving thee, poor worm, writhing in the dazzling effulgence of His Light, and shrivelling beneath the consuming flame of His Loving-kindness!"
Then the leaf was turned, and there before me lay the answer to that first question, "What shall a man do that he may gain the kingdom of Heaven?" There stood the words, plain and clear. But I did not dare to read them, but turning, left that place, shutting the door to behind me. Never have I found that door or entered that room again, but by-and-by I know that I shall find them both once more, and shall then and there read the answer that forever stands written in that book, for it still lies open at the very page, and he upon whose knees it rests is Israfeel, the Angel of Death.

★★★★★★★★

But what of the sequel? Is there a sequel? Are we, then, to suffer ourselves to do evil for the sake of shunning pain in the other world? I trow not! He who sets his foot to climb must never look backward and downward. He who suffers most must reach the highest. There must be another part of the story which lies darkly and dimly behind the letter. One can see, faintly and dimly but nevertheless clearly, what the poor man was to enjoy—the poor man who from without appeared to be so evil, and yet within was not really evil. One can see a vision faint and dim of a simple little house cooled by the dewy shade of green trees forever in foliage; one can see pleasant meadows and gardens forever green, stretching away to the banks of a smooth-flowing river in whose level bosom rests a mirrored image of that which lies beyond its farther bank—a great town with glistering walls and gleaming spires reaching tower above tower and height above height into the blazing blue, the awful serenity of a heavenly sky.

One can know that toward that town the poor man who had sinned and repented would in the evenings gaze and wonder until his soul, now ploughed clean for new seed, might learn the laws that would make it indeed an inhabitant of that place. It is a serene and beautiful vision, but not different from that which all may see, and enjoy even, in part, in this world.

But how was it with that other man—with that good man who had never sinned until his earthly body was stripped away that he might sin and fall in the spirit—sin and fall to a depth so profound that even one furtive look into that awful abysm makes the minds of common men to reel and stagger? When that God-sent blast of fire should have burned out the selfhood that clung to the very vitals of his soul, what then? Who is there that with unwinking eyes may gaze into the effulgent brilliancy of the perfect angelhood? He who sweats drops of salt in his life's inner struggles shall, maybe, eat good bread in the dew of it, but he who sweats drops of blood in agony shall, when his labour is done, sit him, maybe, at the King's table, and feast upon the Flesh of Life and the very Wine of Truth.

Was it so with that man who never sinned until all his hell was let loose at once upon him?

The Little Room

By Madeline Yale Wynne

"How would it do for a smoking-room?"

"Just the very place; only, you know, Roger, you must not think of smoking in the house. I am almost afraid having just a plain common man around, let alone a smoking-man, will upset Aunt Hannah. She is New England—Vermont New England boiled down."

"You leave Aunt Hannah to me; I shall find her tender side. I am going to ask her about the old sea-captain and the yellow calico."

"Not yellow calico—blue chintz."

"Well, yellow *shell*, then."

"No, no! don't mix it up so; you won't know yourself what to expect, and that's half the fun."

"Now you tell me again exactly what to expect; to tell the truth, I didn't half hear about it the other day; I was wool-gathering. It was something queer that happened when you were a child, wasn't it?"

"Something that began to happen long before that, and kept happening, and may happen again; but I hope not."

"What was it?"

"I wonder if the other people in the car can hear us?"

"I fancy not; we don't hear them—not consecutively, at least."

"Well, mother was born in Vermont, you know; she was the only child by a second marriage. Aunt Hannah and Aunt Maria are only half-aunts to me, you know."

"I hope they are half as nice as you are."

"Roger, be still; they certainly will hear us."

"Well, don't you want them to know we are married?"

"Yes, but not just married. There's all the difference in the world."

"You are afraid we look too happy!"

"No; only I want my happiness all to myself."

"Well, the little room?"

"My aunts brought mother up; they were nearly twenty years older than she. I might say Hiram and they brought her up. You see, Hiram was bound out to my grandfather when he was a boy, and when grandfather died Hiram said he 's'posed he went with the farm, 'long o' the critters,' and he has been there ever since. He was my mother's only refuge from the decorum of my aunts. They are simply workers. They make me think of the Maine woman who wanted her epitaph to be, 'She was a *hard* working woman.'"

"They must be almost beyond their working-days. How old are they?"

"Seventy, or thereabouts; but they will die standing; or, at least, on a Saturday night, after all the housework is done up. They were rather strict with mother, and I think she had a lonely childhood. The house is almost a mile away from any neighbours, and off on top of what they call Stony Hill. It is bleak enough up there even in summer.

"When mamma was about ten years old, they sent her to cousins in Brooklyn, who had children of their own, and knew more about bringing them up. She stayed there till she was married; she didn't go to Vermont in all that time, and of course hadn't seen her sisters, for they never would leave home for a day. They couldn't even be induced to go to Brooklyn to her wedding, so she and father took their wedding-trip up there."

"And that's why we are going up there on our own?"

"Don't, Roger; you have no idea how loud you speak."

"You never say so except when I am going to say that one little word."

"Well, don't say it, then, or say it very, very quietly."

"Well, what was the queer thing?"

"When they got to the house, mother wanted to take father right off into the little room; she had been telling him about it, just as I am going to tell you, and she had said that of all the rooms, that one was the only one that seemed pleasant to her. She described the furniture and the books and paper and everything, and said it was on the north side, between the front and back room. Well, when they went to look for it, there was no little room there; there was only a shallow china-closet. She asked her sisters when the house had been altered and a closet made of the room that used to be there. They both said the house was exactly as it had been built—that they had never made any changes, except to tear down the old wood-shed and build a smaller one.

"Father and mother laughed a good deal over it, and when any-thing was lost, they would always say it must be in the little room, and any exaggerated statement was called 'little-roomy.' When I was a child, I thought that was a regular English phrase, I heard it so often.

"Well, they talked it over, and finally they concluded that my mother had been a very imaginative sort of a child, and had read in some book about such a little room, or perhaps even dreamed it, and then had 'made believe,' as children do, till she herself had really thought the room was there."

"Why, of course, that might easily happen."

"Yes, but you haven't heard the queer part yet; you wait and see if you can explain the rest as easily.

"They stayed at the farm two weeks, and then went to New York to live. When I was eight years old my father was killed in the war, and mother was broken-hearted. She never was quite strong afterwards, and that summer we decided to go up to the farm for three months.

"I was a restless sort of a child, and the journey seemed very long to me; and finally, to pass the time, mamma told me the story of the little room, and how it was all in her own imagination, and how there really was only a china-closet there.

"She told it with all the particulars; and even to me, who knew be-forehand that the room wasn't there, it seemed just as real as could be. She said it was on the north side, between the front and back rooms; that it was very small, and they sometimes called it an entry. There was a door also that opened out-of-doors, and that one was painted green, and was cut in the middle like the old Dutch doors, so that it could be used for a window by opening the top part only. Directly opposite the door was a lounge or couch; it was covered with blue chintz—India chintz—some that had been brought over by an old Salem sea-captain as a 'venture.' He had given it to Maria when she was a young girl. She was sent to Salem for two years to school. Grandfather originally came from Salem."

"I thought there wasn't any room or chintz."

"*That is just it.* They had decided that mother had imagined it all, and yet you see how exactly everything was painted in her mind, for she had even remembered that Hiram had told her that Maria could have married the sea-captain if she had wanted to!

"The India cotton was the regular blue-stamped chintz, with the peacock figure on it. The head and body of the bird were in profile, while the tail was full front view behind it. It had seemed to take mamma's fancy, and she drew it for me on a piece of paper as she talked. Doesn't it seem strange to you that she could have made all that up, or even dreamed it?

"At the foot of the lounge were some hanging-shelves with some old books on them. All the books were leather-coloured except one; that was bright red, and was called the *Ladies' Album*. It made a bright break between the other thicker books.

"On the lower shelf was a beautiful pink sea-shell, lying on a mat made of balls of red-shaded worsted. This shell was greatly coveted by mother, but she was only allowed to play with it when she had been particularly good. Hiram had showed her how to hold it close to her ear and hear the roar of the sea in it.

"I know you will like Hiram, Roger, he is quite a character in his way.

"Mamma said she remembered, or *thought* she remembered, having been sick once, and she had to lie quietly for some days on the lounge; then was the time she had become so familiar with everything in the room, and she had been allowed to have the shell to play with all the time. She had had her toast brought to her in there, with make-believe tea. It was one of her pleasant memories of her childhood; it was the first time she had been of any importance to anybody, even herself.

"Right at the head of the lounge was a light-stand, as they called it, and on it was a very brightly polished brass candlestick and a brass tray, with snuffers. That is all I remember of her describing, except that there was a braided rag rug on the floor, and on the wall was a beautiful flowered paper—roses and morning-glories in a wreath on a light-blue ground. The same paper was in the front room."

"And all this never existed except in her imagination?"

"She said that when she and father went up there, there wasn't any little room at all like it anywhere in the house; there was a china-closet where she had believed the room to be."

"And your aunts said there had never been any such room?"

"That is what they said."

"Wasn't there any blue chintz in the house with a peacock figure?"

"Not a scrap, and Aunt Hannah said there had never been any that she could remember; and Maria just echoed her—she always does that. You see, Aunt Hannah is an up-and-down New England woman. She looks just like herself; I mean, just like her character. Her joints move up and down or backward and forward in a plain square fashion. I don't believe she ever leaned on anything in her life, or sat in an easy-chair. But Maria is different; she is rounder and softer; she hasn't any ideas of her own; she never had any. I don't believe she would think it right or becoming to have one that differed from Aunt Hannah's, so what would be the use of having any? She is an echo, that's all.

"When mamma and I got there, of course I was all excitement to see the china-closet, and I had a sort of feeling that it would be the little room after all. So, I ran ahead and threw open the door, crying, 'Come and see the little room.'

"And, Roger," said Mrs. Grant, laying her hand in his, "there really was a little room there, exactly as mother had remembered it. There was the lounge, the peacock chintz, the green door, the shell, the morning-glory and rose paper, *everything exactly as she had described it to me.*"

"What in the world did the sisters say about it?"

"Wait a minute and I will tell you. My mother was in the front hall still talking with Aunt Hannah. She didn't hear me at first, but I ran out there and dragged her through the front room, saying, 'The room *is* here—it is all right.'

"It seemed for a minute as if my mother would faint. She clung to me in terror. I can remember now how strained her eyes looked and how pale she was.

"I called out to Aunt Hannah and asked her when they had had the closet taken away and the little room built; for in my excitement I thought that that was what had been done.

"'That little room has always been there,' said Aunt Hannah, 'ever since the house was built.'

"'But mamma said there wasn't any little room here, only a china-closet, when she was here with papa,' said I.

"'No, there has never been any china-closet there; it has always been just as it is now,' said Aunt Hannah.

"Then mother spoke; her voice sounded weak and far off. She said, slowly, and with an effort, 'Maria, don't you remember that you told me that there had *never been any little room here*? and Hannah said so too, and then I said I must have dreamed it?'

"'No, I don't remember anything of the kind,' said Maria, without the slightest emotion. 'I don't remember you ever said anything about any china-closet. The house has never been altered; you used to play in this room when you were a child, don't you remember?'

"'I know it,' said mother, in that queer slow voice that made me feel frightened. 'Hannah, don't you remember my finding the china-closet here, with the gilt-edge china on the shelves, and then *you* said that the *china-closet* had always been here?'

"'No,' said Hannah, pleasantly but unemotionally—'no, I don't think you ever asked me about any china-closet, and we haven't any gilt-edged china that I know of.'

"And that was the strangest thing about it. We never could make them remember that there had ever been any question about it. You would think they could remember how surprised mother had been before, unless she had imagined the whole thing. Oh, it was so queer! They were always pleasant about it, but they didn't seem to feel any interest or curiosity. It was always this answer: 'The house is just as it was built; there have never been any changes, so far as we know.'

"And my mother was in an agony of perplexity. How cold their grey eyes looked to me! There was no reading anything in them. It just seemed to break my mother down, this queer thing. Many times that summer, in the middle of the night, I have seen her get up and take a candle and creep softly downstairs. I could hear the steps creak under her weight. Then she would go through the front room and peer into the darkness, holding her thin hand between the candle and her eyes. She seemed to think the little room might vanish. Then she would come back to bed and toss about all night, or lie still and shiver; it used to frighten me.

"She grew pale and thin, and she had a little cough; then she did not like to be left alone. Sometimes she would make errands in order to send me to the little room for something—a book, or her fan, or her handkerchief; but she would never sit there or let me stay in there long, and sometimes she wouldn't let me go in there for days together. Oh, it was pitiful!"

"Well, don't talk any more about it, Margaret, if it makes you feel so," said Mr. Grant.

"Oh yes, I want you to know all about it, and there isn't much more—no more about the room.

"Mother never got well, and she died that autumn. She used often to sigh, and say, with a wan little laugh, 'There is one thing I am glad of, Margaret: your father knows now all about the little room.' I think she was afraid I distrusted her. Of course, in a child's way, I thought there was something queer about it, but I did not brood over it. I was too young then, and took it as a part of her illness. But, Roger, do you know, it really did affect me. I almost hate to go there after talking about it; I somehow feel as if it might, you know, be a china-closet again."

"That's an absurd idea."

"I know it; of course, it can't be. I saw the room, and there isn't any china-closet there, and no gilt-edged china in the house, either."

And then she whispered, "But, Roger, you may hold my hand as you do now, if you will, when we go to look for the little room."

"And you won't mind Aunt Hannah's grey eyes?"

"I won't mind *anything*."

It was dusk when Mr. and Mrs. Grant went into the gate under the two old Lombardy poplars and walked up the narrow path to the door, where they were met by the two aunts.

Hannah gave Mrs. Grant a frigid but not unfriendly kiss; and Maria seemed for a moment to tremble on the verge of an emotion, but she glanced at Hannah, and then gave her greeting in exactly the same repressed and non-committal way.

Supper was waiting for them. On the table was the *gilt-edged china*. Mrs. Grant didn't notice it immediately, till she saw her husband smiling at her over his teacup; then she felt fidgety, and couldn't eat. She was nervous, and kept wondering what was behind her, whether it would be a little room or a closet.

After supper she offered to help about the dishes, but, mercy! she might as well have offered to help bring the seasons round; Maria and Hannah couldn't be helped.

So, she and her husband went to find the little room, or closet, or whatever was to be there.

Aunt Maria followed them, carrying the lamp, which she set down, and then went back to the dish-washing.

Margaret looked at her husband. He kissed her, for she seemed troubled; and then, hand in hand, they opened the door. It opened into a *china-closet*. The shelves were neatly draped with scalloped paper; on them was the gilt-edged china, with the dishes missing that had been used at the supper, and which at that moment were being carefully washed and wiped by the two aunts.

Margaret's husband dropped her hand and looked at her. She was trembling a little, and turned to him for help, for some explanation, but in an instant, she knew that something was wrong. A cloud had come between them; he was hurt; he was antagonised.

He paused for an appreciable instant, and then said, kindly enough, but in a voice that cut her deeply:

"I am glad this ridiculous thing is ended; don't let us speak of it again."

"Ended!" said she. "How ended?" And somehow her voice sounded to her as her mother's voice had when she stood there and questioned her sisters about the little room. She seemed to have to drag her words out. She spoke slowly: "It seems to me to have only just begun in my case. It was just so with mother when she—"

"I really wish, Margaret, you would let it drop. I don't like to hear you speak of your mother in connection with it. It—" He hesitated, for was not this their wedding-day? "It doesn't seem quite the thing, quite delicate, you know, to use her name in the matter."

She saw it all now: *he didn't believe her.* She felt a chill sense of withering under his glance.

"Come," he added, "let us go out, or into the dining-room, somewhere, anywhere, only drop this nonsense."

He went out; he did not take her hand now—he was vexed, baffled, hurt. Had he not given her his sympathy, his attention, his belief—and his hand?—and she was fooling him. What did it mean?—she so truthful, so free from morbidness—a thing he hated. He walked up and down under the poplars, trying to get into the mood to go and join her in the house.

Margaret heard him go out; then she turned and shook the shelves; she reached her hand behind them and tried to push the boards away; she ran out of the house on to the north side and tried to find in the darkness, with her hands, a door, or some steps leading to one. She tore her dress on the old rose-tree, she fell and rose and stumbled, then she sat down on the ground and tried to think. What could she think—was she dreaming?

She went into the house and out into the kitchen, and begged Aunt Maria to tell her about the little room—what had become of it, when had they built the closet, when had they bought the gilt-edged china?

They went on washing dishes and drying them on the spotless towels with methodical exactness; and as they worked they said that there had never been any little room, so far as they knew; the china-closet had always been there, and the gilt-edged china had belonged to their mother, it had always been in the house.

"No, I don't remember that your mother ever asked about any little room," said Hannah. "She didn't seem very well that summer, but she never asked about any changes in the house; there hadn't ever been any changes."

There it was again: not sign of interest, curiosity, or annoyance, not a spark of memory.

She went out to Hiram. He was telling Mr. Grant about the farm. She had meant to ask him about the room, but her lips were sealed before her husband.

Months afterwards, when time had lessened the sharpness of their feelings, they learned to speculate reasonably about the phenomenon, which Mr. Grant had accepted as something not to be scoffed away, not to be treated as a poor joke, but to be put aside as something inexplicable on any ordinary theory.

Margaret alone in her heart knew that her mother's words carried a deeper significance than she had dreamed of at the time. "One thing I am glad of, your father knows now," and she wondered if Roger or she would ever know.

Five years later they were going to Europe. The packing was done; the children were lying asleep, with their travelling things ready to be slipped on for an early start.

Roger had a foreign appointment. They were not to be back in America for some years. She had meant to go up to say goodbye to her aunts; but a mother of three children intends to do a great many things that never get done. One thing she had done that very day, and as she paused for a moment between the writing of two notes that must be posted before she went to bed, she said:

"Roger, you remember Rita Lash? Well, she and Cousin Nan go up to the Adirondacks every autumn. They are clever girls, and I have intrusted to them something I want done very much."

"They are the girls to do it, then, every inch of them."

"I know it, and they are going to."

"Well?"

"Why, you see, Roger, that little room—"

"Oh—"

"Yes, I was a coward not to go myself, but I didn't find time, because I hadn't the courage."

"Oh! *that* was it, was it?"

"Yes, just that. They are going, and they will write us about it."

"Want to bet?"

"No; I only want to know."

★★★★★★★★

Rita Lash and Cousin Nan planned to go to Vermont on their way to the Adirondacks. They found they would have three hours between trains, which would give them time to drive up to the Keys farm, and they could still get to the camp that night. But, at the last minute, Rita was prevented from going. Nan had to go to meet the Adirondack party, and she promised to telegraph her when she arrived at the camp. Imagine Rita's amusement when she received this message:

"Safely arrived; went to the Keys farm; it is a little room."

Rita was amused, because she did not in the least think Nan had been there. She thought it was a hoax; but it put it into her mind to carry the joke further by really stopping herself when she went up, as she meant to do the next week.

She did stop over. She introduced herself to the two maiden ladies, who seemed familiar, as they had been described by Mrs. Grant.

They were, if not cordial, at least not disconcerted at her visit, and willingly showed her over the house. As they did not speak of any other stranger's having been to see them lately, she became confirmed in her belief that Nan had not been there.

In the north room she saw the roses and morning-glory paper on the wall, and also the door that should open into—what?

She asked if she might open it.

"Certainly," said Hannah; and Maria echoed, "Certainly."

She opened it, and found the china-closet. She experienced a certain relief; she at least was not under any spell. Mrs. Grant left it a china-closet; she found it the same. Good.

But she tried to induce the old sisters to remember that there had at various times been certain questions relating to a confusion as to whether the closet had always been a closet. It was no use; their stony eyes gave no sign.

Then she thought of the story of the sea-captain, and said, "Miss Keys, did you ever have a lounge covered with India chintz, with a figure of a peacock on it, given to you in Salem by a sea-captain, who brought it from India?"

"I dun'no' as I ever did," said Hannah. That was all. She thought Maria's cheeks were a little flushed, but her eyes were like a stone-wall.

She went on that night to the Adirondacks. When Nan and she were alone in their room she said. "By-the-way, Nan, what did you see at the farmhouse? and how did you like Maria and Hannah?"

Nan didn't mistrust that Rita had been there, and she began excitedly to tell her all about her visit. Rita could almost have believed Nan had been there if she hadn't known it was not so. She let her go on for some time, enjoying her enthusiasm, and the impressive way in which she described her opening the door and finding the "little room." Then Rita said: "Now, Nan, that is enough fibbing. I went to the farm myself on my way up yesterday, and there is *no* little room, and there *never* has been any; it is a china-closet, just as Mrs. Grant saw it last."

She was pretending to be busy unpacking her trunk, and did not look up for a moment; but as Nan did not say anything, she glanced at her over her shoulder. Nan was actually pale, and it was hard to say whether she was most angry or frightened. There was something of both in her look. And then Rita began to explain how her telegram had put her in the spirit of going up there alone. She hadn't meant to cut Nan out. She only thought—Then Nan broke in: "It isn't that; I am sure you can't think it is that. But I went myself, and you did not go; you can't have been there, for *it is a little room*."

Oh, what a night they had! They couldn't sleep. They talked and argued, and then kept still for a while, only to break out again, it was so absurd. They both maintained that they had been there, but both felt sure the other one was either crazy or obstinate beyond reason. They were wretched; it was perfectly ridiculous, two friends at odds over such a thing; but there it was—"little room," "china-closet,"—"china-closet," "little room."

The next morning Nan was tacking up some tarlatan at a window to keep the midges out. Rita offered to help her, as she had done for the past ten years. Nan's "No, thanks," cut her to the heart.

"Nan," said she, "come right down from that stepladder and pack your satchel. The stage leaves in just twenty minutes. We can catch the afternoon express train, and we will go together to the farm. I am either going there or going home. You better go with me."

Nan didn't say a word. She gathered up the hammer and tacks, and was ready to start when the stage came round.

It meant for them thirty miles of staging and six hours of train, besides crossing the lake; but what of that, compared with having a lie lying round loose between them! Europe would have seemed easy to accomplish, if it would settle the question.

At the little junction in Vermont they found a farmer with a wagon full of meal-bags. They asked him if he could not take them up to the old Keys farm and bring them back in time for the return train, due in two hours.

They had planned to call it a sketching trip, so they said, "We have been there before, we are artists, and we might find some views worth taking, and we want also to make a short call upon the Misses Keys."

"Did ye calculate to paint the old *house* in the picture?"

They said it was possible they might do so. They wanted to see it, anyway.

"Waal, I guess you are too late. The *house* burnt down last night, and everything in it."

The Bringing of the Rose

By Harriet Lewis Bradley

For certain subjects one of the most valuable works of reference in all Berlin was Miss Olivia Valentine's *Adress-buch,* the contents of which were self-collected, self-tested, and abounded in extensive information concerning hotels and pensions, apartments and restaurants, families offering German home life with the language, instructors, and courses of lectures, doctors, dentists, dressmakers, milliners, the most direct way to Mendelssohn's grave in the Alte Dreifaltigkeits-Kirchhof, how to find lodgings in Baireuth during the Wagner festival, where to stay in Oberammergau, if it happened to be the year of the Passion Play, and so on, indefinitely.

Miss Valentine herself was a kind-hearted, middle-aged woman, who, as the result of much sojourning in foreign lands, possessed an intelligent knowledge of subjects likely to be of use to other sojourners, and who was cordially ready to share the same, according to the needs of the season. If it were November, people came asking in what manner they could take most profitable advantage of a Berlin winter; if it were approaching spring, they wanted addresses for Paris or Switzerland or Italy. It was March now and Sunday afternoon. Mr. Morris Davidson sat by Miss Valentine's table, the famous *Adress-buch* in his hand. "I suppose you don't undertake starting parties for heaven?" he said, opening the book. "Ah! here it is—'*Himmel und Hoelle.*' I might have known it, you are so thorough."

"If you read a little further," remarked Miss Valentine, "you will see that '*Himmel und Hoelle*' is a German game."

"Oh yes, I remember now; we play it at our pension. It's that game where you say 'thou' to the you-people, and 'you' to the thou-people, and are expected to address strange ladies whom you are meeting for the first time as Klara and Charlotte and Wilhelmine, with most embarrassing familiarity, and it is very stupid if the game happens to send you to heaven. I wonder if there really is such a locality? I've been thinking lately I should like to go there; things don't seem to agree with me very well here. I've closed my books, walked the Thiergarten threadbare, sleep twelve hours out of twenty-four, do everything I've been told to do, with no result whatever except to grow duller." The young man yawned as he spoke. "Do excuse me; I've come to such a pass that I'm not able to look any one in the face without yawning. All things considered, I am afraid I shouldn't be any better off in heaven. I'm afraid I couldn't stand the people, there must be so many of them. I want to get away from people."

"I know exactly where to send you," said Miss Valentine. "I was thinking about it when you came in. It isn't heaven, but it is very near it, and it also begins with H; and you are sure to like it—that is, unless you object to the ghost."

"Oh, not in the least; only is the rest of it all right? Things are not, generally; either the drainage is bad or there is a haunted room, and everyone who sleeps in it dies, and of course one cannot help sleeping in it, just to see how it is going to work."

"Nothing of the kind," returned Miss Valentine; "the drainage is excellent; and as for the haunted room, I once shared it half a summer with a niece and namesake of mine, and we were never troubled by any unusual occurrence, and we are both in excellent health and likely to remain so. The ghost is reported to have a Mona Lisa face, to be dressed in black, with something white and fluffy at the neck and sleeves, gold bracelets, a necklace and ring of black pearls, and she carries a rose. If her appearance means death or misfortune, the rose is white; if she is only straying about in a friendly way, the rose is red.

"The place is called the Halden—the Hillside. I have taken the precaution to state vaguely that it is in the neighbourhood of Zurich; I want to do all in my power to keep the spot unspoiled. There is so little left in Switzerland that is not tired of being looked at—the trees are tired, and the grass, and the waterfalls; but here is a sweet hidden-away nook, where everything is as fresh as before the days of foreign travel. I am going to provide you with the directions for finding it."

She sat down by the writing-desk, and presently gave a slip of paper to Morris Davidson, who put it carefully in his pocket-book.

"The castle of the Halden," Miss Valentine continued, "belonged to a certain countess, by name Maria Regina. There is a tradition that one night a mist coming down from the mountain concealed the castle from the village, and when it lifted, behold! the countess and her entire household had vanished forever, and not a word was ever heard from them again. The ghost-lady is supposed to be a sister of the Countess Maria Regina, and in some way connected with the death of a young Austrian officer who figures as a lover in the story; just whose lover no one seems to know, but it is surmised of Maria Regina's daughter, said to be a very aristocratic and haughty young person. The castle remained closed after this mysterious occurrence for about two hundred years, and then an enterprising Swiss-German had it put in order for a summer hotel. What are you doing? I believe you are making extracts from my '*Adress-buch.*' Now that is something I never allow. I like to give out information discriminately, with personal explanations."

The young man showed what he had written. "Just a hint or two for Italy," he said. "I may go down there next week. If I do, I shall certainly turn aside and tarry a little at your Halden. I should like to try whether your ghost-lady would lead me into any adventure."

Miss Valentine did not see Morris Davidson again, but a few weeks later she received a letter bearing a Swiss postmark:

Dear Miss Valentine—I am here, and in order to give complete proof of it I sacrifice my prejudice and write on ruled paper, with purple ink and an unpleasant pen, that it may be all of the Halden. The place is exactly what I wanted and needed. I am so delighted to have it to myself. I am the only guest in the castle, the only stranger in the town. I came to stay a day; I intend now to stay a week. Yesterday, my first whole day, was perfect. I went by train to Muehlehorn, and walked from there to Wallenstadt, came back for dinner, and in the afternoon climbed the hill to Amden, where I found a *hepatica* in bloom, and had a beautiful view of the sunset. This morning there is a mist on the mountains, which is slowly rising, so I am using the time for letter-writing. Mountain-climbing is not yet inviting, owing to the snow; but, on the whole, the season of the year is not at all unfavourable.

The loneliness is what I like best. The people do not interest me; I avoid them, and must appear in their eyes even more deluded than I am to come to this secluded spot at this unseasonable moment and be satisfied with my own society—no, not my own society, but that of these kind brotherly mountains. From a prosaic pedant I can almost feel myself becoming an ecstatical hermit, and my soul getting ready to—

. . . smooth itself out a long cramped scroll.
Freshening and fluttering in the wind.

—What a solid satisfaction it is to have a few days free from railroad travel! I have made a roundabout journey, coming here by way of Dresden, Leipsic, Cologne, Bonn, Frankfort, Heidelberg, Strasburg, Freiburg, Basel, and Zurich. It was all pleasant, but I am glad it is over. Please never advertise the Halden as a health-resort; let it remain a complete secret between us two, so that when we wish to leave everything and hermitise we may have the opportunity. If it were not for betraying this secret, I should like to recommend the castle for its generosity.

At breakfast I have put beside my plate a five-pound loaf of bread, one slice of which is fifteen inches long by six wide, and thick *ad libitum* dimensions, the delicacy of which even a Prussian soldier would call into question.

I haven't attempted to tell you what I think of your Halden. It is impossible. I simply give myself over to a few days of happiness and rest; all too soon I shall have to face the busy world again.

> Most gratefully yours,
>
> Morris Davidson.

P.S.—I have not yet seen the ghost-lady. I thought I heard her footstep last night in the hall and a rustling at my door. I opened it, half expecting to find a rose upon the threshold. I found nothing, saw nothing.

The letter was dated March 13th, and contained a pressed *hepatica*. Some two months later another letter came. It said:

I am still here. My Italian journey melted into a Swiss sojourn. If I stay much longer, I shall not dare to go away, I feel so safe under the care of these wonderful mountains. What words has one to describe them, with their fulness of content, of majesty and mystery? I go daily up the time-worn steps behind the castle, throw myself on the grass, count the poplar-trees rising from the plain below, try to make out where earth ends and heaven begins as the white May clouds meet the snowdrifts on the mountain-tops. I am working a little again, but tramping a good deal more. I have not been so happy since I was a boy. In a certain sense I have died here, unaided by the apparition with the rose, unless, indeed, she has come in my sleep, and that of course would not count.

I have died, because surely all that death can ever mean is the putting away of something no longer needed, and therefore we die daily—one day most of all. But although I have never seen the ghost-lady, I have every reason to have perfect faith in her existence. I was talking with our landlord's aged mother about it today. She carefully closed the door when the conversation turned in this direction, begging me never to mention the subject before the servants, and then in a half-whisper she gave me exactly the same description that you did in Berlin.

Early in June a third letter came:

Will you believe me when I say I have not only seen *Her*, but *Them*; that I have sat with Them, and talked with Them—the lost ladies of the Hill-side—with the Countess Maria Regina, the proud daughter, the mysterious sister? No, certainly you will not believe me.

I write nothing here of the physical results of my stay. Enough that I am ready for work; that I love my fellow-men; that I no longer dread to go to heaven for fear of their society; that I have formed an intimate friendship with the village weaver and priest and postmaster; that when we part, as we shall tomorrow, it will be affectionately and regretfully.

All this you know, or have guessed. What I am about to tell, you do not know, and can never guess.

It had been raining for a week. You remember what it is like here when it rains—how damp, sticky, discouraging; how cold the stone floor; how wet the fountain splashes when one goes through the court to dinner. I was driven to taking walks in the hall outside my room by way of exercise, and thus discovered in a certain dark corner a low door to which I eventually succeeded in finding a key.

This door led me into an unused tower dimly lighted, hung with cobwebs, and filled with old red velvet furniture. I sat down on a sofa, and before long became conscious that I was being gazed upon by a haughty young woman, with an aristocratic nose, large dark eyes, hair caught back by tortoise-shell combs under a peculiar head-dress, having a gleam of gold directly on the top. Her gown was of dark green, with white puffs let into the sleeves below the elbows; around her tapering waist was a narrow belt of jewels; the front of her corsage was also trimmed with jewels.

But the most distinctive feature of her costume consisted in a floating scarf of old-rose, worn like the frontispiece lady in some volume of *Keepsake* or *Token*. Imagine meeting such a being as this unexpectedly in the long-closed tower-room of a castle after a week of Swiss rain! I forgot time, weather, locality, individuality; I began to think, in fact, that I myself might be the young Austrian officer who was murdered. Presently I noticed that my haughty young woman had a chaperon—a lady wearing a light green picturesquely shaped hood; a kerchief of the same shade bordered with golden tassels; a necklace of dark beads, from which hung a crucifix. She was not pretty, but had very plump red cheeks, and held a little dog. I learned, on nearer acquaintance, that this was the Countess Maria Regina, and as she then appeared so she had looked in the year 1695.

We sat for a while silently regarding each other, Maria Regina's cheek seeming all the time to grow deeper in colour, the point in which the green hood terminated more and more distinct, the little dog making ready to bark, the daughter with the floating scarf prouder and prouder, and I, as the Austrian officer, hardly daring to move, lest the sister with the rose should join the group, and that perhaps be the end of me, when I had the happy thought of going in search of her, and thus breaking the spell, and preventing the mischief which might occur should she come uninvited. I left the sofa and peered about, and could scarcely believe my eyes as I came upon her standing by the tower window, pearls, black gown, lace frills, and rose in hand, all there, although very indistinct and shadowy, the Mona Lisa face looking discreetly towards the wall.

Now, my dear Miss Valentine, having related this remarkable adventure, I am about to relate one even more remarkable. It occurred this very evening, between seven and eight o'clock. I had been off for the day with the village goat-boy and his flock—the dear creatures, who have never had their bells removed to be painted over with Swiss landscapes and offered for sale as souvenir *bric-a-brac*. I had patted the goats goodnight and goodbye, and going up to my room, thrown myself into a reclining-chair, deliciously tired as one can only be after a long day of Swiss mountain life. The door was open, the room full of pleasant twilight, the three ladies safe in their tower close by. I was thinking and wondering about them, when I heard a rustling at the opposite end of the room. Now, as you know, the place being spacious as a banqueting-hall, objects at a distance, especially in the half-light, might easily deceive one. This was what I thought as I saw by the window a girlish form in black, with something white at the neck and sleeves. I rubbed my hands across my eyes, looked again, and, lo! my vision had vanished completely, noiselessly, without moving from the spot; for there had not been time to move. I sprang up and crossed the room. On the window-ledge was a rose, and the rose was red. Another curious thing—the ghost-lady of the tower, according to her own authority, was forty-nine in the year 1698. I don't know how ghosts manage about their age, but my ghost of this evening couldn't have been over nineteen.

Well, I have told my story. I wait for you to suggest the explanation of the second part; the first will explain itself when I bring to you, in a few days at most, and with the hearty consent and approval of the castle's present proprietor, the Countess Maria Regina, the haughty daughter, the ghost-lady herself, as found on the rainy day in the tower.

I am so well, so happy, so rich in life and thoughts and hopes! I owe it all to you, and I thank you again and still again, and sign my last letter from the Halden with the sweet salutation of the country, '*Grüss' Gott!*'

> Devotedly yours,
>
> Morris Davidson.

Midnight, June the first.

In the same mail Miss Valentine received a letter from her niece and namesake, who was travelling with friends from Munich to Geneva.

My Dearest Aunt,—I can't possibly go to sleep without telling you about this beautiful day. Of course, you knew we were going through Zurich, but you did not know we were going to give ourselves the joy of stopping for a little glimpse of the Halden country.

We took a very early train this morning, and without waiting at the village, went directly on that glorious ten-mile walk to Obstalden, and dined at the inn 'Zum Hirschen.'

You remember it—there where we tried to express ourselves once in verse:

The pasture-lands stretched far overhead,
And blooming pathways heavenward led,
As on the best of the land we fed
At the pleasant inn 'Zum Hirschen.'

Above us, a sky of wondrous blue;
Below, a lake of marvellous hue;
And glad seemed life—the whole way through,
That day as we dined 'Zum Hirschen.'

And that was how life seemed today, but we were wise enough not to attempt poetry. When we got back to the village at night, we climbed up to the castle for supper. I did so hope to see your Mr. Davidson; unfortunately, he had gone off for a long tramp. You should hear *die alte Grossmutter* talk about him; she can't begin to say flattering things enough. And where do you think I went, Aunt Olivia? Into our old room, to be sure—your Mr. Davidson's room now—the door was open, and so I entered.

Oh, the view from that window!—the snow-tipped mountain over across the quiet lake, the little village, the castle garden, with its terraces and bowers! I wanted you so much!

Suddenly I had a feeling as if someone were coming, and very gently I pushed aside the panel door, closed it behind me, and descended in the dark—not a minute too soon, as it proved, because, firstly, when I looked back there was a light in the room above; and secondly, the rest of the party had gone to the station, expecting to find me there, and I arrived just in time to prevent us from missing the train.

And, oh, dear Aunt Olivia, your Mr. Davidson has made some wonderful discovery. *Die alte Grossmutter* couldn't resist telling me, although she wouldn't tell me what it was; she said he was intending to bring it, or them, to you as a present, and he might be wishing to make it a surprise, and it wasn't for her to go and spoil it all. Now what do you suppose it can be? I am consumed with curiosity, and could shed tears of envy. He doesn't know a word about the secret stairway. *Die alte Grossmutter* hadn't thought to mention it. Imagine that! So exactly like people who possess unusual things not to appreciate them. When you build your house do put in a secret stairway, they are so convenient.

The castle garden today was a perfect wilderness of roses; we brought as many as we could back to Zurich, and one I left on the window-ledge of our old room—an unsigned offering from a past to a present occupant. It was a red rose too, and therefore of particularly good omen at the Halden. I wonder if your Mr. Davidson has found it yet, and is asking himself how it came?

And now, my dearest Aunt Olivia, I kiss you goodnight, and end my letter with the sweet salutation which we have been hearing all day from peasant folk—'*Grüss' Gott!*'

Lovingly, your namesake niece,

Olivia.

Midnight, June the first.

Perdita

By Hildegarde Hawthorne

1: ALFALFA RANCH

Alfalfa Ranch, low, wide, with spreading verandas all overgrown by roses and woodbine, and commanding on all sides a wide view of the rolling alfalfa-fields, was a most bewitching place for a young couple to spend the first few months of their married life. So, Jack and I were naturally much delighted when Aunt Agnes asked us to consider it our own for as long as we chose. The ranch, in spite of its distance from the nearest town, surrounded as it was by the prairies, and without a neighbour within a three-mile radius, was yet luxuriously fitted with all the modern conveniences.

Aunt Agnes was a rich young widow, and had built the place after her husband's death, intending to live there with her child, to whom she transferred all the wealth of devotion she had lavished on her husband. The child, however, had died when only three years old, and Aunt Agnes, as soon as she recovered sufficient strength, had left Alfalfa Ranch, intending never to visit the place again. All this had happened nearly ten years ago, and the widow, relinquishing all the advantages her youth and beauty, quite as much as her wealth, could give her, had devoted herself to work amid the poor of New York.

At my wedding, which she heartily approved, and where to a greater extent than ever before she cast off the almost morbid quietness which had grown habitual with her, she seemed particularly anxious that Jack and I should accept the loan of Alfalfa Ranch, apparently having an old idea that the power of our happiness would somehow lift the cloud of sorrow which, in her mind, brooded over the place. I had not been strong, and Jack was overjoyed at such an opportunity of taking me into the country. High as our expectations were, the beauty of the place far exceeded them all. What colour! What glorious sunsets! And the long rides we took, seeming to be utterly tireless in that fresh sweet air!

One afternoon I sat on the veranda at the western wing of the house. The veranda here was broader than elsewhere, and it was reached only by a flight of steps leading up from the lawn on one side, and by a door opposite these steps that opened into Jack's study. The rest of this veranda was enclosed by a high railing, and by wire nettings so thickly overgrown with vines that the place was always very shady. I sat near the steps, where I could watch the sweep of the great shadows thrown by the clouds that were sailing before the west wind. Jack was inside, writing, and now and then he would say something to me through the open window. As I sat, lost in delight at the beauty of the view and the sweetness of the flower-scented air, I marvelled that Aunt Agnes could ever have left so charming a spot. "She must still love it," I thought, getting up to move my chair to where I might see still further over the prairies, "and some time she will come back——"

At this moment I happened to glance to the further end of the veranda, and there I saw, to my amazement, a little child seated on the floor, playing with the shifting shadows of the tangled creepers. It was a little girl in a daintily embroidered white dress, with golden curls around her baby head. As I still gazed, she suddenly turned, with a roguish toss of the yellow hair, and fixed her serious blue eyes on me.

"Baby!" I cried. "Where did you come from? Where's your mamma, darling?" And I took a step towards her.

"What's that, Silvia?" called Jack from within. I turned my head and saw him sitting at his desk.

"Come quick, Jack; there's the loveliest baby—" I turned back to the child, looked, blinked, and at this moment Jack stepped out beside me.

"Baby?" he inquired. "What on earth are you talking about, Silvia dearest?"

"Why, but—" I exclaimed. "There *was* one! How did she get away? She was sitting right there when I called."

"A *baby*!" repeated my husband. "My dear, babies don't appear and disappear like East-Indian magicians. You have been napping, and are trying to conceal the shameful fact."

"Jack," I said, decisively, "don't you suppose I know a baby when I see one? She was sitting right there, playing with the shadows, and I—It's certainly very queer!"

Jack grinned. "Go and put on your habit," he replied; "the horses will be here in ten minutes. And remember that when you have

92

accounted for her disappearance, her presence still remains to be explained. Or perhaps you think Wah Sing produced her from his sleeve?"

I laughed. Wah Sing was our Chinese cook, and more apt, I thought, to put something up his sleeve than to take anything out.

"I suppose I *was* dreaming," I said, "though I could almost as well believe I had only dreamed our marriage."

"Or rather," observed Jack, "that our marriage had only dreamed us."

2: Shadows

About a week later I received a letter from Aunt Agnes. Among other things, chiefly relating to New York's slums, she said:

"I am in need of rest, and if you and Jack could put up with me for a few days, I believe I should like to get back to the old place. As you know, I have always dreaded a return there, but lately I seem somehow to have lost that dread. I feel that the time has come for me to be there again, and I am sure you will not mind me."

Most assuredly we would not mind her. We sat in the moonlight that night on the veranda, Jack swinging my hammock slowly, and talked of Aunt Agnes. The moon silvered the waving alfalfa, and sifted through the twisted vines that fenced us in, throwing intricate and ever-changing patterns on the smooth flooring. There was a hum of insects in the air, and the soft wind ever and *anon* blew a fleecy cloud over the moon, dimming for a moment her serene splendour.

"Who knows?" said Jack, lighting another cigar. "This may be a turning-point in Aunt Agnes's life, and she may once more be something like the sunny, happy girl your mother describes. She is beautiful, and she is yet young. It may mean the beginning of a new life for her."

"Yes," I answered. "It isn't right that her life should always be shadowed by that early sorrow. She is so lovely, and could be so happy. Now that she has taken the first step, there is no reason why she shouldn't go on."

"We'll do what we can to help her," responded my husband. "Let me fix your cushions, darling; they have slipped." He rose to do so, and suddenly stood still, facing the further end of the veranda. His expression was so peculiar that I turned, following the direction of his eyes, even before his smothered exclamation of "Silvia, look there!" reached me.

Standing in the fluttering moonlight and shadows was the same little girl I had seen already. She still wore white, and her tangled curls floated shining around her head. She seemed to be smiling, and slightly shook her head at us.

"What does it mean, Jack?" I whispered, slipping out of the hammock.

"How did she get there? Come!" said he, and we walked hastily towards the little thing, who again shook her head. Just at this moment another cloud obscured the moon for a few seconds, and though in the uncertain twilight I fancied I still saw her, yet when the cloud passed, she was not to be found.

3: Perdita

Aunt Agnes certainly did look as though she needed rest. She seemed very frail, and the colour had entirely left her face. But her curling hair was as golden as ever, and her figure as girlish and graceful. She kissed me tenderly, and kept my hand in hers as she wandered over the house and took long looks across the prairie.

"Isn't it beautiful?" she asked, softly. "Just the place to be happy in! I've always had a strange fancy that I should be happy here again someday, and now I feel as though that day had almost come. You are happy, aren't you, dear?"

I looked at Jack, and felt the tears coming to my eyes. "Yes, I am happy. I did not know one could be so happy," I answered, after a moment.

Aunt Agnes smiled her sweet smile and kissed me again. "God bless you and your Jack! You almost make me feel young again."

"As though you could possibly feel anything else," I retorted, laughing. "You little humbug, to pretend you are old!" and slipping my arm round her waist, for we had always been dear friends, I walked off to chat with her in her room.

We took a ride that afternoon, for Aunt Agnes wanted another gallop over that glorious prairie. The exercise and the perfect afternoon brought back the colour to her cheeks.

"I think I shall be much better tomorrow," she observed, as we trotted home. "What a country this is, and what horses!" slipping her hand down her mount's glossy neck. "I did right to come back here. I do not believe I will go away again." And she smiled on Jack and me, who laughed, and said she would find it a difficult thing to attempt.

We all three came out on the veranda to see the sunset. It was always a glorious sight, but this evening it was more than usually magnificent. Immense rays of pale blue and pink spread over the sky, and the clouds, which stretched in horizontal masses, glowed rose and golden. The whole sky was luminous and tender, and seemed to tremble with light.

We sat silent, looking at the sky and at the shadowy grass that seemed to meet it. Slowly the colour deepened and faded.

"There can never be a lovelier evening," said Aunt Agnes, with a sigh.

"Don't say that," replied Jack. "It is only the beginning of even more perfect ones."

Aunt Agnes rose with a slight shiver, "It grows chilly when the sun goes," she murmured, and turned lingeringly to enter the house. Suddenly she gave a startled exclamation. Jack and I jumped up and looked at her. She stood with both hands pressed to her heart, looking—

"The child again," said Jack, in a low voice, laying his hand on my arm.

He was right. There in the gathering shadow stood the little girl in the white dress. Her hands were stretched towards us, and her lips parted in a smile. A belated gleam of sunlight seemed to linger in her hair.

"Perdita!" cried Aunt Agnes, in a voice that shook with a kind of terrible joy. Then, with a stifled sob, she ran forward and sank before the baby, throwing her arms about her. The little girl leaned back her golden head and looked at Aunt Agnes with her great, serious eyes. Then she flung both baby arms round her neck, and lifted her sweet mouth—

Jack and I turned away, looking at each other with tears in our eyes. A slight sound made us turn back. Aunt Agnes had fallen forward to the floor, and the child was nowhere to be seen.

We rushed up, and Jack raised my aunt in his arms and carried her into the house. But she was quite dead. The little child we never saw again.

At La Glorieuse

By M. E. M. Davis

Madame Raymonde-Arnault leaned her head against the back of her garden chair, and watched the young people furtively from beneath her half-closed eyelids. "He is about to speak," she murmured under her breath; "she, at least, will be happy!" and her heart fluttered violently, as if it had been her own thin bloodless hand which Richard Keith was holding in his; her dark sunken eyes, instead of Félice's brown ones, which drooped beneath his tender gaze.

Marcelite, the old *bonne*, who stood erect and stately behind her mistress, permitted herself also to regard them for a moment with something like a smile relaxing her sombre yellow face; then she too turned her turbaned head discreetly in another direction.

The plantation house at La Glorieuse is built in a shining loop of Bayou L'Eperon. A level grassy lawn, shaded by enormous live-oaks, stretches across from the broad stone steps to the sodded levee, where a flotilla of small boats, drawn up among the flags and lily-pads, rise and fall with the lapping waves. On the left of the house the white cabins of the quarter show their low roofs above the shrubbery; to the right the plantations of cane, following the inward curve of the bayou, sweep southward field after field, their billowy blue-green reaches blending far in the rear with the indistinct purple haze of the swamp.

The great square house, raised high on massive stone pillars, dates back to the first quarter of the century; its sloping roof is set with rows of dormer-windows, the big red double chimneys rising oddly from their midst; wide galleries with fluted columns enclose it on three sides; from the fourth is projected a long narrow wing, two stories in height, which stands somewhat apart from the main building, but is connected with it by a roofed and latticed passageway. The lower rooms of this wing open upon small porticos, with balustrades of wrought ironwork rarely fanciful and delicate. From these you may

97

step into the rose garden—a tangled *pleasaunce* which rambles away through alleys of wild-peach and magnolia to an orange grove, whose trees are gnarled and knotted with the growth of half a century.

The early shadows were cool and dewy there that morning; the breath of damask-roses was sweet on the air; brown, gold-dusted butterflies were hovering over the sweet-peas abloom in sunny corners; birds shot up now and then from the leafy aisles, singing, into the clear blue sky above; the chorus of the negroes at work among the young cane floated in, mellow and resonant, from the fields. The old mistress of La Glorieuse saw it all behind her drooped eyelids. Was it not April too, that long-gone unforgotten morning? And were not the bees busy in the hearts of the roses, and the birds singing, when Richard Keith, the first of the name who came to La Glorieuse, held her hand in his, and whispered his love-story yonder, by the ragged thicket of crepe-myrtle? Ah, Félice, my child, thou art young, but I too have had my sixteen years; and yellow as are the curls on the head bent over thine, those of the first Richard were more golden still. And the second Richard, he who—

Marcelite's hand fell heavily on her mistress's shoulder. Madame Arnault opened her eyes and sat up, grasping the arms of her chair. A harsh grating sound had fallen suddenly into the stillness, and the shutters of one of the upper windows of the wing which overlooked the garden were swinging slowly outward. A ripple of laughter, musical and mocking, rang clearly on the air; at the same moment a woman appeared, framed like a portrait in the narrow casement. She crossed her arms on the iron window-bar, and gazed silently down on the startled group below. She was strangely beautiful and young, though an air of soft and subtle maturity pervaded her graceful figure.

A glory of yellow hair encircled her pale oval face, and waved away in fluffy masses to her waist; her full lips were scarlet; her eyes, beneath their straight dark brows, were grey, with emerald shadows in their luminous depths. Her low-cut gown, of some thin, yellowish-white material, exposed her exquisitely rounded throat and perfect neck; long, flowing sleeves of spidery lace fell away from her shapely arms, leaving them bare to the shoulder; loose strings of pearls were wound around her small wrists, and about her throat was clasped a strand of blood-red coral, from which hung to the hollow of her bosom a single translucent drop of amber. A smile at once daring and derisive parted her lips; an elusive light came and went in her eyes.

Keith had started impatiently from his seat at the unwelcome interruption. He stood regarding the intruder with mute, half-frowning inquiry.

Félice turned a bewildered face to her grandmother. "Who is it, *mère?*" she whispered. "Did—did you give her leave?"

Madame Arnault had sunk back in her chair. Her hands trembled convulsively still, and the lace on her bosom rose and fell with the hurried beating of her heart. But she spoke in her ordinary measured, almost formal tones, as she put out a hand and drew the girl to her side. "I do not know, my child. Perhaps Suzette Beauvais has come over with her guests from Grandchamp. I thought I heard but now the sound of boats on the bayou. Suzette is ever ready with her pranks. Or perhaps—"

She stopped abruptly. The stranger was drawing the batten blinds together. Her ivory-white arms gleamed in the sun. For a moment they could see her face shining like a star against the dusky glooms within; then the bolt was shot sharply to its place.

Old Marcelite drew a long breath of relief as she disappeared. A smothered ejaculation had escaped her lips, under the girl's intent gaze; an ashen grey had overspread her dark face. "Mam'selle Suzette, she been an' dress up one o' her young ladies jes fer er trick," she said, slowly, wiping the great drops of perspiration from her wrinkled forehead.

"Suzette?" echoed Félice, incredulously. "She would never dare! Who *can* it be?"

"It is easy enough to find out," laughed Keith. "Let us go and see for ourselves who is masquerading in my quarters."

He drew her with him as he spoke along the winding violet-bordered walks which led to the house. She looked anxiously back over her shoulder at her grandmother. Madame Arnault half arose, and made an imperious gesture of dissent; but Marcelite forced her gently into her seat, and leaning forward, whispered a few words rapidly in her ear.

"Thou art right, Marcelite," she acquiesced, with a heavy sigh. "'Tis better so."

They spoke in *nègre*, that mysterious *patois* which is so uncouth in itself, so soft and caressing on the lips of women. Madame Arnault signed to the girl to go on. She shivered a little, watching their retreating figures. The old *bonne* threw a light shawl about her shoulders, and crouched affectionately at her feet. The murmur of their voices as they talked long and earnestly together hardly reached beyond the shadows of the wild-peach-tree beneath which they sat.

"How beautiful she was!" Félice said, musingly, as they approached the latticed passageway.

"Well, yes," her companion returned, carelessly. "I confess I do not greatly fancy that style of beauty myself." And he glanced significantly down at her own flower-like face.

She flushed, and her brown eyes drooped, but a bright little smile played about her sensitive mouth. "I cannot see," she declared, "how Suzette could have dared to take her friends into the ballroom!"

"Why?" he asked, smiling at her vehemence.

She stopped short in her surprise. "Do you not know, then?" She sank her voice to a whisper. "The ballroom has never been opened since the night my mother died. I was but a baby then, though sometimes I imagine that I remember it all. There was a grand ball there that night. La Glorieuse was full of guests, and everybody from all the plantations around was here. *Mère* has never told me how it was, nor Marcelite; but the other servants used to talk to me about my beautiful young mother, and tell me how she died suddenly in her ball dress, while the ball was going on. My father had the whole wing closed at once, and no one was ever allowed to enter it.

"I used to be afraid to play in its shadow, and if I did stray anywhere near it, my father would always call me away. Her death must have broken his heart. He rarely spoke; I never saw him smile; and his eyes were so sad that I could weep now at remembering them. Then he too died while I was still a little girl, and now I have no one in the world but dear old *mère*." Her voice trembled a little, but she flushed, and smiled again beneath his meaning look. "It was many years before even the lower floor was reopened, and I am almost sure that yours is the only room there which has ever been used."

They stepped, as she concluded, into the hall.

"I have never been in here before," she said, looking about her with shy curiosity. A flood of sunlight poured through the wide arched window at the foot of the stair. The door of the room nearest the entrance stood open; the others, ranging along the narrow hall, were all closed.

"This is my room," he said, nodding towards the open door.

She turned her head quickly away, with an impulse of girlish modesty, and ran lightly up the stair. He glanced downward as he followed, and paused, surprised to see the flutter of white garments in a shaded corner of his room. Looking more closely, he saw that it was a glimmer of light from an open window on the dark polished floor.

The upper hall was filled with sombre shadows; the motionless air was heavy with a musty, choking odour. In the dimness a few tattered hangings were visible on the walls; a rope, with bits of crumbling evergreen clinging to it, trailed from above one of the low windows. The panelled double door of the ballroom was shut; no sound came from behind it.

"The girls have seen us coming," said Félice, picking her way daintily across the dust-covered floor, "and they have hidden themselves inside."

Keith pushed open the heavy valves, which creaked noisily on their rusty hinges. The gloom within was murkier still; the chill dampness, with its smell of mildew and mould, was like that of a funeral vault.

The large, low-ceilinged room ran the entire length of the house. A raised dais, whose faded carpet had half rotted away, occupied an alcove at one end; upon it four or five wooden stools were placed; one of these was overturned; on another a violin in its baggy green baize cover was lying. Straight high-backed chairs were pushed against the walls on either side; in front of an open fireplace with a low wooden mantel two small cushioned divans were drawn up, with a claw-footed table between them.

A silver salver filled with tall glasses was set carelessly on one edge of the table; a half-open fan of sandal-wood lay beside it; a man's glove had fallen on the hearth just within the tarnished brass fender. Cobwebs depended from the ceiling, and hung in loose threads from the mantel; dust was upon everything, thick and motionless; a single ghostly ray of light that filtered in through a crevice in one of the shutters was weighted with grey lustreless motes. The room was empty and silent. The visitors, who had come so stealthily, had as stealthily departed, leaving no trace behind them.

"They have played us a pretty trick," said Keith, gayly. "They must have fled as soon as they saw us start towards the house." He went over to the window from which the girl had looked down into the rose garden, and gave it a shake. The dust flew up in a suffocating cloud, and the spiked nails which secured the upper sash rattled in their places.

"That is like Suzette Beauvais," Félice replied, absently. She was not thinking of Suzette. She had forgotten even the stranger, whose disdainful eyes, fixed upon herself, had moved her sweet nature to something like a rebellious anger. Her thoughts were on the beautiful young mother of alien race, whose name, for some reason, she was forbidden to speak. She saw her glide, gracious and smiling, along the smooth floor; she heard her voice above the call and response of the violins; she breathed the perfume of her laces, backward-blown by the swift motion of the dance!

She strayed dreamily about, touching with an almost reverent finger first one worm-eaten object and then another, as if by so doing she could make the imagined scene more real. Her eyes were downcast; the blood beneath her rich dark skin came and went in brilliant flushes on her cheeks; the bronze hair, piled in heavy coils on her small, well-poised head, fell in loose rings on her low forehead and against her white neck; her soft grey gown, following the harmonious lines of her slender figure, seemed to envelop her like a twilight cloud.

"She is adorable," said Richard Keith to himself.

It was the first time that he had been really alone with her, though this was the third week of his stay in the hospitable old mansion where his father and his grandfather before him had been welcome guests. Now that he came to think of it, in that bundle of yellow, time-worn letters from Félix Arnault to Richard Keith, which he had found among his father's papers, was one which described at length a ball in this very ballroom. Was it in celebration of his marriage, or of his home-coming after a tour abroad? Richard could not remember. But he idly recalled portions of other letters, as he stood with his elbow on the mantel watching Félix Arnault's daughter.

"*Your son and my daughter,*" the phrase which had made him smile when he read it yonder in his Maryland home, brought now a warm glow to his heart. The half-spoken avowal, the question that had trembled on his lips a few moments ago in the rose garden, stirred impetuously within him.

Félice stepped down from the dais where she had been standing, and came swiftly across the room, as if his unspoken thought had called her to him. A tender rapture possessed him to see her thus drawing towards him; he longed to stretch out his arms and fold her to his breast. He moved, and his hand came in contact with a small object on the mantel. He picked it up. It was a ring, a band of dull worn gold, with a confused tracery graven upon it. He merely glanced at it, slipping it mechanically on his finger. His eyes were full upon hers, which were suffused and shining.

"Did you speak?" she asked, timidly. She had stopped abruptly, and was looking at him with a hesitating, half-bewildered expression.

"No," he replied. His mood had changed. He walked again to the window and examined the clumsy bolt. "Strange!" he muttered. "I have never seen a face like hers," he sighed, dreamily.

"She was very beautiful," Félice returned, quietly. "I think we must be going," she added. "*Mère* will be growing impatient." The flush had died out of her cheek, her arms hung listlessly at her side. She shuddered as she gave a last look around the desolate room. "They were dancing here when my mother died," she said to herself.

He preceded her slowly down the stair. The remembrance of the woman began vaguely to stir his senses. He had hardly remarked her then, absorbed as he had been in another idea. Now she seemed to swim voluptuously before his vision; her tantalising laugh rang in his ears; her pale perfumed hair was blown across his face; he felt its filmy strands upon his lips and eyelids. "Do you think," he asked, turning eagerly on the bottom step, "that they could have gone into any of these rooms?"

She shrank unaccountably from him. "Oh no," she cried. "They are in the rose garden with *mère*, or they have gone around to the lawn. Come"; and she hurried out before him.

Madame Arnault looked at them sharply as they came up to where she was sitting. "No one!" she echoed, in response to Keith's report. "Then they really have gone back?"

"*Madame* knows dat we is hear de boats pass up de bayou whilse *m'sieu* an' *mam'selle* was inside," interposed Marcelite, stooping to pick up her mistress's cane.

"I would not have thought Suzette so—so indiscreet," said Félice. There was a note of weariness in her voice.

Madame Arnault looked anxiously at her and then at Keith. The young man was staring abstractedly at the window, striving to recall the vision that had appeared there, and he felt, rather than saw, his hostess start and change colour when her eyes fell upon the ring he was wearing. He lifted his hand covertly, and turned the trinket around in the light, but he tried in vain to decipher the irregular characters traced upon it.

"Let us go in," said the old *madame*. "Félice, my child, thou art fatigued."

Now when in all her life before was Félice ever fatigued? Félice, whose strong young arms could send a *pirogue* flying up the bayou for miles; Félice, who was ever ready for a tramp along the rose-hedged lanes to the swamp lakes when the water-lilies were in bloom; to the sugar-house in grinding-time, down the levee road to St. Joseph's, the little brown ivy-grown church, whose solitary spire arose slim and straight above the encircling trees.

Marcelite gave an arm to her mistress, though, in truth, she seemed to walk a little unsteadily herself. Félice followed with Keith, who was silent and self-absorbed.

The day passed slowly, a constraint had somehow fallen upon the little household. Madame Arnault's fine high-bred old face wore its customary look of calm repose, but her eyes now and then sought her guest with an expression which he could not have fathomed if he had observed it. But he saw nothing. A mocking red mouth; a throat made for the kisses of love; white arms strung with pearls—these were ever before him, shutting away even the pure sweet face of Félice Arnault.

"Why did I not look at her more closely when I had the opportunity, fool that I was?" he asked himself, savagely, again and again, revolving in his mind a dozen pretexts for going at once to the Beauvais plantation, a mile or so up the bayou. But he felt an inexplicable shyness at the thought of putting any of these plans into action, and so allowed the day to drift by. He arose gladly when the hour for retiring came—that hour which he had hitherto postponed by every means in his power. He kissed, as usual, the hand of his hostess, and held that of Félice in his for a moment; but he did not feel its trembling, or see the timid trouble in her soft eyes.

His room in the silent and deserted wing was full of fantastic shadows. He threw himself on a chair beside a window without lighting his lamp. The rose garden outside was steeped in moonlight; the magnolia bells gleamed waxen-white against their glossy green leaves; the vines on the tall trellises threw a soft network of dancing shadows on the white-shelled walks below; the night air stealing about was loaded with the perfume of roses and sweet-olive; a mocking-bird sang in an orange-tree, his mate responding sleepily from her nest in the old summer-house.

"Tomorrow," he murmured, half aloud, "I will go to Grandchamp and give her the ring she left in the old ballroom."

He looked at it glowing dully in the moonlight; suddenly he lifted his head, listening. Did a door grind somewhere near on its hinges? He got up cautiously and looked out. It was not fancy. She was standing full in view on the small balcony of the room next his own. Her white robes waved to and fro in the breeze; the pearls on her arms glistened. Her face, framed in the pale gold of her hair, was turned towards him; a smile curved her lips; her mysterious eyes seemed to be searching his through the shadow. He drew back, confused and trembling, and when, a second later, he looked again, she was gone.

He sat far into the night, his brain whirling, his blood on fire. Who was she, and what was the mystery hidden in this isolated old plantation house? His thoughts reverted to the scene in the rose garden, and he went over and over all its details. He remembered Madame Arnault's agitation when the window opened and the girl appeared; her evident discomfiture—of which at the time he had taken no heed, but which came back to him vividly enough now—at his proposal to visit the ballroom; her startled recognition of the ring on his finger; her slurring suggestion of visitors from Grandchamp; the look of terror on Marcelite's face. What did it all mean? Félice, he was sure, knew nothing. But here, in an unused portion of the house, which even the members of the family had never visited, a young and beautiful girl was shut up a prisoner, condemned perhaps to a life-long captivity.

"Good God!" He leaped to his feet at the thought. He would go and thunder at Madame Arnault's door, and demand an explanation. But no; not yet. He calmed himself with an effort. By too great haste he might injure her. "Insane?" He laughed aloud at the idea of madness in connection with that exquisite creature.

It dawned upon him, as he paced restlessly back and forth, that although his father had been here more than once in his youth and manhood, he had never heard him speak of La Glorieuse nor of Félix Arnault, whose letters he had read after his father's death a few months ago—those old letters whose affectionate warmth indeed had determined him, in the first desolation of his loss, to seek the family which seemed to have been so bound to his own. Morose and taciturn as his father had been, surely he would sometimes have spoken of his old friend if—Worn out at last with conjecture; beaten back, bruised and breathless, from an enigma which he could not solve; exhausted by listening with strained attention for some movement in the next room, he threw himself on his bed, dressed as he was, and fell into a heavy sleep, which lasted far into the forenoon of the next day.

When he came out (walking like one in a dream), he found a gay party assembled on the lawn in front of the house. Suzette Beauvais and her guests, a bevy of girls, had come from Grandchamp. They had been joined, as they rowed down the bayou, by the young people from the plantation houses on the way. Half a dozen boats, their long paddles laid across the seats, were added to the home fleet at the landing. Their stalwart black rowers were basking in the sun on the levee, or lounging about the quarter. At the moment of his appearance, Suzette herself was indignantly disclaiming any complicity in the jest of the day before.

"Myself, I was making orange-flower conserve," she declared; "an' anyhow I wouldn't go in that ballroom unless *madame* send me."

"But who was it, then?" insisted Félice.

Mademoiselle Beauvais spread out her fat little hands and lifted her shoulders. "*Moi pas connais*," she laughed, dropping into *patois*.

Madame Arnault here interposed. It was but the foolish conceit of some teasing neighbour, she said, and not worth further discussion. Keith's blood boiled in his veins at this calm dismissal of the subject, but he gave no sign. He saw her glance warily at himself from time to time.

"I will sift the matter to the bottom," he thought, "and I will force her to confess the truth, whatever it may be, before the world."

The noisy chatter and meaningless laughter around him jarred upon his nerves; he longed to be alone with his thoughts; and presently, pleading a headache—indeed his temples throbbed almost to bursting, and his eyes were hot and dry—he quitted the lawn, seeing but not noting until long afterwards, when they smote his memory like a two-edged knife, the pain in Félice's uplifted eyes, and the little sorrowful quiver of her mouth. He strolled around the corner of the house to his apartment. The blinds of the arched window were drawn, and a hazy twilight was diffused about the hall, though it was mid-afternoon outside. As he entered, closing the door behind him, the woman at that moment uppermost in his thoughts came down the dusky silence from the further end of the hall. She turned her inscrutable eyes upon him in passing, and flitted noiselessly and with languid grace up the stairway, the faint swish of her gown vanishing with her. He hesitated a moment, overpowered by conflicting emotion; then he sprang recklessly after her.

He pushed open the ballroom door, reaching his arms out blindly before him. Once more the great dust-covered room was empty. He strained his eyes helplessly into the obscurity. A chill reaction passed over him; he felt himself on the verge of a swoon. He did not this time even try to discover the secret door or exit by which she had disappeared; he looked, with a hopeless sense of discouragement, at the barred windows, and turned to leave the room. As he did so, he saw a handkerchief lying on the threshold of the door. He picked it up eagerly, and pressed it to his lips. A peculiar delicate perfume which thrilled his senses lurked in its gossamer folds. As he was about thrusting it into his breast-pocket, he noticed in one corner a small bloodstain fresh and wet. He had then bitten his lip in his excitement.

"I need no further proof," he said aloud, and his own voice startled him, echoing down the long hall. "She is beyond all question a prisoner in this detached building, which has mysterious exits and entrances. She has been forced to promise that she will not go outside of its walls, or she is afraid to do so. I will bring home this monstrous crime. I will release this lovely young woman who dares not speak, yet so plainly appeals to me." Already he saw in fancy her starlike eyes raised to his in mute gratitude, her white hand laid confidingly on his arm.

The party of visitors remained at La Glorieuse overnight. The negro fiddlers came in, and there was dancing in the old-fashioned double parlours and on the moonlit galleries. Félice was unnaturally gay. Keith looked on gloomily, taking no part in the amusement.

"*Il est bien bête*, your yellow-haired Marylander," whispered Suzette Beauvais to her friend.

He went early to his room, but he watched in vain for some sign from his beautiful neighbour. He grew sick with apprehension. Had Madame Arnault—But no; she would not dare. "I will wait one more day," he finally decided; "and then—"

The next morning, after a late breakfast, someone proposed impromptu charades and tableaux. Madame Arnault good-naturedly sent for the keys to the tall presses built into the walls, which contained the accumulated trash and treasure of several generations. Mounted on a stepladder, Robert Beauvais explored the recesses, and threw down to the laughing crowd embroidered shawls and scarfs yellow with age, soft muslins of antique pattern, stiff big-flowered brocades, scraps of gauze ribbon, gossamer laces. On one topmost shelf he came upon a small wooden box inlaid with mother-of-pearl. Félice reached up for it, and, moved by some undefined impulse, Richard came and stood by her side while she opened it.

A perfume which he recognised arose from it as she lifted a fold of tissue-paper. Some strings of Oriental pearls of extraordinary size, and perfect in shape and colour, were coiled underneath, with a coral necklace, whose pendant of amber had broken off and rolled into a corner. With them—he hardly restrained an exclamation, and his hand involuntarily sought his breast-pocket at sight of the handkerchief with a drop of fresh blood in one corner! Félice trembled without knowing why. Madame Arnault, who had just entered the room, took the box from her quietly, and closed the lid with a snap. The girl, accustomed to implicit obedience, asked no questions; the others, engaged in turning over the old-time finery, had paid no attention.

"Does she think to disarm me by such puerile tricks?" he thought, turning a look of angry warning on the old *madame*; and in the steady gaze which she fixed on him he read a haughty defiance.

He forced himself to enter into the sports of the day, and he walked down to the boat-landing a little before sunset to see the guests depart. As the line of boats swept away, the black rowers dipping their oars lightly in the placid waves, he turned with a sense of release, leaving Madame Arnault and Félice still at the landing, and went down the levee road towards St. Joseph's. The field gang, whose red, blue, and brown blouses splotched the squares of cane with colour, was preparing to quit work; loud laughter and noisy jests rang out on the air; high-wheeled plantation wagons creaked along the lanes; negro children, with dip-nets and fishing-poles over their shoulders, ran homeward along the levee, the dogs at their heels barking joyously; a schooner, with white sail outspread, was stealing like a fairy bark around a distant bend of the bayou; the silvery waters were turning to gold under a sunset sky.

It was twilight when he struck across the plantation, and came around by the edge of the swamp to the clump of trees in a corner of the home field which he had often remarked from his window. As he approached, he saw a woman come out of the dense shadow, as if intending to meet him, and then draw back again. His heart throbbed painfully, but he walked steadily forward. It was only Félice. *Only Félice!* She was sitting on a flat tombstone. The little spot was the Raymonde-Arnault family burying-ground. There were many marble headstones and shafts, and two broad low tombs side by side and a little apart from the others.

A tangle of rose-briers covered the sunken graves, a rank growth of grass choked the narrow paths, the little gate interlaced and overhung with honeysuckle sagged away from its posts, the fence itself had lost a picket here and there, and weeds flaunted boldly in the gaps. The girl looked wan and ghostly in the lonely dusk.

"This is my father's grave, and my mother is here," she said, abruptly, as he came up and stood beside her. Her head was drooped upon her breast, and he saw that she had been weeping. "See," she went on, drawing her finger along the mildewed lettering:

Félix Marie-Joseph Arnault . . . âgé de trente-quatre ans' . . . 'Hélène Pallacier, épouse de Félix Arnault . . . décédée a l'âgé de dix-neuf ans.

Nineteen years old," she repeated, slowly. "My mother was one year younger than I am when she died—my beautiful mother!"

Her voice sounded like a far-away murmur in his ears. He looked at her, vaguely conscious that she was suffering. But he did not speak, and after a little she got up and went away. Her dress, which brushed him in passing, was wet with dew. He watched her slight figure, moving like a spirit along the lane, until a turn in the hedge hid her from sight. Then he turned again towards the swamp, and resumed his restless walk.

Some hours later he crossed the rose garden. The moon was under a cloud; the trunks of the crepe-myrtles were like pale spectres in the uncertain light. The night wind blew in chill and moist from the swamp. The house was dark and quiet, but he heard the blind of an upper window turned stealthily as he stepped into the latticed arcade.

"The old *madame* is watching me—and her," he said to himself.

His agitation had now become supreme. The faint familiar perfume that stole about his room filled him with a kind of frenzy. Was this the chivalric devotion of which he had so boasted? this the desire to protect a young and defenceless woman? He no longer dared question himself. He seemed to feel her warm breath against his cheeks. He threw up his arms with a gesture of despair. A sigh stirred the deathlike stillness. At last! She was there, just within his doorway; the pale glimmer of the veiled moon fell upon her. Her trailing laces wrapped her about like a silver mist; her arms were folded across her bosom; her eyes—he dared not interpret the meaning which he read in those wonderful eyes. She turned slowly and went down the hall.

He followed her, reeling like a drunkard. His feet seemed clogged, the blood ran thick in his veins, a strange roaring was in his ears. His hot eyes strained after her as she vanished, just beyond his touch, into the room next his own. He threw himself against the closed door in a transport of rage. It yielded suddenly, as if opened from within. A full blaze of light struck his eyes, blinding him for an instant; then he saw her. A huge four-posted bed with silken hangings occupied a recess in the room. Across its foot a low couch was drawn.

She had thrown herself there. Her head was pillowed on crimson gold-embroidered cushions; her diaphanous draperies, billowing foamlike over her, half concealed, half revealed her lovely form; her hair waved away from her brows, and spread like a shower of gold over the cushions. One bare arm hung to the floor; something jewel-like gleamed in the half-closed hand; the other lay across her forehead, and from beneath it her eyes were fixed upon him. He sprang forward with a cry. . . .

At first, he could remember nothing. The windows were open; the heavy curtains which shaded them moved lazily in the breeze; a shaft of sunlight that came in between them fell upon the polished surface of the marble mantel. He examined with languid curiosity some trifles that stood there—a pair of Dresden figures, a blue Sevres vase of graceful shape, a bronze clock with gilded rose-wreathed Cupids; and then raised his eyes to the two portraits which hung above. One of these was familiar enough—the dark melancholy face of Félix Arnault, whose portrait by different hands and at different periods of his life hung in nearly every room of La Glorieuse.

The blood surged into his face and receded again at sight of the other. Oh, so strangely like! The yellow hair, the slumberous eyes, the full throat clasped about with a single strand of coral. Yes, it was she! He lifted himself on his elbow. He was in bed. Surely this was the room into which she had drawn him with her eyes. Did he sink on the threshold, all his senses swooning into delicious faith? Or had he, indeed, in that last moment thrown himself on his knees by her couch? He could not remember, and he sank back with a sigh.

Instantly Madame Arnault was bending over him. Her cool hands were on his forehead. "*Dieu merci!*" she exclaimed, "thou art thyself once more, *mon fils.*"

He seized her hand imperiously. "Tell me, *madame*," he demanded—"tell me, for the love of God! What is she? Who is she? Why have you shut her away in this deserted place? Why—"

She was looking down at him with an expression half of pity, half of pain.

"Forgive me," he faltered, involuntarily, all his darker suspicions somehow vanishing; "but—oh, tell me!"

"Calm thyself, Richard," she said, soothingly, seating herself on the side of the bed, and stroking his hand gently. Too agitated to speak, he continued to gaze at her with imploring eyes. "Yes, yes, I will relate the whole story," she added, hastily, for he was panting and struggling for speech. "I heard you fall last night," she continued, relapsing for greater ease into French; "for I was full of anxiety about you, and I lingered long at my window watching for you. I came at once with

Marcelite, and found you lying insensible across the threshold of this room. We lifted you to the bed, and bled you after the old fashion, and then I gave you a *tisane* of my own making, which threw you into a quiet sleep. I have watched beside you until your waking. Now you are but a little weak from fasting and excitement, and when you have rested and eaten—"

"No," he pleaded; "now, at once!"

"Very well," she said, simply. She was silent a moment, as if arranging her thoughts. "Your grandfather, a Richard Keith like yourself," she began, "was a college-mate and friend of my brother, Henri Raymonde, and accompanied him to La Glorieuse during one of their vacations. I was already betrothed to Monsieur Arnault, but I—No matter! I never saw Richard Keith afterwards. But years later he sent your father, who also bore his name, to visit me here. My son, Félix, was but a year or so younger than his boy, and the two lads became at once warm friends. They went abroad, and pursued their studies side by side, like brothers. They came home together, and when Richard's father died, Félix spent nearly a year with him on his Maryland plantation. They exchanged, when apart, almost daily letters. Richard's marriage, which occurred soon after they left college, strengthened rather than weakened this extraordinary bond between them. Then came on the war. They were in the same command, and hardly lost sight of each other during their four years of service.

"When the war was ended, your father went back to his estates. Félix turned his face homeward, but drifted by some strange chance down to Florida, where he met *her*"—she glanced at the portrait over the mantel. "Helene Pallacier was Greek by descent, her family having been among those brought over some time during the last century as colonists to Florida from the Greek islands. He married her, barely delaying his marriage long enough to write me that he was bringing home a bride. She was young, hardly more than a child, indeed, and marvellously beautiful"—Keith moved impatiently; he found these family details tedious and uninteresting—"a radiant soulless creature, whose only law was her own selfish enjoyment, and whose coming brought pain and bitterness to La Glorieuse.

"These were her rooms. She chose them because of the rose garden, for she had a sensuous and passionate love of nature. She used to lie for hours on the grass there, with her arms flung over her head, gazing dreamily on the fluttering leaves above her. The pearls—which she always wore—some coral ornaments, and a handful of amber beads were her only dower, but her caprices were the insolent and extravagant caprices of a queen. Félix, who adored her, gratified them at whatever expense; and I think at first, she had a careless sort of regard for him. But she hated the little Félice, whose coming gave her the first pang of physical pain she had ever known. She never offered the child a caress. She sometimes looked at her with a suppressed rage which filled me with terror and anxiety.

"When Félice was a little more than a year old, your father came to La Glorieuse to pay us a long-promised visit. His wife had died some months before, and you, a child of six or seven years, were left in charge of relatives in Maryland. Richard was in the full vigour of manhood, broad-shouldered, tall, blue-eyed, and blond-haired, like his father and like you. From the moment of their first meeting Helene exerted all the power of her fascination to draw him to her. Never had she been so whimsical, so imperious, so bewitching! Loyal to his friend, faithful to his own high sense of honour, he struggled against a growing weakness, and finally fled. I will never forget the night he went away. A ball had been planned by Félix in honour of his friend. The ballroom was decorated under his own supervision.

"The house was filled with guests from adjoining parishes; everybody, young and old, came from the plantations around. Helene was dazzling that night. The light of triumph in her cheeks; her eyes shone with a softness which I had never seen in them before. I watched her walking up and down the room with Richard, or floating with him in the dance. They were like a pair of radiant godlike visitants from another world. My heart ached for them in spite of my indignation and apprehension; for light whispers were beginning to circulate, and I saw more than one meaning smile directed at them. Félix, who was truth itself, was gayly unconscious.

"Towards midnight I heard far up the bayou the shrill whistle of the little packet which passed up and down then, as now, twice a week; and presently she swung up to our landing. Richard was standing with Helene by the fireplace. They had been talking for some time in low earnest tones. A sudden look of determination came into his eyes. I saw him draw from his finger a ring which she had one day playfully bade him wear, and offer it to her. His face was white and strained; hers wore a look which I could not fathom. He quitted her side abruptly, and walked rapidly across the room, threading his way among the dancers, and disappeared in the press about the door.

"A few moments later a note was handed me. I heard the boat

steam away from the landing as I read it. It was a hurried line from Richard. He said that he had been called away on urgent business, and he begged me to make his *adieux* to Madame Arnault and Félix. Félix was worried and perplexed by the sudden departure of his guest. Helene said not a word, but very soon I saw her slipping down the stair, and I knew that she had gone to her room. Her absence was not remarked, for the ball was at its height. It was almost daylight when the last dance was concluded, and the guests who were staying in the house had retired to their rooms.

"Félix, having seen to the comfort of all, went at last to join his wife. He burst into my room a second later almost crazed with horror and grief. I followed him to this room. She was lying on a couch at the foot of the bed. One arm was thrown across her forehead, the other hung to the floor, and in her hand, she held a tiny silver bottle with a jewelled stopper. A handkerchief, with a single drop of blood upon it, was lying on her bosom. A faint curious odour exhaled from her lips and hung about the room, but the poison had left no other trace.

"No one save ourselves and Marcelite ever knew the truth. She had danced too much at the ball that night, and she had died suddenly of heart-disease. We buried her out yonder in the old Raymonde-Arnault burying-ground. I do not know what the letter contained which Félix wrote to Richard. He never uttered his name afterwards. The ballroom, the whole wing, in truth, was at once closed. Everything was left exactly as it was on that fatal night. A few years ago, the house being unexpectedly full, I opened the room in which you have been staying, and it has been used from time to time as a guestroom since. My son lived some years, prematurely old, heart-broken, and desolate. He died with her name on his lips."

Madame Arnault stopped.

A suffocating sensation was creeping over her listener. Only in the past few moments had the signification of the story begun to dawn upon him. "Do you mean," he gasped, "that the girl whom I—that she is—was—"

"Hélène, the dead wife of Félix Arnault," she replied, gravely. "Her restless spirit has walked here before. I have sometimes heard her tantalising laugh echo through the house, but no one had ever seen her until you came—so like the Richard Keith she loved!"

"When I read your letter," she went on, after a short silence, "which told me that you wished to come to those friends to whom your father had been so dear, all the past arose before me, and I felt that I ought to forbid your coming. But I remembered how Félix and Richard had loved each other before she came between them. I thought of the other Richard Keith whom I—I loved once; and I dreamed of a union at last between the families. I hoped, Richard, that you and Félice—"

But Richard was no longer listening. He wished to believe the whole fantastic story an invention of the keen-eyed old *madame* herself. Yet something within him confessed to its truth. A tumultuous storm of baffled desire, of impotent anger, swept over him. The ring he wore burned into his flesh. But he had no thought of removing it—the ring which had once belonged to the beautiful golden-haired woman who had come back from the grave to woo him to her!

He turned his face away and groaned.

Her eyes hardened. She rose stiffly. "I will send a servant with your breakfast," she said, with her hand on the door. "The down boat will pass La Glorieuse this afternoon. You will perhaps wish to take advantage of it."

He started. He had not thought of going—of leaving her—*her*! He looked at the portrait on the wall and laughed bitterly.

Madame Arnault accompanied him with ceremonious politeness to the front steps that afternoon.

"Mademoiselle Félice?" he murmured, inquiringly, glancing back at the windows of the sitting-room.

"Mademoiselle Arnault is occupied," she coldly returned. "I will convey to her your farewell."

He looked back as the boat chugged away. Peaceful shadows enwrapped the house and overspread the lawn. A single window in the wing gleamed like a balefire in the rays of the setting sun.

The years that followed were years of restless wandering for Richard Keith. He visited his estate but rarely. He went abroad and returned, hardly having set foot to land; he buried himself in the fastnesses of the Rockies; he made a long, aimless sea-voyage. Her image accompanied him everywhere. Between him and all he saw hovered her faultless face; her red mouth smiled at him; her white arms enticed him. His own face became worn and his step listless. He grew silent and gloomy. "He is madder than the old colonel, his father, was," his friends said, shrugging their shoulders.

One day, more than three years after his visit to La Glorieuse, he found himself on a deserted part of the Florida seacoast. It was late in November, but the sky was soft and the air warm and balmy. He bared his head as he paced moodily to and fro on the silent beach. The waves rolled languidly to his feet and receded, leaving scattered half-wreaths of opalescent foam on the snowy sands. The wind that fanned his face was filled with the spicy odours of the sea. Seized by a capricious impulse, he threw off his clothes and dashed into the surf. The undulating billows closed around him; a singular lassitude passed into his limbs as he swam; he felt himself slowly sinking, as if drawn downward by an invisible hand. He opened his eyes. The waves lapped musically above his head; a tawny glory was all about him, a luminous expanse in which he saw strangely formed creatures moving, darting, rising, falling, coiling, uncoiling.

"You was jes on de eedge er drowndin', Mars Dick," said Wiley, his black body-servant, spreading his own clothes on the porch of the little fishing-hut to dry. "In de name o' Gawd whar mek you wanter go in swimmin' dis time o' de yea', anyhow? Ef I hadn' er splunge in an' fotch you out, dey'd er been mo'nin' yander at de plantation, sho!"

His master laughed lazily. "You are right, Wiley," he said; "and you are going to smoke the best tobacco in Maryland as long as you live." He felt buoyant. Youth and elasticity seemed to have come back to him at a bound. He stretched himself on the rough bench, and watched the blue rings of smoke curl lightly away from his cigar. Gradually he was aware of a pair of wistful eyes shining down on him. His heart leaped. They were the eyes of Félice Arnault! "My God, have I been mad!" he muttered. His eyes sought his hand. The ring, from which he had never been parted, was gone. It had been torn from his finger in his wrestle with the sea. "Get my traps together at once, Wiley," he said. "We are going to La Glorieuse."

"Now you *talkin'*, Mars Dick," assented Wiley, cheerfully.

It was night when he reached the city. First of all, he made inquiries concerning the little packet. He was right; the *Assumption* would leave the next afternoon at five o'clock for Bayou L'Eperon. He went to the same hotel at which he had stopped before when on his way to La Glorieuse. The next morning, too joyous to sleep, he rose early, and went out into the street. A grey uncertain dawn was just struggling into the sky. A few people on their way to market or to early mass were passing along the narrow banquettes; sleepy-eyed women were unbarring the shutters of their tiny shops; high-wheeled milk-carts were rattling over the granite pavements; in the vine-hung court-yards, visible here and there through iron *grilles*, parrots were scolding on their perches; children pattered up and down the long, arched corridors; the prolonged cry of an early clothes-pole man echoed, like the note of a winding horn, through the close alleys. Keith sauntered carelessly along.

"In so many hours," he kept repeating to himself, "I shall be on my way to La Glorieuse. The boat will swing into the home landing; the negroes will swarm across the gang-plank, laughing and shouting; Madame Arnault and Félice will come out on the gallery and look, shading their eyes with their hands. Oh, I know quite well that the old *madame* will greet me coldly at first. Her eyes are like steel when she is angry. But when she knows that I am once more a sane man—And Félice, what if she—But no! Félice is not the kind of woman who loves more than once; and she did love me, God bless her! unworthy as I was."

A carriage, driven rapidly, passed him; his eyes followed it idly, until it turned far away into a side street. He strayed on to the market, where he seated himself on a high stool in *L'Appel du Matin* coffee stall. But a vague, teasing remembrance was beginning to stir in his brain. The turbaned woman on the front seat of the carriage that had rolled past him yonder, where had he seen that dark, grave, wrinkled face, with the great hoops of gold against either cheek? *Marcelite!* He left the stall and retraced his steps, quickening his pace almost to a run as he went. Félice herself, then, might be in the city. He hurried to the street into which the carriage had turned, and glanced down between the rows of white-eaved cottages with green doors and batten shutters. It had stopped several squares away; there seemed to be a number of people gathered about it. "I will at least satisfy myself," he thought.

As he came up, a bell in a little cross-crowned tower began to ring slowly. The carriage stood in front of a low red brick house, set directly on the street; a silent crowd pressed about the entrance. There was a hush within. He pushed his way along the banquette to the steps. A young nun, in a brown serge robe, kept guard at the door. She wore a wreath of white artificial roses above her long coarse veil. Something in his face appealed to her, and she found a place for him in the little convent chapel.

Madame Arnault, supported by Marcelite, was kneeling in front of the altar, which blazed with candles. She had grown frightfully old and frail. Her face was set, and her eyes were fixed with a rigid stare on the priest who was saying mass. Marcelite's dark cheeks were streaming with tears. The chapel, which wore a gala air with its lights and flowers, was filled with people. On the left of the altar, a bishop,

116

in gorgeous robes, was sitting, attended by priests and acolytes; on the right, the wooden panel behind an iron grating had been removed, and beyond, in the nun's choir, the black-robed sisters of the order were gathered. Heavy veils shrouded their faces and fell to their feet. They held in their hands tall wax-candles, whose yellow flames burned steadily in the semi-darkness. Five or six young girls knelt, motionless as statues, in their midst. They also carried tapers, and their rapt faces were turned towards the unseen altar within, of which the outer one is but the visible token. Their eyelids were downcast. Their white veils were thrown back from their calm foreheads, and floated like wings from their shoulders.

He felt no surprise when he saw Félice among them. He seemed to have foreknown always that he should find her thus on the edge of another and mysterious world into which he could not follow her.

Her skin had lost a little of its warm rich tint; the soft rings of hair were drawn away under her veil; her hands were thin, and as waxen as the taper she held. An unearthly beauty glorified her pale face.

"Is it forever too late?" he asked himself in agony, covering his face with his hands. When he looked again the white veil on her head had been replaced by the sombre one of the order. "If I could but speak to her!" he thought; "if she would but once lift her eyes to mine, she would come to me even now!"

Félice! Did the name break from his lips in a hoarse cry that echoed through the hushed chapel, and silenced the voice of the priest? He never knew. But a faint colour swept into her cheeks. Her eyelids trembled. In a flash the rose-garden at La Glorieuse was before him; he saw the turquoise sky, and heard the mellow chorus of the field gang; the smell of damask-roses was in the air; her little hand was in his, he saw her coming swiftly towards him across the dusk of the old ballroom; her limpid innocent eyes were smiling into his own . . . she was standing on the grassy lawn; the shadows of the leaves flickered over her white gown. . . .

At last the quivering eyelids were lifted. She turned her head slowly, and looked steadily at him. He held his breath. A cart rumbled along the cobble-stones outside; the puny wail of a child sounded across the stillness; a handful of rose leaves from a vase at the foot of the altar dropped on the hem of Madame Arnault's dress. It might have been the gaze of an angel in a world where there is no marrying nor giving in marriage, so pure was it, so passionless, so free of anything like earthly desire.

As she turned her face again towards the altar the bell in the tower above ceased tolling; a triumphant chorus leaped into the air, borne aloft by joyous organ tones. The first rays of the morning sun streamed in through the small windows. Then light penetrated into the nuns' choir, and enveloped like a mantle of gold Sister Mary of the Cross, who in the world had been Félicité Arnault.

A Faded Scapular

By F. D. Millet

We are seldom able to trace our individual superstitions to any definite cause, nor can we often account for the peculiar sensations developed in us by the inexplicable and mysterious incidents in our experience. Much of the timidity of childhood may be traced to early training in the nursery, and sometimes the moral effects of this weakness cannot be eradicated through a lifetime of severe self-control and mental suffering. The complicated disorders of the imagination which arise from superstitious fears can frequently be accounted for only by inherited characteristics, by peculiar sensitiveness to impressions, and by an overpowering and perhaps abnormally active imagination. I am sure I am confessing to no unusual characteristic when I say that I have felt from childhood a certain sentiment or sensation in regard to material things which I can trace to no early experience, to the influence of no literature, and to no possible source, in fact, but that of inherited disposition.

The sentiment I refer to is this: whatever has belonged to or has been used by any person seems to me to have received some special quality, which, though often invisible and still oftener indefinable, still exists in a more or less strong degree according to the amount of the impressionable power, if I may call it so, which distinguished the possessor. I am aware that this sentiment may be stigmatised as of the schoolgirl order; that it is, indeed, of the same kind and class with that which leads an otherwise honest person to steal a rag from a famous battle flag, a leaf from a historical laurel wreath, or even to cut a signature or a title-page from a precious volume; but with me the feeling has never taken this turn, else I should never have confessed to the possession of it. Whatever may be said or believed, however, I must refer to it in more or less comprehensible terms, because it may explain the conditions, although it will not unveil the causes, of the incidents

I am about to describe with all honesty and frankness.

Nearly twenty years ago I made my first visit to Rome, long before it became the centre of the commercial and political activity of Italy, and while it was yet unspoiled for the antiquarian, the student, the artist, and the traveller. Never shall I forget the first few hours I spent wandering aimlessly through the streets, so far as I then knew a total stranger in the city, with no distinct plan of remaining there, and with only the slight and imperfect knowledge of the place that one gains from the ordinary travellers' descriptions. The streets, the houses, the people, the strange sounds and stranger sights, the life so entirely different from what I had hitherto seen, all this interested me greatly. Far more powerful and far more vivid and lasting, however, was the impression of an inconceivable number of presences—I hesitate to call them spirits—not visible, of course, nor tangible, but still oppressing me mentally and morally, exactly the same as my physical self is often crushed and overpowered in a great assembly of people.

I walked about, visited the *cafés* and concert halls, and tried in various ways to shake off the uncomfortable feeling of ghostly company, but was unsuccessful, and went to my lodgings much depressed and nervous. I took my note-book, and wrote in it: "Rome has been too much lived in. Among the multitude of the dead there is no room for the living." It seemed then a foolish memorandum to write, and now, as I look at the half-effaced pencil lines, I wonder why I was not ashamed to write it. Yet there it is before me, a witness to my sensations at the time, and the scrawl has even now the power to bring up to me an unpleasantly vivid memory of that first evening in Rome.

After a few days passed in visiting the galleries and the regular sights of the town, I began to look for a studio and an apartment, and finally found one in the upper storey of a house on the Via di Ripetta. Before moving into the studio, I met an old friend and fellow-artist, and as there was room enough for two, gladly took him in with me.

The studio, with apartment, in the Via di Ripetta was by no means unattractive. It was large, well-lighted, comfortably and abundantly furnished. It was, as I have said, at the top of the house, the studio overlooked the Tiber, and the sitting-room and double-bedded sleeping-room fronted the street. The large studio window was placed rather high up, so that the entrance door—a wide, heavy affair, with large hinges and immense complicated lock and a "judas"—opened from the obscurity of the hall directly under the large window into the full light of the studio. The roof of the house slanted from back to front, so that the two rooms were lower studded than the studio, and an empty space or low attic opening into the studio above them was partly concealed by an ample and ragged curtain.

The fireplace was in the middle of the left wall as you entered the studio; the door into the sitting-room was in the further right-hand corner, and the bedroom was entered by a door on the right-hand wall of the sitting-room, so that the bedroom formed a wing of the studio and sitting-room, and from the former, looking through two doors, the bedroom window and part of the street wall could be seen. Both the beds were hidden from sight of anyone in the studio, even when the doors were open.

The apartment was furnished in a way which denoted a certain amount of liberality, but everything was faded and worn, though not actually shabby or dirty. The carpets were threadbare, the damask-covered sofa and chairs showed marks of the springs, and the gimp was fringed and torn off in places. The beds were not mates; the basin and ewer were of different patterns; the few pictures on the wall were, like everything else in the place, curiously grey and dusty-looking, as if they had been shut up in the darkened rooms for a generation. Beyond the fireplace in the studio, the corner of the room was partitioned off by a dingy screen, six feet high or more, fixed to the floor for the space of two yards, with one wing which shut like a door, enclosing a small space fitted up like a miniature scullery, with a curious and elaborate collection of pots and pans and kitchen utensils, all hung in orderly rows, but every article with marks of service on it, and more recent and obtrusive trace of long disuse.

In one of the first days of my search for a studio I had found and inspected this very place, but it had given me such a disagreeable feeling—it had seemed so worn out, so full of relics of other people—that I could not make up my mind to take it. After a thorough search and diligent inquiry, however, I came to the conclusion that there was absolutely no other place in Rome at that busy season where I could set up my easel, and after having the place recommended to me by all the artists I called upon as a well-known and useful studio, and a great find at the busy season of the year, I took a lease of the place for four months.

My friend and I moved in at the same time, and I will not deny that I planned to be supported by the presence of my friend at the moment of taking possession. When we arrived and had our traps all deposited in the middle of the studio, there came over the spirits of us both a strange gloom, which the bustle and confusion of settling did not in the least dispel. It was nearly dark that winter afternoon before we had finished unpacking, and the street lights were burning before we reached the little restaurant in the Via Quattro Fontano, where we proposed to take our meals. There was a cheerful company of artists and architects assembled there that evening, and we sat over our wine long after dinner. When the jolly party at last dispersed, it was well past midnight.

How gloomy the outer portal of the high building looked as we crossed the dimly lighted street and pushed open the black door! A musty, damp smell, like the atmosphere of the catacombs, met us as we entered. Our footsteps echoed loud and hollow in the empty corridor, and the large wax match I struck as we came in gave but a flickering light, which dimly shadowed the outline of the stone stairway, and threw the rest of the corridor into a deep and mysterious gloom. We tramped up the five long flights of stone stairs without a word, the echo of our footsteps sounding louder and louder, and the murky space behind us deepening into the damp darkness of a cavern. At last, after what seemed an interminable climb, we came to the studio entrance.

I put the large key in the lock, turned it, and pushed open the door. A strong draught, like the lifeless breath from the mouth of a tunnel, extinguished the match and left us in darkness. I hesitated an instant, instinctively dreading to enter, and then went in, followed by my friend, who closed the door behind us. The heavy hinges creaked, the door shut into the jambs with a solid thud, the lock sprang into place with a sharp click, and a noise like the clanging of a prison gate resounded and re-echoed through the corridor and through the spacious studio. I felt as if we were shut in from the whole world.

Lighting all the candles at hand and stirring up the fire, we endeavoured to make the studio look cheerful, and neither of us being inclined to go to bed, we sat for a long time talking and smoking. But even the bright fire and the soothing tobacco smoke did not wholly dispel the gloom of the place, and when we finally carried the candles into the bedroom, I felt a vague sense of dismal anticipation and apprehension. We left both doors open, so that the light from our room streamed across the corner of the sitting-room, and threw a great square of strong reflection on the studio carpet. While undressing, I found that I had left my match-box on the studio table, and thought I would return for it. I remember now what a mental struggle I went through before I made up my mind to go without a candle.

I glanced at my friend's face, partly to see if he noticed any indication of nervousness in my expression, and partly because I was conscious of a kind of psychological sympathy between us. But fear that he would laugh at me made me effectually conceal my feelings, and I went out of the room without speaking. As I walked across the non-resonant, carpeted stone floor I had the most curious set of sensations I have ever experienced. At nearly every step I took I came into a different stratum or perpendicular layer of air. First it was cool to my face, then warm, then chill again, and again warm. Thinking to calm my nervous excitement, I stood still and looked around me. The great window above my head dimly transmitted the sky reflection, but threw little light into the studio. The folds of the curtain over the open space above the sitting-room appeared to wave slightly in the uncertain light, and the easels and lay-figure stood gaunt and ghostly along the further wall.

I waited there and reasoned with myself, arguing that there was no possible cause for fear, that a strong man ought to control his nerves, that it was silly at my time of life to begin to be afraid of the dark, but I could not get rid of the sensation. As I went back to the bedroom, I experienced the same succession of physical shocks; but whether they followed each other in the same order or not I was unable to determine.

It was some time before I could get to sleep, and I opened my eyes once or twice before I lost consciousness. From the bedroom window there was a dim, very dim light on the lace curtains, but the window itself was visible as a square mass, and did not appear to illuminate the room in the least. Suddenly, after a dreamless sleep of some duration, I awoke as completely as if I had been startled by a loud noise. The lace curtains were now quite brilliantly lighted from somewhere, I could not tell where, but the window itself seemed to be as little luminous as when I went to sleep. Without moving my head, I turned my eyes in the direction of the studio, and could see the open door as a dark patch in the grey wall, but nothing more.

Then, as I was looking again at the curious illumination of the curtains, a moving mass came into the angle of my vision out of the corner of the room near the head of the bed, and passed slowly into full view between me and the curtain. It was unmistakably the figure of a man, not unlike that of the better type of Italian, and was dressed in the commonly worn soft hat and ample cloak. His profile came out clearly against the light background of the lace curtain, and showed him to be a man of considerable refinement of feature. He did not make an actually solid black silhouette against the light, neither was the figure translucent, but was rather like an object seen through a vapor or through a sheet of thin ground glass.

I tried to raise my head, but my nerve force seemed suddenly to fail me, and while I was wondering at my powerlessness, and reasoning at the same time that it must be a nightmare, the figure had moved slowly across in front of the window, and out through the open door into the studio.

I listened breathlessly, but not a sound did I hear from the next room. I pinched myself, opened and shut my eyes, and noticed that the breathing of my roommate was irregular, and unlike that of a sleeping man. I am unable to understand why I did not sit up or turn over or speak to my friend to find out if he was awake. I was fully conscious that I ought to do this, but something, I know not what, forced me to lie perfectly motionless watching the window. I heard my roommate breathing, opened and shut my eyes, and was certain, indeed, that I was really awake. As I reasoned on the phenomenon, and came naturally to the unwilling conclusion that my hallucination was probably premonitory of malaria, my nerves grew quiet, I began to think less intensely, and then I fell asleep.

The next morning, I awoke with a feeling of disagreeable anticipation. I was loath to rise, even though the warm Italian sunlight was pouring into the room and gilding the dingy interior with brilliant reflections. In spite of this cheering glow of sunshine, the rooms still had the same dead and uninhabited appearance, and the presence of my friend, a vigorous and practical man, seemed to bring no recognisable vitality or human element to counteract the oppressiveness of the place. Every detail of my waking dream or hallucination of the night before was perfectly fresh in my mind, and the sense of apprehension was still strong upon me.

The distracting operations of settling the studio, and the frequent excursions to neighbouring shops to buy articles necessary to our meagre housekeeping, did much towards taking my mind off the incident of the night, but every time I entered the sitting-room or the bedroom it all came up to me with a vividness that made my nerves quiver. We explored all the corners and cupboards of the place. We even crawled up over the sitting-room behind the dingy curtain, where a large quantity of disused frames and old stretchers were packed away. We familiarized ourselves, in fact, with every nook and cranny of each room; moved the furniture about in a different order; hung up draperies and sketches, and in many ways changed the character of the interior.

The faded, weary-looking widow from whom I hired the place, and who took care of the rooms, carried away to her own apartment many of the most obnoxious trifles which encumbered the small tables, the *etagere*, and the wall spaces. She sighed a great deal as we were making the rapid changes to suit our own taste, but made no objection, and we naturally thought it was the regular custom of every new occupant to turn the place upside down.

Late in the afternoon I was alone in the studio for an hour or more, and sat by the fire trying to read. The daylight was not gone, and the rumble of the busy street came plainly to my ears. I say "trying to read," for I found reading quite impossible. The moment I began to fix my attention on the page, I had a very powerful feeling that someone was looking over my shoulder. Do what I would, I could not conquer the unreasonable sensation. Finally, after starting up and looking about me a dozen times, I threw down the book and went out. When I returned, after an hour in the open air, I found my friend walking up and down in the studio with open doors and two guttering candles alight.

"It's a curious thing," he said, "I can't read this book. I have been trying to put my mind on it a whole half-hour, and I can't do it. I always thought I could get interested in Gaborieau in a moment under any circumstances."

"I went out to walk because I couldn't manage to read," I replied, and the conversation ended.

We went to the theatre that evening, and afterwards to the *café* Greco, where we talked art in half a dozen languages until midnight, and then came home. Our entrance to the house and the studio was much the same as on the previous night, and we went to bed without a word. My mind naturally reverted to the experience of the night before, and I lay there for a long time with my eyes open, making a strong effort of the imagination to account for the vision by the dim shapes of the furniture, the lace curtains, and the suggestive and shadowy perspective. But, although the interior was weird enough, by reason of the dingy hangings and the diffused light, I was unable to trace the origin of the illusion to any object within the range of my vision, or to account for the strange illumination which had startled me. I went to sleep thinking of other things, and with my nerves comparatively quiet.

Sometime in the early morning, about three o'clock, as near as I could judge, I slowly awoke, and saw the lace curtains illuminated as before. I found myself in an expectant frame of mind, neither calm nor excited, but rather in that condition of philosophical quiet which best prepared me for an investigation of the phenomenon which I confidently expected to witness. Perhaps this is assuming too eagerly the position of a philosopher, but I am certain no element of fear disturbed my reason, that I was neither startled nor surprised at awakening as I did, and that my mind was active and undoubtedly prepared for the investigation of the mystery.

I was therefore not at all shocked to observe the same shape come first into the angle of my eye, and then into the full range of my vision, next appear as a silhouette against the curtains, and finally lose itself in the darkness of the doorway. During the progress of the shape across the room I noticed the size and general aspect of it with keen attention to detail and with satisfactory calmness of observation. It was only after the figure had passed out of sight, and the light on the window curtains grew dim again, much as an electric light loses its brilliancy with the diminution of the strength of the current, that it occurred to me to consider the fact that during the period of the hallucination I had been utterly motionless. There was not the slightest doubt of my being awake. My friend in the adjoining bed was breathing regularly, the ticking of my watch was plainly audible, and I could feel my heart beating with unusual rapidity and vigour.

The strange part of the whole incident was this incapacity of action, and the more I reasoned about it the more I was mystified by the utter failure of nerve force. Indeed, while the mind was actively at work on this problem the physical torpor continued, a languor not unlike the incipient drowsiness of anaesthesia came gradually over me, and, though mentally protesting against the helpless condition of the body, and struggling to keep awake, I fell asleep, and did not stir till morning.

With the bright clear winter's day returned the doubts and disappointments of the day before—doubts of the existence of the phenomenon, disappointment at the failure of any solution of the hallucination. A second day in the studio did little towards dispelling the mental gloom which possessed us both, and at night my friend confessed that he thought we must have stumbled into a malarial quarter.

At this distance of time it is absolutely incomprehensible to me how I could have gone on as I did from day to day, or rather from night to night—for the same hallucination was repeated nightly—without speaking to my friend, or at least taking some energetic steps towards an investigation of the mystery. But I had the same experience every night for fully a week before I really began to plan serious means of discovering whether it was a hallucination, a nightmare, or a flesh-and-blood intruder. First, I had some curiosity each night to see whether there would be a repetition of the incident. Second, I was eager to note any physical or mental symptom which would serve as a clue to the mystery. Pride, or some other equally authoritative sentiment, continued to keep me from disclosing my secret to my friend, although I was on the point of doing so on several occasions.

My first plan was to keep a candle burning all night, but I could invent no plausible excuse to my comrade for this action. Next, I proposed to shut the bedroom door, and on speaking of it to my friend, he strongly objected on the ground of the lack of ventilation, and was not willing to risk having the window open on account of the malaria. After all, since this was an entirely personal matter, it seemed to me the only thing to do was to depend on my own strength of mind and moral courage to solve this mystery unaided. I put my loaded revolver on the table by the bedside, drew back the lace curtain before going to bed, and left the door only half open, so I could not see into the studio.

The night I made these preparations I awoke as usual, saw the same figure, but, as before, could not move a hand. After it had passed the window, I tried hard to bring myself to take my revolver, and find out whether I had to deal with a man or a simulacrum. But even while I was arguing with myself, and trying to find out why I could not move, sleep came upon me before I had carried out my purposed action.

The shock of the first appearance of the vision had been nearly overbalanced by my eagerness to investigate, and my intense interest in the novel condition of mind or body which made such an experience possible. But after the utter failure of all my schemes and the collapse of my theories as to evident causes of the phenomenon, I began to be harassed and worried, almost unconsciously at first, by the ever-present thought, the daily anticipation, and the increasing dread of the hallucination. The self-confidence that first supported me in my nightly encounter diminished on each occasion, and the curiosity which stimulated me to the study of the phenomenon rapidly gave way to the sentiment akin to terror when I proved myself incapable of grappling with the mystery.

The natural result of this preoccupation was inability to work and little interest in recreation, and as the long weeks wore away, I grew morose, morbid, and hypochondriacal. The pride which kept me from sharing my secret with my friend also held me at my post and nerved me to endure the torment in the rapidly diminishing hope of finally exorcising the spectre or recovering my usual healthy tone of mind. The difficulty of my position was increased by the fact that the apparition failed to appear occasionally, and while I welcomed each failure as a sign that the visits were to cease, they continued spasmodically for weeks, and I was still as far away from the interpretation of the problem as ever.

Once I sought medical advice, but the doctor could discover nothing wrong with me except what might be caused by tobacco, and, following his advice, I left off smoking. He said I had no malaria; that I needed more exercise, perhaps; but he could not account for my insomnia, for I, like most patients, had concealed the vital facts in my case, and had complained of insomnia as the cause of my anxiety about my health.

The approach of spring tempted me out-of-doors, and in the warm villa gardens and the sun-bathed Campagna I could sometimes forget the nightmare that haunted me. This was not often possible unless I was in the company of cheerful companions, and I grew to dread the hour when I was to return to the studio after an excursion into the country among the soothing signs of returning summer. To shut the clanging door of the studio was to place an impenetrable barrier between me and the outside world, and the loneliness of that interior seemed to be only intensified by the presence of my companion, who was apparently as much depressed in spirits as myself.

We made various attempts at the entertainment of friends, but they all lacked that element of spontaneous fun which makes such occasions successful, and we gave it up. On pleasant days we threw open the windows on the street to let in the warm air and sunshine, but this did not seem to drive away the musty odours of the interior. We were much too high up to feel any neighbourly proximity to the people on the other side of the street. The chimneypots and irregular roofs below and beyond were not very cheerful objects in the view, and the landlady, who, as far as we knew, was the only other occupant of the upper storey, did not give us a great sense of companionship. Never once did I enter the studio without feeling the same curious sensation of alternate warm and cool *strata* of air. Never for a quarter of an hour did I succeed in reading a book or a newspaper, however interesting it might be. We frequently had two models at a time, and both my friend and myself made several beginnings of pictures, but neither of us carried the work very far.

On one occasion a significant remark was made by a lady friend who came to call. She will undoubtedly remember now when she reads these lines that she said, on leaving the studio: "This is a curiously draughty place. I feel as if it had been blowing hot and cold on me all the time I have been here, and yet you have no windows open."

At another time my comrade burst out as I was going away one evening about eleven o'clock to a reception at one of the palaces: "I wish you wouldn't go in for society so much. I can't go to the *café*; all the fellows go home about this time of the evening. I don't like to stay here in this dismal hole all cooped up by myself. I can't read, I can't sleep, and I can't think."

It occurred to me that it was a little queer for him to object to being left alone, unless he, like myself, had some disagreeable experiences there, and I remembered that he had usually gone out when I had, and was seldom, if ever, alone in the studio when I returned. His tone was so peevish and impatient that I thought discussion was injudicious, and simply replied, "Oh, you're bilious; I'll be home early," and went away. I have often thought since that it was the one occasion when I could have easily broached the subject of my mental trouble, and I have always regretted I did not do so.

Matters were brought to a climax in this way: My friend was summoned to America by telegraph a little more than two months after we took the studio, and left me at a day's notice. The amount and kind of moral courage I had to summon up before I could go home alone the first evening after my comrade left me can only be appreciated by those who have undergone some similar torture. It was not like the bracing up a man goes through when he has to face some imminent known danger, but was of a more subtle and complex kind.

"There is nothing to fear," I kept saying to myself, and yet I could not shake off a nameless dread. "You are in your right mind and have all your senses," I continually argued, "for you see and hear and reason clearly enough. It is a brief hallucination, and you can conquer the mental weakness which causes it by persistent strength of will. If it be a simulacrum, you as a practical man, with good physical health and sound enough reasoning powers, ought to investigate it to the best of your ability." In this way I endeavoured to nerve myself up, and went home late, as usual. The regular incident of the night occurred. I felt keenly the loss of my friend's companionship, and suffered accordingly, but in the morning, I was no nearer to the solution of the mystery than I was before.

For five weary, torturing nights did I go up to that room alone, and, with no sound of human proximity to cheer me or to break the wretched feeling of utter solitude, I endured the same experience. At last I could bear it no longer, and determined to have a change of air and surroundings. I hastily packed a travelling-bag and my colour-box, leaving all my extra clothes in the wardrobes and the bureau drawers, told the landlady I should return in a week or two, and paid her for the remainder of the time in advance. The last thing I did was to take my travelling-cap, which hung near the head of my bed. A break in the wallpaper showed that there was a small door here. Pulling the knob which had held my cap, the door was readily opened, and disclosed a small niche in the wall. Leaning against the back of the niche was a small crucifix with a rude figure of Christ, and suspended from the neck of the image by a small cord was a triangular object covered with faded cloth. While I was examining with some interest the hiding-place of these relics, the landlady entered.

"What are these?" I asked.

"Oh, *signore!*" she said, half sobbing as she spoke. "Those are relics of my poor husband. He was an artist like yourself, *signore*. He was—he was—ill, very ill—and in mind as well as body, *signore*. May the Blessed Virgin rest his soul! He hated the crucifix, he hated the scapular, he hated the priests. *Signore*, he—he died without the sacrament, and cursed the holy water. I have never dared to touch those relics, *signore*. But he was a good man, and the best of husbands"; and she buried her face in her hands.

I took the first train for Naples, and have never been in Rome since.

At the Hermitage
By E. Levi Brown

The October sun was shining hot, but it was cool and pleasant inside the mill. The brown water in Sawny Creek lapped softly
against the rocks in its bed, and the sycamore and cottonwood trees,
which grew from the water's edge up the steep, muddy banks, stood
straight and motionless in the warm sunny air, no touch of autumn
upon them yet; only the sweet-gums were turning slightly yellow, and
the black-gums were tinging red. It wanted two hours of sunset, but
blackbirds were on their way home, and the thickets were noisy with
their crying.

Inside the moss-grown old mill there was music and dancing going
on, for, comfortably reclining on a pile of cotton seed in the rough
ginning-room, with thick festoons of cobwebs everywhere, and bits
of dusty lint clinging to every splinter in its walls, a young man was
playing a banjo, and two others, with naked feet, were dancing as if for
their lives. A slim dark girl in a blue and white homespun dress, her
head turbaned with a square of the same, sat on a bag of seed cotton
watching them.

"Now, boys, a breakdown," called out the player, "and then I must
gin out Religion's cotton; come, now, lively."

And they went lively enough.

You bake the bread, and gimme the crus';
You sift the meal, and gimme the husk;
You bile the pot, and gimme the grease;
I have the crumbs, and you have the feast—
But mis' gwine gimme the ham-bone.

The loose boards shook and trembled under the heavy feet, the
scattered cotton seed whirled away in little eddies, and baskets of cotton standing about tipped a little break-down of their own. Even the

girl on the bag, whose sober, earnest face seemed out of keeping with the gayety, beat time with her bare feet. But by the time the miller threw his banjo aside, its strings still quivering, she was standing up, and the look of interest had given place to the old gravity. She had not a pretty feature, not even the usual pretty teeth. She was a homely black girl.

"See here, Religion," said the miller, "this here's Saturday evenin', and I keeps holiday like everybody else but you; can't you git along without that little tum of cotton? It ain't wuth ginnin'."

"I'm 'bliged to have it," she answered. "I didn't give nary day's work for rent this week; will pay the week's rent and git sumpin beside. We doesn't draw no ration."

"It's a mighty small heap o' ration you'll git out'n that tum of cotton after you pay fifty cents for your week's rent. Don't you find it cheaper to work out the week's rent than to pay it?"

"I git fifty cents a hundred for pickin'," she answered, simply, "and I kin pick two hundred and fifty a day, and scrap twenty-five more. We doesn't git but fifty cents fur a whole day's work on the plantation."

He looked at her admiringly, at the thin supple body and long light arms that could reach so far among the cotton bolls. He untied the bags and proceeded to fill the gin. A girl who could pick two hundred and seventy-five pounds of cotton a day was a person of some consequence.

The gin stopped its whir, and the clerk weighed the cotton. Religion watched him sharply, and counted the checks he handed her twice.

"If you pass 'em at the Hermitage," he said, "tell 'em to give you another five-cent check; I'm short tonight."

"I ain't goin' to the Hermitage store; I'm goin' to the ferry. They give me cash there for the checks."

"What do they take off?"

"They takes one cent out'n every five. But I'm 'bliged to have the hard money. We has to pay for a good many things we git for Min in hard money." She had taken up the empty bags, but still waited. "I wish you'd please, sir, see if you 'ain't got another check nowhere."

"You're a sight, Religion," he said, good-naturedly. "Here's a nickel."

With her bags on her arm she went out across the dry grass to where a little black mule, not much larger than a goat, was standing. Beck greeted her with a bray astonishing for one of her size, and a switch with her rope of a tail. Unheeding the cheerful greeting, Religion gave all her attention to untying the halter, and soon they were going along the sandy road straight through the woods.

The rickety box-wagon and the chain traces rattled noisily. Religion cracked her whip—it was a stick with a plaited leather string on the end. Beck was in a hurry to get home, and the wagon bumped along over roots and stumps until it was a wonder how Religion kept herself on the board which served for a seat. All the swamps and woods in Sawny were in bad repute. There was an old cemetery, rambling over many acres, lost in ivy and briers and immense trees, but abundant in ghost stories. There was the swamp through which Sherman's soldiers had cut a road, and nearby was the hillside where many sunken hollows marked their graves. A "spirit" could be raised there at a thought's notice. Beck flew past these unpleasant places, and her little hoofs were clattering over the loose bridge at the foot of the hill, where, the cemetery ending, the plantation road began, when she backed suddenly—so suddenly that the board tipped up and dropped Religion into the bottom of the wagon.

Beck had some tricks like all of her kind, and thinking this was one, Religion was scrambling up and readjusting her seat when she saw a face bending over her that she never forgot—a strange evil face, the lower part hidden by a short bushy beard, the upper by many thin braids of hair curling at the ends. Between the two crops of hair she saw a pair of small red eyes, dull and sleepy, but with a curious gleam in them like the eyes of the snakes in the swamp, and thick widespread nostrils. She only had time to note these features and the thick rings of gold in the great ears when the face disappeared, and, as if they floated in the air, she heard the words:

"I am the seventh son of the seventh daughter. I know all things. I can tell you what is killing your sister."

Religion pulled up her rope reins, and Beck flew up the road as if all Sherman's army were after her; nor did she slacken until she reached the great gateway which turned into the Hermitage. Only a flat-topped post remained of the gate, and a boy of twelve, with a face like Religion's, was perched on it.

"Hi, dar, 'Ligion! Ho, Beck!" he cried. "Take me in an' give me a piece of a ride anyway," and with a twinkle of his long ashy legs he landed safely in the wagon.

"What you doin' here, Bud?" questioned his sister. "Why ain't you to home with mammy and Min?"

"Min done had one o' she wussest spells, an' mammy sent me to Miss Tina fur calomel. I heerd youna comin', an' I waited; 'kase ridin' beats walkin' black and blue."

He looked up at her with a sly giggle, and crammed his mouth with persimmons. He expected a scolding for delaying with the calomel, but his sister only said:

"Quit eatin' them 'simmons. Pres'n'y we'll have to git calomel for youna."

They were passing through the quarter now, where everyone was getting supper. The air was full of the appetising odour of frying cornbread and bacon and boiling coffee. Men sat on the doorsteps or smoked in groups under the fine oaks which grew in the middle of the street, waiting for the call to supper. Up at the end of the row of houses, and separated a little from them by a wild-plum thicket, stood a house like a black stump just seen above the green around it. It had what none of the others possessed, a porch in front, but the rotten frame-work had dropped off piece by piece, until it was a mystery how the heavy scuppernong vine that grew upon it was supported. There were lilies and roses in the clean bit of front yard, and on a box was a number of geraniums flourishing in tin cans. There were boxes of violets, and a thick honeysuckle was hugging a post and sending out sweet yellow sprays. Beck drew up before the house with a jerk that had determination in it. Bud jumped out with a boyish shout, but his sister caught his arm.

"Hush, Bud! Don't you hear Min?"

"Min made up that piece today," responded Bud, in a roaring whisper. "Maw an' me's been scared pretty nigh to death. Miss Tina say it ain't Min singin', but that spell workin' on her."

The voice was sweet and rich, with an undercurrent of sadness running through that went to the heart. It seemed to wait and tremble, then float and float away, dying into softest melody. It was not the untaught music of the plantation singers; it was a voice exquisitely trained.

"Lord! Lord!" ejaculated Religion. The words held a heartful of trouble. She lowered the shafts gently and led Beck round the house.

"That you, Religion?" inquired a voice from somewhere in the yard.

She could hear milk straining into a pail, and the tramp of some animal over dry shucks.

"It's me, maw, an' I got enough to pay the rent, and there'll be

134

some over."

"Youna mus' had good luck. Min'll be more'n middlin' glad of a few crackers. I thought sure the gal was gone today, Religion," and a tall form rose up from beside the cow and came towards the girl. "I sut'n'y thought she was gone today," continued the mother. "She just died off, and didn't 'pear to have no more life in her than a dead bird. I was mighty scared."

"Why youna didn't send fur me?"

"Chile, I didn't want to worry youna. Then the neighbours come in, 'kase I did a big piece o' hollerin', an' they worked on her and fotched her back; I 'ain't been no 'count since. See how my hand trembles now."

She placed her hand on her daughter's arm. It was large and hard, but all the ploughing, hoeing, and wood-cutting that she had done had not destroyed its fine shape. It was cold and trembling.

Religion took it between her own square thick ones. "Never mind, maw; she's better now, 'kase she's singin' a new piece. I'll go an' eat and do the errands, so as to git back. You won't feel so bad when I'm here."

The single thing which made the room she entered different from all the other rooms in the quarter was a white bed. The two other beds had the usual patchwork quilts and yellow slips. Religion touched a light-wood splinter to the fire, and holding the light above her head, went up to the white bed. The face on the pillow was of that pure lustrous whiteness which is sometimes seen in very young children; the features were perfect. She seemed a creature of an entirely different sphere—as different from Religion as a butterfly from a grub, and yet there was an indefinable likeness between the two.

"I was waiting for you, 'Ligion," she said, opening her eyes; "I want to tell you something; come close, so ma and Bud won't hear. A woman has been here, a little old woman, and she sat on the bed and told me some things. She told me that Tina had cut off a piece of my hair and hid it in a gum-tree in the swamp, and that I never would be well till my hair was found.

"I remember the night she combed my hair, and how Mauma Amy said it was bad luck to comb hair after dark; it was so thick and long then, and it has come out so since." She drew the long thin brown braid between her fingers. "Why should Tina want to hurt me? The only harm I ever did her was to love her."

She burst into tears, and Religion hugged her in mute sympathy; that was her only way to comfort. When Min was quiet, she stirred up the pillows and smoothed out the white spread. Then she took a tin cup full of clabber, poured a little syrup upon it, and ate it heartily. A plate of greens was hot on the hearth, and a corncake was browning beautifully in the bake-kettle. But there was no time to eat the dainties.

John Robinson, the owner of Hermitage, was a single man. He was old, feeble, and notoriously grasping, yet the dirty, ill-smelling room which Religion entered was strewn with choicest books, sheets of music lay on the table and chairs, and several rare violins lay on a piano, whose mother-of-pearl keys glowed in the red firelight.

"Who's that?" he called, in a cracked old voice, the instant he heard Religion's footsteps. He was wrapped in a cloak and sunk in an armchair before the fire.

"Me, Marse John—Minnie's Religion. I've come to pay the rent."

"Oh, come in, girl! Down, Bull!" he piped to a great hound that was slowly rising from a sheepskin. "It's fifty cents. Sure you've got it all, and no nickels with holes in them?"

She placed a little tobacco-bag in his hand, and he leaned forward to the light to count the money. He had a sharp, pinched old face surrounded by shaggy white hair. A portrait of him taken in a long-past day hung over the fireplace. In that he was a handsome man, with thick chestnut-brown hair. His hands shook so that the pieces of money dropped from them and rolled upon the brick hearth. A tall *mulatto* woman came from a near room and picked them up.

"Count it over again, Tina," he commanded, "and see if it's all there and no holes in it. You can't trust Religion herself with money. How's your sister?"

"Min ain't no better; she ain't never going to be no better in this world."

"Tut, tut!" he muttered. "There should be some strength of will in that girl. But, pshaw! she had a mother and a line of nonentities behind her. I forgot that. Is that money all right, Tina?"

"It's all right, Marse John."

Tina was a beautiful woman, with the smoothest brown skin, and black hair coiled many times around a perfectly shaped head.

The renters never waited long in Mr. Robinson's presence when their business was ended. But Religion only moved back a little and lingered. Tina, bringing a cup of cocoa, at last noticed her.

"Why, Religion, you're not gone."

"And why ain't you gone!" screamed the old man.

"I—I'm waiting for the receipt, sir."

"Waiting for the receipt?" he shrieked. "God and fury! things have come to a pretty pass that a slave wench should wait in my house for a receipt. Get out of this, or—Bull!"

"Stand still, Religion," cried Tina, as the dog leaped up. "Down, Bull! Marse John"—and her voice sank to a sweet, soothing tone—"you'd better not upset yourself so; you'll be sick."

She stroked his face and hair tenderly, and when he lay back quiet in his chair, worn out with his passion, she beckoned to Religion to follow her. They went into one of the rooms. The candle burning in it showed a bed, with posts reaching to the ceiling, and an ancient mahogany chest. A handful of fire burned in the deep fireplace, and before it crouched Mack, an old slave of Mr. Robinson's—a miserable idiot, with just mind enough to perform a very few menial services.

"Trick yer! trick yer!" he piped, in a high thin voice, like an old woman's. "Done got de blacksnake's head an' de dead baby's hand right hyar. Trick yer! trick yer! Git out quick!" He kept up the cry while Tina wrote the receipt, and when she led the way to the door he pattered after them. "Git out quick, 'fore Tina trick yer. I done hope Tina trick Min."

Religion turned fiercely. "Has you tricked my sister and brung her to what she is?"

Tina laughed contemptuously. "Who says I put a spell on Min?"

"Min says it, an' Mack says it, an' I b'lieves it. You always was jealous of her, 'kase Marse John taught her, and made more of her than he did of you."

"Then it's likely this *spell* will put her out of my way," said Tina, all the sweetness gone out of her voice and face, and nothing but venom left. She turned to go in, but Religion dropped on her knees and clasped her feet.

"Oh, Tina! if you did put a spell on Min, take it off, for Christ's sake. Nobody kin do it but you. Our pooty, pooty Min! she be dyin' there before our eyes, and we-uns can't do nothin'. Take the ban off, an' I'll work for you the longest day I live."

Tina dragged herself away and shut the door heavily.

****

Religion was in the field scattering pine straw, and Beck was there too, harnessed in company with a very lean Texas pony. Her mother and Bud were in the same occupation, but Mollie, the old brown cow, drew their wagon.

Religion was crooning a solemn old ditty, as she always did when alone and thinking.

"I just made up my mind this mornin' that I'd got to do sumpin when Mr. Frye come for we-uns to scatter this straw. An' I wish I knowed what to do. Oh, Lord, don't I wish I knowed what to do. There's Min been down on that air bed one whole year come Christmas, and nobody can't say what is the matter with her. Sich a heap o' calomel, and quinine, and turpentine, and doctor's stuff as she has took, and 'tain't done no good. I can't count the times I been to the tavern. I know I brung off more'n two gallons of the best whiskey, an' it's been mixed up with pine-top, an' snakeroot, an' mullein, an' I dun'no' what all, an' none of it 'ain't done no good. An' Min is dyin' just as fast as she can die. Oh, Lord!"

A fine mule, drawing a light road-cart, trotted past. The driver was a short, squat man, his face almost hidden in hair. It was Dr. Buzzard. He was known for miles as a successful "conjurer" and giver of "hands." Most of the people around had perfect faith in his cures and revelations, and had advised Religion to try him, but the girl objected, vaguely questioning reason and conscience, and Min was getting worse. It was despair, not belief, which made her whisper to herself, "I'm goin' to see him this very night."

"Great day! 'ain't we-uns had trouble! Lord, Lord! I b'lieve one-half this wurl' has all the trouble fur all the rest, anyhow!"

Religion was on her way, and thinking over the family record as she walked. The sun had set, the cotton-pickers were in, and odours of supper were afloat. Religion was eating hers as she walked and thought—it was a finely browned ash-cake, richly flavoured with the cabbage leaves in which it was baked.

The Beckets had always been very poor, hard-working people, without any especial grace or finer touch of nature about them. The two brothers had married two sisters, and such marriages were considered unlucky.

When Religion was a little girl her father broke his contract with his employer, and to escape imprisonment he ran away. Religion remembered his stolen visits at night, and his silent caresses of her. After a while the visits stopped. They heard of him in a distant city, but he never came back. His brother had died long before.

The widowed sisters stayed on the plantation, and both were favourites of Mr. Robinson. Min and Tina were half-sisters. They were as opposite in character as they were in appearance; everybody loved

Min; she sang like a bird, and her voice had been carefully trained, and some especial provision had been made for its further cultivation when this strange sickness overtook her.

Good nursing was unknown on the plantations, or perhaps the slight cold, which was the beginning of the end with Min, might have been cured. Since no member of the family had died with consumption, it was not believed that she could have it.

When all the home remedies and doctors' prescriptions failed, there was but one verdict, Min was "hurt." It was known that her half-sister was not very friendly nor over-scrupulous, and it was believed that Tina, out of jealousy, had thrown an evil spell.

The light was still lingering when Religion, turning out of the road, ran down a narrow lane bordered with turpentine woods on one side, and on the other by a field of dead pines. Away back among the latter was a substantial log house, with good brick chimneys at either end. There were several smaller buildings in the yard, and in one a woman was stooping over the fire frying cakes, a young man was thrumming a banjo, and a little boy in scantiest jeans was careening around to the inspiring strains of "Old Joe kicking up behind and before."

Inside, the large low-ceiled room was in a blaze of light. There was a tumbled bed in one corner, a table covered with dusty dishes and glassware in another, and a large case filled with bottles, jugs, and bundles occupied a third. Walls and ceiling were hidden by packages of herbs and strings of roots, while over the fireplace were three shelves piled high with cigar-boxes, carefully labelled.

Half buried in a great chair, his breast bare, his sleeves rolled up above his elbows, the veins in his arms standing out like cords, his legs wrapped in a blanket and resting upon a stool, sat Dr. Buzzard, to all appearances in a deep sleep. On the floor, close to the hearth, was a most evil-looking old crone, continually stirring a pot bubbling on the coals. She threw one glance at Religion, and went on stirring. The doctor never moved. A splendid-looking *mulatto* noiselessly brought a box, and the girl subsided upon it.

There were other visitors. A young man wanted help to get money that was due him; another sought assistance in settling a difficulty. A woman with a child in her arms wanted to charm her recreant husband back to her; a sick one desired relief from the spell which was making her cough her life out.

But the great man slumbered on with a gentle snore, and the old woman stirred the pot. There was not a sound in the room save his snore, the swish of the spoon, and the occasional dropping of a coal. Everyone sat in silent, intense expectation, waiting for—they knew not what.

The oaken logs had died down to a bed of glowing coals when suddenly a red glare flashed from it. Religion closed her eyes, blinded by the light. When she opened them, the doctor was sitting upright, his head hanging back, his eyes wide open and staring upward, and his breast heaving as if in pain. His wife was in the room holding whispered consultations with each person. The men stated their complaints briefly, but the women detained her longer. When she had been the round she glided back to the side of the doctor.

Then in a low chant, sweet and sorrowful, she repeated the story which each had told her, running them into a continuous recitative. The old woman rose from the floor, and joining in the chant in a quavering croon, sprinkled salt at the thresholds of the doors and at the feet of every person, ending by throwing a large handful up the chimney. It fell back and sputtered and cracked in the fire. Seizing one of the cigar-boxes, she sprinkled a pinch of its contents over the fire. A dense grey vapor rose. The doctor raised his arms, and let them fall slowly, three times.

"The fire holds many secrets," he uttered, in a hollow, unnatural voice, like one talking in his sleep; "he who would see his enemy about his work of destruction, let him look in the fire."

With eyes ready to start from her head, Religion with the rest bent forward to look. She saw, or thought she saw, in the curling grey cloud a woman's face. It seemed to take shape and expression, as she gazed, until it grew familiar. The forsaken woman, who had seen the face of a successful rival, sank heavily upon the floor. Some of the others screamed, some moaned and prayed. The cloud over the fire was repeated many times, and dissolving into fantastic shapes, pictured to the excited fancy of the others their enemies and distresses. At last the exhibition ended, and the visitors were sent from the room, and called in again, separately, to receive directions, medicines, and charms against further evil.

Religion found the doctor sitting at the table, surrounded by jugs, bottles, and boxes, his wife and the old woman standing on either side. He still slept, breathing heavily. His hands were on the table.

"A girl named Religion Becket inquiring for her sister," spoke the doctor in the same strange voice. "The sister seems to be dying."

"Say yes close to his right ear," instructed the wife, and Religion did so.

"The doctors know nothing about the case," responded the conjurer. "A red scorpion is inside her body feeding on her vitals. I see a woman hiding something in a black-gum tree that hangs over running water. It is at the hour when spirits walk. The first creature that runs over the cleft where the hand is hidden is the one to torment your sister. That first creature is a red scorpion. Its young one lives in your sister's side. I, even I, can withdraw it."

Like one moved by some power outside of himself, his hands moved in the array before him, lightly touching this or that bottle and bundle until he found what he sought. And like a careful druggist he deliberately measured each ingredient, giving clear directions at the same time. When Religion came out, she had a large bottle of medicine, several huge plasters, and orders for a bewildering list of root teas, with a promise of an early visit from the great man himself.

★★★★★★★★

Religion was feeding the cane-mill. Bud was on the other side drawing out the crushed cane; the mother was under the shed stirring the boiling syrup. Beck was travelling round and round doing the grinding. The sun was set. It would soon be time to stop work. Religion seemed to be expecting someone; she never stooped to pick up an armful of stalks without glancing up the road.

"What you keep lookin' up the road for, 'Ligion?" inquired her mother, her body swaying back and forth as she drew or pushed the long wooden ladle.

"Nuthin'. I ain't lookin' fur nuthin'."

"I b'lieve there's a spell on youna too," said her mother, surveying her anxiously. "I wish youna'd be more keerful and not put your fingers so close to the teeth."

"It's time to quit, anyhow," put in Bud; "the sun's 'way down, an' I'm more'n middlin' hungry."

"You kin take the mule out an' go home an' make the fire. Will you go an' git supper, Religion, or stay an' stir?"

"I reckon I'll stay and stir. You kin bring me some supper when you come. We'll be here half the night."

With another look up the road, where the sunlight was fast fading, she took up the wet bags which protected her dress, and passed under the shed, glad to sit down and rest her aching limbs. The shed was a primitive affair, but everything was convenient for syrup-boiling, and the two long boilers were full of the golden-brown liquid. There was nothing to do but to stir continually and keep a steady fire.

The short autumn twilight had died out, and the fields and woods were slipping into gloom. The cane-mill was in the overseer's yard, and back of it the quarter began. A multitude of sounds came up to Religion's ear—the crying of babies, the laughing of children, the barking of dogs, the whistle of the boys rubbing off the mules, the scolding and calling of women for wood and water. Night was closing in. Religion stirred and thought.

All Dr. Buzzard's instructions had been carefully followed. He had come many times, performed a variety of strange operations, frightened and gladdened them all one day by declaring that the red scorpion had passed out of her body through her foot and run into the fire, that now all danger was passed, pocketed thirty dollars which Minnie and Religion had obtained by giving a lien on Beck, the old cow, all the corn in the crib, and every article of furniture their cabin held; and still Min was no better—was worse, indeed, with the worry of it all.

Someone was coming. "Is that you, Bud?" she called.

The unnatural laugh that answered her could belong to no one but Mack. Lifting a blazing stick above her head, she peered out into the darkness.

"Come fur youna," he mumbled. "Miss Tina goin' on drefful; come fur youna quick."

"You go, Religion," said a woman who had come unperceived. "The Lord's gwine to cl'ar up some t'ings what's took place in this quarter. You go, an' I'll stay an' stir."

Religion hurried away. She found Tina tossing about in a pretty white bed, her hands and feet bound in onions, her whole body swathed in red flannel saturated with turpentine, and her head bandaged with dock leaves wet with vinegar. There was a hot fire, and the room was crowded with men and women.

Dr. Buzzard was there, with a black calico bag, from which he frequently drew a black bottle, examined it sharply at the lamp, then gravely replaced it, after which he always looked at and pinched Tina's fingers.

"Mother," he said at last, addressing himself to Tina's mother, "the time has come for me to show you the cause of your daughter's illness. She has been hurt. She was too beautiful and well-loved to suit all I could name. An evil hand was laid on her."

He took out his watch, looked at it gravely, and laid it upon the table. Removing his coat, he turned back the cuffs of his brown shirt, then took off the bandages from Tina's hands and feet.

He rubbed each arm from the shoulder to the end of the fingers with one sweep, first lightly, then harder, snapping his fingers violently after every stroke. Tina writhed under the treatment, then screamed loudly, and tried to leap from the bed. He called two men to hold her, and the rubbing went on.

With each stroke he grew more and more excited. He lifted his arms high above his head, and bore down upon Tina painfully. His eyes were burning, and the perspiration pouring down his face. He broke into a low humming, and the women took it up, moaning in concert, and rocking their bodies in sympathy.

Suddenly he yelled out, "Ah! there it is; see there, see there; there he goes into the fire, the miserable lizard, which was purposely put into Tina's drink, and has grown in her, and poisoned her blood until I came to drive it out!"

Everyone jumped to see the lizard, and saw nothing but the glowing logs. There was a faint smell of burning flesh. The women fell back into their seats, staring fearfully into each other's faces. Tina sprang upright in bed.

"Min is down by the Black Run calling me, an' I'm goin' to her. He told me to put her hair and some stuff he give me into a hole in the black-gum that hangs over the stone, and I did it. Before God! I never meant to hurt her. I hated her because Marse thought more of her than he did me. He taught her, but he never taught me, and we was both his children. But I never meant to hurt her. Tell Religion so. I'm comin', Min; yes, I'm comin'; wait for me!"

She leaped upon the floor, but the unnatural strength supplied by the delirium of fever had fled. She dropped at Religion's feet with a cry like a wounded dog.

Daylight found Religion in the lonely swamp: only great pools of thick black water and leaning trees shrouded in long grey moss. The water lay still in those levels until the sun dried it up. In just one place was there the slightest movement. A short descent sent a stream slowly curling away under masses of green briers.

The only stone known to be in the whole swamp was at the head of the stream, on a tiny hillock formed of logs and the debris of many freshets. It was known as Cuffee's Stone, and the story was that a slave escaping from his master, and hiding in the swamp, had carried the stone there to build his fire upon. Close by, its sprawling roots washed by the running water, was an immense black-gum, in the branches of which the same Cuffee had built himself a covert of branches, from which he watched his pursuers in their vain hunt for him. Had Cuffee's shade, which was said still to haunt the tree, been abroad at that hour, it would have seen a girl narrowly scanning the rough stem, to find some crack or cleft in which anything might be hidden.

And she found a small crevice which would have escaped any but her searching eyes. They lit up as if she had found a rare treasure. Inserting the point of a knife, she drew out a little bag wet and mouldy. She never stopped to examine it, but leaped from log to log through the briers and water out of the swamp.

"Here's your hair, Min. Curl it round your finger three times and throw it in the fire. Oh, Min, now youna'll get well!"

A light shone in the sick girl's eyes. "Yes, I shall get well. Come out and listen to the music, Religion."

"There isn't any music, Min. See the hair."

"Yes, I see the hair; but, oh, the beautiful music! If I could only learn it!"

Religion clasped her close in her arms. The water-oaks were in a golden-brown haze, and the room was full of rich light. But it swam in darkness before the exhausted girl.

A moment after she recovered herself, but Min was well.

The Reprisal
By H. W. McVickar

1

It was the 17th of March, yet the sun shone brilliantly, and the air was soft and balmy as on any July day. Even the good St. Patrick could have found no possible cause for complaint.

Most of the invalids about the hotel had ventured forth upon the terrace, and sat in groups of twos and threes basking in the sunshine. Their more fortunate brethren who were sojourning merely for rest after the arduous duties of a social season had long since taken themselves off to the pursuits best suited to their inclinations and livers.

One exception, however, there was to this general rule. A young man of some thirty years of age, who, seated upon the first step of a series leading from the terrace to the road, seemed quite content to enjoy the warmth and sunshine in a purely passive way.

To some of those seated in their invalid-chairs it seemed as if he had not moved or changed his position for hours, and after a while his absolute repose rather irritated them.

Nevertheless, he sat there with his elbows resting on his knees and a cigarette between his lips. The cigarette had long gone out, but to all appearances he was blissfully unconscious of the fact.

A pair of rather attractive eyes were gazing into space, and at times there was a fine, sensitive expression about his lips, but the rest of his features were commonplace, neither good nor bad. His face being smooth-shaven gave him from a distance a decidedly boyish appearance.

There was something, however, about him which might be termed interesting, something a trifle different from his neighbours. Even his clothes had that slight difference that hardly can be explained.

After a while his attention was drawn to a very smart-looking trap, half dog and half training cart, which for the past fifteen minutes had

145

been driven up and down by the most diminutive of grooms. Slowly he took in every detail, the high-actioned hackney, the handsome harness, the livery of the groom, even the wicker basket under the seat with its padlock hanging on the hasp. Lazily he attempted to decipher the monogram on the cart's shining sides, but without success. Five minutes more passed, and still up and down drove the groom. Was its owner never coming? he thought. Surely it must be a woman to keep it waiting such a time. Little by little he became more interested in the vehicle, and incidentally in its mistress, and he found himself conjecturing as to what manner of person this was. Was she tall or short, fat or lean, good figure or bad. On the whole, he thought she must be "horsy." That probably expressed it all.

How long these conjectures would have lasted it would be hard to say, had not just then the owner of the trap and horse and diminutive groom herself put in an appearance. She came out of the hotel entrance drawing on one tan-coloured glove about three times too big for a rather pretty hand. She wore a light-coloured driving-coat which reached to her heels, and adorned with mother-of-pearl buttons big enough to be used for saucers. As she passed down the steps, he had a good opportunity to take her in, and when she stopped to give the horse a lump of sugar, a still better chance for observation was afforded.

He could hardly say whether she was good-looking or not; he was inclined to think she was. She had a very winning smile—this he noticed as she gave some instructions to the groom. On the whole his verdict was rather flattering than otherwise, for she impressed him as being decidedly smart, and that with him covered a multitude of sins.

At last she took up her skirts and stepped into the cart, gathered up the lines, and drew the whip from its socket. The groom scrambled up somehow, and after a little preliminary pawing of the air, the horse and cart, driver and groom, disappeared down the road.

"Hello, Jack! What are you doing here sitting in the sun? Come along and have a game of golf with me."

"Thanks! By-the-bye, do you know who that young woman is who has just driven off?"

"Certainly; Miss Violet Easton, of Washington; very fond of horses; keeps a lot of hunters; rich as mud. Would you like to know her?"

"Yes. Much obliged for the information. Oh, play golf? No; it's a very overrated game; you had better count me out this morning."

An hour later, when she returned, had she taken the trouble to notice, she would have seen him still sitting at the top of the same flight of steps, seemingly absorbed in nothing.

2

Three weeks had now passed since that 17th day of March, and Jack Mordaunt had been introduced to Miss Easton; had walked and driven with Miss Easton; had ridden Miss Easton's horses to the hunt three times a week—in fact, had been seen so much in the society of the young woman that gossips had already begun to couple their names.

If, however, Miss Easton and Mr. Mordaunt were aware of this fact, it seemed in no wise to trouble them, nor to cause their meetings to be less frequent. A very close observer might, if he had taken the trouble to observe, have noticed that on these various occasions Miss Easton's colour would be slightly accentuated, and that there was a perceptible increase in the interest she was wont to vouchsafe to the ordinary public. But then there were no close observers, or if there were they had other things to interest them.

On this particular day—it was then about 2 p.m.—Jack Mordaunt leaned lazily against the office desk, deeply absorbed in the perusal of a letter. The furrow that was quite distinct between his eyes would seem to indicate that the contents of the same were far from agreeable.

Twice already had he read the epistle, and was now engaged in going over it for the third time.

He was faultlessly attired in his hunting things, this being Saturday and the run of the week. Whatever disagreeableness may have occurred, Jack Mordaunt was at least a philosopher, and had no intention of missing a meet so long as Miss Easton was willing to see that he was well mounted. His single-breasted pink frock-coat was of the latest cut, and his white moleskin breeches and black pink-top boots were the best that London makers could turn out. His silk hat and gloves lay upon the office desk beside him.

"You seem vastly absorbed in that letter, Mr. Mordaunt; this is the second time I have tried to attract your attention, but with little success. I trust the contents are more than interesting."

Jack whirled round to find himself face to face with Miss Easton. Try as he would, the tell-tale blood slowly mounted to his tanned cheeks, suffusing his entire face with a ruddy hue. Instinctively he crumpled up the letter in his hand and thrust it into his coat-pocket, then, with a poor attempt at a smile, answered her question. "Yes; the letter contains disagreeable news, at least so far as I am concerned. In fact, I will have to return to New York Sunday morning."

"But you are coming back?"

He shook his head. "I fear it will be 'goodbye.'"

Did he observe the quiver of her lips? Perhaps so. Still, no one would have known it as he stood there, swinging his hunting-crop like a pendulum from one finger.

And she—well, the quiver did not last long, and with a little laugh and shrug she continued: "I suppose most pleasant times come to an end, and perhaps it is better that they should come too soon than too late. But, Mr. Mordaunt, we must be going—that is, if we are to be in time for the meet."

"Where is it to be?"

"At Farmingdale, and that is twelve miles away."

Together they walked down the wide corridor, and many an admiring glance was bestowed upon them as they passed, and many an insinuating wink and shrug was given as soon as their backs were turned.

Together they passed through the hotel door on to the terrace and down the steps—those same steps upon which Jack Mordaunt had sat just three weeks ago and watched her drive away. There was the same trap waiting, the same diminutive-looking groom standing at the horse's head. He helped her in, a trifle more tenderly, perhaps, than was absolutely necessary. Then he mounted to the seat beside her, and away they drove, the groom behind hanging on as by his eyelids.

All during those twelve miles they talked together of anything and everything, save on the one subject which was uppermost in their minds. Religiously they abstained from discussing themselves, and yet they knew that sooner or later that subject would have to be broached. Instinctively, however, they both avoided it, as if in their hearts they knew that from it no good could come.

At Farmingdale, as they drove into the stable-yard behind the little country tavern, all thoughts but of the hunt were banished, at least for the moment. They were both too keen about the sport not to feel their pulses quicken at the familiar scene and sounds.

All the hunters had been sent over in the morning, and stood ready in the adjoining stalls and sheds; grooms were taking off and folding blankets, tightening girths and straps preparatory to the start. In the middle of the stable-yard, O'Rourke, the first whip, was struggling with all his might and main to get into his pink coat, which had grown a trifle tight, and was giving the finishing touches to his toilet, gazing at himself in a broken piece of looking-glass that a friendly groom was patiently holding up before him.

Gentlemen and grooms were going and coming, giving and receiving their final instructions. The baying of the hounds, and the dashes here and there of colour from pink coats, all went to make up a most charming and exhilarating picture.

Into the midst of this noise and bustle came Miss Easton and Jack. The groom scrambled down from his perch, and the two got out. In an instant she was surrounded by three or four men, all talking at the same time and upon the same subject: "Was not the day superb?" "Did she know which way the hounds were to run?" "Was she going to ride Midnight?" "What a beauty he was!" and a great deal more of the same kind.

She was gracious to all, and when at last Jack returned, followed by a groom leading her horse, not one man of that group but felt that Miss Easton was simply charming, and anyone who married her was indeed in luck.

Jack stood aside to let young Martin give her a lift into the saddle, and watched him somewhat wistfully as he arranged her straps and skirt. At the final call everyone sought his horse, mounted, and away they went, chattering and laughing.

The run was one of the best of the season, and after it was over Jack found himself riding by Miss Easton on their homeward journey.

Perhaps the others had ridden quite fast, or perchance these two had gone at a snail's pace, but when half-way home they looked about them and found that they were alone.

As far as the eye could reach along the wooded road no living thing was to be seen. The sun was setting like a globe of fire, and the red shafts of light penetrated between the straight trunks of the tall trees, bringing them out black against the evening sky, while the soft breeze moaned through their branches laden with the odours of hemlock and pine.

And this was the end. Another twenty minutes and the hotel would loom up before them, and the little farce, comedy, or tragedy, whichever it might be, would be finished. The curtain would fall, and the two principal actors would disappear.

No art could have given a finer setting to this the last act.

Neither cared to break the spell, and so they rode in silence until it seemed as if the intense stillness could no longer be borne. It was she who first spoke:

"And so, it is really goodbye?"

For a long time, he did not answer, but gazed steadily ahead of him, looking into space.

"Yes," he said at length, "it is goodbye; and it were better had it been goodbye three weeks ago."

"Why?"

He gave a little start, merely repeating the word after her in a queer absent-minded way.

"Yes, why?"

"Oh, I don't know."

Again, silence fell upon them both.

"Violet," it was the first time he had ever used that name.

Violet Easton turned in her saddle and looked straight at him, trying to read something in those dreamy eyes. He met her gaze quietly.

"Why do you call me Violet?"

"Because—because—" He drew in his breath sharply, and hesitated.

"Because—" and she looked inquiringly in his face.

"Don't ask me; please don't ask me. I believe I am mad."

Again, she let her eyes rest upon him with the same earnest look of inquiry.

He turned away, and gazed absently into the trees and underbrush.

In a few minutes she again spoke. "Is this all you have to say, especially—especially"—and she paused a moment as if searching for a word—"if this is the end?"

Again, he turned and looked at her. Their horses were now walking side by side, and very close; one ungloved hand lay upon her knee.

He leaned over and took it, and attempted to draw her towards him.

"No, no, not that; please not that."

"Why?"

"Can't you see—can't you understand? You and I are going to part—this very night, in fact, and—and—Oh, please do not."

He paid little heed to what she was saying, but drew her closer to him. The blood rushed to her cheeks, suffusing them with a deep red glow. Nearer and nearer he drew her, until, half-resisting, half-willing, her lips met his. It was but for an instant, and then all was over. She drew herself away from him, and the blood faded from her face until it was very white. Two tears welled up into her big blue eyes, overflowed, and ran down her cheeks.

"Oh, why did you do it? Otherwise we might have remained friends. But now," and she looked him fair in the face, while her words came slowly and distinctly, "you belong to me, for you are the only man that has ever kissed my lips."

A little shiver passed over Jack as he heard her speak. He could find no explanation for the feeling.

The next day Miss Easton found on her plate at breakfast a big bunch of red roses. Attached to them was a card, and on it the single word "*Adieu!*"

3

A month later Violet Easton sat at the writing-desk in her little private parlour. Her elbows were on the table, and her head rested on her hands. Scalding tears were in her eyes, and try as she would they forced themselves down her cheeks. Before her lay a letter, which she had read for the twentieth time.

It was a simple, commonplace note at best, and seemed hardly worthy of calling forth such feeling. It ran as follows, and was in a man's handwriting:

My Dear Miss Easton—Remembering that you told me you expected this week to run up to New York, I write in behalf of my wife to ask if you will give us both the pleasure of your company at dinner on Thursday evening.

If you like, we can go afterwards to the play.

How is Midnight, and is he still performing as brilliantly as ever?

Sincerely,   J. Mordaunt.

At last, with a great effort, she stopped her tears, and wiping her eyes with her soaking handkerchief, drew out a piece of note-paper from the blotter and began to write.

The first three attempts were evidently failures, for she tore them up and threw the pieces into a scrap-basket; the fourth effort, however, seemed to prove satisfactory.

My Dear Mr. Mordaunt—Many thanks for your and your wife's kind invitation. I have altered my plans, and no longer expect to go to New York.

Midnight is a friend I have never found wanting.

Very sincerely,   Violet Easton.

She read this over carefully, folded, and placed it in an envelope. Upon it she wrote the name of John Mordaunt, Esq., and the address, and ringing a bell, delivered the letter to a hall-boy to mail.

Long after midnight she was still sitting there, gazing seemingly into space.

★★★★★★★★

Jack Mordaunt looked for an instant at the calendar which stood in front of him upon his office desk.

In large numbers were printed 17, and underneath the month of March was registered. He stopped writing for a moment. Somehow that date had forced his mind back just one year, and as he sat there, he was going over again the incidents of that time. They were all so vivid—too vivid, in fact, to be altogether pleasing. Had he forgotten Violet Easton? He had tried to forget her, but his attempts were vain. Since they parted, he had never heard from or of her save that one short note, and yet at odd intervals her remembrance would force itself upon his mind. Her parting words, "You belong to me," haunted him.

And now, just as he was imagining that the little incident was to be forever forgotten, that date had brought up freshly and distinctly every detail of those three weeks. After all, what had he done? A passing flirtation with an attractive girl! To be sure, he had omitted to say that he was married, but after all it was not absolutely necessary for him to proclaim his family history to every passing acquaintance.

Somehow today the recollection of it all irritated him. He felt out of sorts and angry with himself, and inclined to place the blame on others. He shrugged his shoulders and went on with his work. He would dismiss it all now and forever, and yet, try as he would, it would persist in coming back.

He threw down his pen and left the table, going over to the window. The outlook was far from encouraging, the March wind blew in eddies along the street, and now and then the rain came down in sheets, so that the opposite buildings were hardly visible. He shivered slightly; the room felt cold. He went back to his desk and rang the bell. One of the clerks answered it at once.

"Jones, I wish you would turn on the steam heat. The room seems chilly."

"Sorry, sir, but the steam is on full blast. Is there anything else that you wish?"

"No; you can go."

He sat down, and for the next hour again tried to concentrate his mind upon his work. It seemed useless. He looked at his watch; it was a quarter to six. "I think I will have to go home," he muttered to himself. "I don't feel very well, somehow."

John, the office-boy, here put in an appearance. "I beg pardon, Mr. Mordaunt, if you don't want me any more tonight, may I go? All the other clerks have gone."

"Yes." And John disappeared into the outer office.

A few minutes later he again put in his head. "Mr. Mordaunt, a lady wishes to see you; shall I show her in?"

"Certainly."

The door was flung open, and Violet Easton entered.

So sudden and unexpected was her appearance that Jack had to grasp the desk to steady himself. Really, he thought, my nerves must be frightfully unstrung. I think I must take a holiday. Aloud, he said: "Why, Miss Easton, this is a most unexpected pleasure. Won't you be seated? Can I be of any service to you?"

He drew a chair up for her, and she took it, and he sank back into his own.

And now for the first time he had an opportunity to look at her, for she had pushed up the heavy veil that covered her face.

She looked ghastly white, and heavy black rings were round her eyes, "Miss Easton, you look ill. Can I get you anything?"

"Oh no. I am not ill."

He said no more, but waited for her to speak. At last she did. "Mr. Mordaunt, I thought a long time before troubling you, but I decided that as it was purely a matter of business you would not object. I desire you to draw out my will, and, as I am contemplating leaving the city tomorrow, it would be a great convenience if you could do it now and let me sign it. Then perhaps you would be good enough to keep it for me. I have my reasons—"

"I can assure you that I shall be more than pleased to do anything you request."

"Then will you kindly write as I dictate? Of course, I wish you to put it in legal form, as," and she smiled, "I prefer to avoid litigation."

He drew towards him several sheets of legal cap, and began to write as she dictated.

He read it over to her when it was finished, and she nodded approval.

"And now, if you will execute it, I will try and get the janitor and his wife to acknowledge the instrument. I regret to say all my clerks have gone home."

He got up and left the room, returning in a short time with the janitor and his spouse. Miss Easton took the pen from Jack's hand and wrote her name, Violet Easton, in a clear, distinct manner. The janitor subscribed his name as one of the witnesses, and his wife did the same.

Jack thanked them both for their trouble, and they departed. He took the document, and having placed it in an envelope, sealed it with his own seal, and put it away in the safe.

"I don't know how I can thank you, Mr. Mordaunt. If you will kindly send your account to me in Washington, it will be paid."

Jack protested. "I could not think of taking any pay for such a trifling service, I assure you."

"Yes, but if I insist?"

"Oh, very well; I will do as you wish."

"And now I must be going." She rose from her chair and began drawing on her gloves, while he sat and watched her. Suddenly an irresistible desire seemed to take possession of him. A desire in some way to make amends for the past.

He pushed back his chair and stood facing her. Several times he attempted to speak, but no sound would come from his parched and burning lips. He stretched forth his hand and took her ungloved one, the same as he had done a year ago. It seemed to him that it was icy cold. Again, he tried in vain to say something. Slowly he drew her close, still closer to him, until their lips again met in one long kiss.

Her lips were cold, while his were burning hot. It seemed a long, long time before she gently disengaged herself from his embrace. A sweet smile flitted across her pale face.

"Yes," she said, as if speaking to herself, "this is the second time, but it will be the last. And now I must be going. *Adieu!*"

He went with her into the hall and down to the elevator, and saw her into the cab. He forgot to ask her where she was staying. His brain seemed to be on fire.

The next morning, he felt far from well, and at the breakfast-table his wife remarked upon his looks.

"Oh, it's nothing, dear; I think I am a little overworked. As soon as I can dispose of the Farley case I shall try and get away, but it is too important to leave before it is decided. Is there any news in this morning's paper?"

"Nothing very startling, except I see the death of your friend Miss

Easton, in Washington."

"What!" Jack fairly grasped the table for support. "Impossible! There is some mistake." He was now deathly white.

"Perhaps there is some mistake; but here is the notice," and she handed him the paper.

Hurriedly he ran his eye along the death notices until he came to this one:

Easton, Violet—On the 17th day of March, at the residence of her father, K Street, Washington, of diphtheria, aged twenty-three years. Notice of funeral hereafter.

For some time, he sat there as if stunned, until his wife broke in upon his thoughts.

"It seems to me," she said, "that you take this matter very much to heart."

He did not answer her, but soon excused himself, and left the table.

He went straight to his office and into his private room. With trembling fingers, he made out the combination of the safe, and opened the heavy iron doors. There, where he had placed it the night before, lay the sealed envelope. Beads of perspiration stood out upon his forehead, and he was shaking like an aspen leaf. Surely, he thought, I must be ill or mad. He took the envelope and tore it open; his hands were trembling so that he found it difficult to unfold the document. There, at the bottom, in her clear handwriting, was the signature of Violet Easton. There, also, were the signatures of the janitor and his wife. In feverish haste he read the will. It was just as he had written it the night before. It left all her money to her father with the exception of a few gifts.

Midnight had been left to him. He remembered protesting, but she had told him that she was sure he would always be kind to the animal.

He rang the bell, and John appeared.

"Did you show a lady in here last night just before you went home?"

"No, sir."

"Are you positive?"

"Yes, sir."

"Go and get the janitor, and tell him I wish to speak to him."

In a few minutes that dignitary put in an appearance.

"Is that your signature?" and Jack handed him the will.

"Yes, sir; I signed it last night at your request, and so did my wife."

"Was there a lady here at the time?"

"No, sir."

Jack put his hand up to his forehead. "My God!" he muttered, "I must be going mad." Suddenly everything began to whirl about him, and he sank exhausted into his chair.

"John," he said, "send for a cab; I am feeling very ill, and must go home."

Four days later he was dead. The family doctor pronounced the case one of malignant diphtheria.

The Sequel to the Little Room

By Madeline Yale Wynne

'For the land's sake! What'll Maria do now!'

'That's just what Hiram said—"What'll Maria do now!" It ain't as if she had folks belongin' to her, and now the house is burnt, and Hannah is *as* she is, it does seem as if Maria'd find it hard gittin' on alone and doin' her own thinkin'.'

'There wan't nothin' saved, I s'pose.'

'Next door to nothin'; one washtub, I believe, and the old grey horse that was out to pasture, that's about all; I did hear, though, something about the menfolk's having saved a blue-chintz sofy—'twas the only thing they could get out of the house before the roof fell in; they couldn't seem to get a holt of anythin' else, 'twas so hot, and the old house burnt like tinder; Hannah she was that scairt she seemed dazed, and this mornin' Miss Fife, she that married Ben Fife down on the Edge farm, at the foot of the hill, they took 'em in and did for 'em; and when Lucindy Fife went to call 'em to breakfast at five o'clock, there was Maria cryin' like a baby, and Hannah lyin', like an image, with her eyes starin' wide open; she must a had a shock in the night.'

'Fur the land's sake!' said the other woman again.

'Yes, and Miss Fife she tried to get Maria to eat somethin', but she wouldn't eat a thing; she just sat and cried; you know she was always sort of a shadder to Hannah, and now she's just like a baby.'

'I declair! I believe I'll go up to Miss Fife's; I hate to lose the time, I ought to stir butter today; but just as likely as not lots of folks'll drop in, and I sort of want to hear it all at first hand.'

'I believe you're right, and if you'll set a while, I'll hurry up these doughnuts and be ready in no time; it's a sort of lonesome walk up there.'

The Widder Luke turned the light side of a doughnut under, the

157

fat sizzled, and Jane Peebles said: 'Did you hear what sofy 'twas that they saved?'

'I don't rightly know myself which one 'twas. Miss Culver she said it was the blue chintz one, but I don't recollect as they had no blue sofy; I don't seem to know exactly what they did have. Hannah never was just the same to me after we had that tiff over the raspberry jam she and I made for the church sale; but I aint goin' to bring that up agin her, now she's laid low; I shall go up there just the same in their time of trouble.'

'I s'pose the sofy must have been a new one, or they wouldn't have been so keen to save it.'

'I guess 'twas;—seems as if these doughnuts wouldn't never brown; it's always so when you're in a hurry.'

'I guess I'll ask Maria about that sofy,' said Jane; 'it's likely that she'll tell all she knows when she gets used to the situation; I always thought Maria was a sight nicer than she seemed. I know once she came near tellin' me how they made that soft soap, that special kind you know, so white, and it keeps like jell, year after year; 'twas at a sewin'-bee, and Maria she warmed up and was just goin' to tell me, when Hannah she came in, and Maria she shet up as quick as anythin'. It was sort of curious how she knuckled down to Hannah. Did you ever think Hannah was sort of set?' added Jane, in a low, mysterious tone.

'Hannah *set*! She was sotter'n a meetin'-house, and you know it, Jane Peebles, for all you sided with her about that raspberry jam.'

Widder Luke's eyes flashed as she lifted the kettle of hot fat. She got in a good stroke on an old score, and Jane did not dare to retort. Soon after twelve she and Jane Peebles were walking through the lane towards the Fifes'—there was a Sunday air about their dresses, but a Monday decision in their faces; the reporting in hill towns is done mostly by such volunteers, and one must 'git up airly' for the first news.

Widder Luke carried a plate of doughnuts as a neighbourly tribute to the occasion.

At the Corners the women paused a moment; they could see from where they stood the black skeleton of the burned barn silhouetted against the sky, beyond 'Huckleberry Hill.'

Just then Si Briggs came along in his spring wagon, with two strange ladies on the back seat. They took the right-hand road that led to the old Keys place, and as they passed, Mr. Briggs drew his reins with an osh-sh-sh to his horse.

'Won't you get in and ride up the hill?'

Widder Luke and Miss Peebles decorously hesitated a moment, and then climbed over the wheel and sat on either side of Mr. Briggs, who settled himself leisurely between the two women with neighbourly familiarity. Then pointing backward with the butt-end of his whip to indicate and introduce his passengers, he said: 'These ladies were pretty well disappointed to find the Keys house burnt up; they come all the way from—where did you say 'twas you come from?'

'We came down from the Adirondacks,' said Rita. 'We wanted to call on Miss Hannah and Maria, and if possible, to get a sketch of the house, to paint a picture of it.'

'You don't say so! well I declair for it, it's too bad!' said the Widder Luke; 'but there's sights of houses older'n that one you might paint; there's the Fife house, where they are stoppin' now; that's as old agin and more tumble-down, if that's what you want. I read a piece in the *Greentown Gazette* about artists; it said they always took the worst-lookin' houses to paint, though it does seem queer to me.'

'Did you know the Keys house very well, and can you tell us how the rooms were built?'

'Why, certain!' said Mr. Briggs. 'I've been in it a hundred times if I have once.'

Rita and Nan bent forward to listen; the horse jogged slowly up the hill, Mr. Briggs flicking his whip from side to side to encourage the steady walk.

'There was a hall a-runnin' right through the middle, from front to back—an awful waste of space to my thinkin'; when my brother Joel built his house, he sot out to have just such a hall, and I said to him, sez I: "While you're about it why don't you build a house, or else build a hall and let it out for dancin'?" Joel was dead set agin dancin' and it kind of stuck in his mind, so he built his'n without any hall; you jest step right out of doors into the settin'-room; it's nice in summer, but a *leetle* cold in winter.'

'Yes, I should think it might be. What were the other rooms in the Keys house?'

'Wall, there was the family settin'-room, on the right-hand side of the hall, and back of that the bed-room for the old folks; Hannah she's slep' there for some years now; on the north side there was the keepin'-room, and back of that the dinin'-room, though I'll be blessed if I know why it wasn't a kitchen, that is, if a kitchen is where folks cook. Them Keyses, way back to Jonathan Keys, was always folks for high-flyin' names, 'specially Hannah.'

'Was that all the rooms there were in the lower part?'

'Pretty much all, except a shed they used for a kitchen in old times.'

'Wasn't there a little room between the front and back rooms on the north side?' asked Nan, a little hesitatingly, while Rita gave her a pinch of excitement.

'I don'no' as there was,' said Mr. Briggs.

Jane Peebles spoke up:

'I believe there was some sort of a room there. I remember once Maria said she kept that north door a leetle crack open in fly-time, and it did seem to rid the little room of flies considerble.'

'I don't recollect,' said Mr. Briggs, 'as there was a door on the north side, but I ain't sure; them pine-trees was so dark and the rose-bushes so thick; I can't remember as I've been round there lately; it didn't seem any special place to go to.'

'Well!' said Jane Peebles, decisively, 'I guess there ain't nobody in Titusville that knows any more about that house than I do, unless it's the Keyses themselves; and I *know* there was a little room.'

'Now Jane!' said Widder Luke (Jane wilted a little); 'if there was a little room there, where was the door to it—on the inside I mean? I guess I haven't been to the Baptist Sewing Circle for forty years for nothin', and the Keyses have had it once every year, in January; and I venture to say I've set and sewed in that front room scores of times, and the only door in the front room was the door into the china-closet, except, of course, the door into the hall-way; and as to the dinin'-room, as they called it' (Si Briggs was a widower, and this was a subtle compliment to him), 'there wan't no door at all on that side of the room, just blank wall, with them black pictures of the family done in ink, under glass.

'I always was struck with that one of Jonathan Keys, it did look exactly like Hannah—just so set and stubborn about the mouth. Poor Hannah, she has had her day though. I have often heard my mother say that Hannah was the prettiest girl in Titusville when she was sixteen, though she was always that stiff. She was sixteen just before she went down to Salem.'

Here was an opening, and Nan plunged in.

'I heard something about that: didn't she meet an old sea-captain down there and come near marrying him?'

'I don't know how near she came to marrying him, I know he never came to Titusville. Now I wonder how you ever came to hear that old story; it seems a hundred years ago since my mother told me.'

'Here we be!' called out Mr. Briggs, as he stopped his horse with the soothing down-east osh-sh-sh.

Beyond them yawned the black pit where the cellar of the Keys house had been; the ashes still guarded the mystery of the Little Room.

'My! but don't it look mournful!' ejaculated Widder Luke, and then she continued: 'My mother said 'twas rumoured round Titusville that Hannah had caught a *beau* down to Salem. Of course, that made a stir and folks wanted to know all the particulars, but all they could find out by hook or by crook was that 'twas a sea-captain, and that he was after his third wife, having buried his two others, and that he had asked Hannah to marry him; he gave her lots of heathenish stuff that he had brought from India for his first wife. They couldn't seem to find out much more than that, when suddenly Hannah came home, without any warnin'; she brought an extry trunk back with her, but she did look dreadful peakid; she was sort of pale, and her eyes had a look just like her Grandfather Keys'; she hadn't never looked like any of the Keyses before.

'She didn't let on that anything had happened, and she went everywhere just the same, and nobody knew what she had brought home in that extry trunk, till one day, when the family had all gone to meetin', Nancy Stack—she was Hannah's mother's sister—she went and peeked in the trunk and she saw a lot of trash, seashells and queer sorts of calico; but just as she went to lift the tray to see what else there was, she heard the folks comin', so she shut it up quicker'n lightnin'; 'twas a snap-lock and her apron got caught; she couldn't take time to open it, so she just tore off a piece of the hem to get away, meanin' to go and get the scrap out some other time; but Hannah must have been in the habit of goin' to that trunk, and before night she found the checked gingham caught in the lid, and Nancy Stark she left very sudden that afternoon and didn't never set foot in the house again. It's queer how it all comes back to me. I s'pose it's seein' the house gone and knowin' how Hannah was took last night.'

'Oh, do tell us more,' said Rita, breathlessly. 'We know Mrs. Grant, their niece, and it is all so interesting.'

'Wall, folks *is* generally interested in what they are interested in, but I don't know that there's much more to tell. The captain he never turned up to get his third wife. Nancy Stark, she died, and Hannah and Maria here always lived up there alone since the old folks died, and a pretty lonesome spot it was, to be sure.'

'Did anybody ever dare to ask Miss Hannah about the captain?'

'No, I guess not; folks up here mind their own business pretty much.'

There was a silence after this rebuke; but Nan, who always began to hold on when other people let go, said:

'I heard once that they had some beautiful china in the china-closet, some that had belonged to their grandmother.'

Nobody volunteered any remark about this. Mr. Briggs had got out and was poking round with a stick in the ashes.

Nan persisted:

'Did you ever see the china?'

'*I* did' said Jane Peebles, 'sights of times.'

'What kind was it?'

'Oh, just blue willer pattern,—but there was sights of it.'

'Then they didn't have any other kind, white with a gilt edge, for instance?'

'Wall, up *here*, blue willer, *if* it's the real old kind, is considered good 'nough for most folks.'

'Why, of course; I only wish I had any half so nice,' said Rita, politely.

'Be you a chaney collector?' asked Widder Luke, with a defiant note.

'Not at all, oh no; but I do wish we could find out whether they ever did have a gilt-edged set.'

'Sakes alive! if you really want to know particular, I shouldn't make any bones myself about asking Maria. I should like her to know I don't bear any grudge against 'em, though we did have a fallin'-out about that jam, Hannah and me, come ten years ago next August. I shouldn't mind showin' I had friendly interest in them—now, they're in trouble.'

The ruins of the old house looked small and insignificant in the broad sunshine. The poplars were shrivelled by the fire, and the thicket of roses was blackened and trampled; it was as dehumanized as if no one had lived there for a century.

Mr. Briggs came back to the wagon and said, briskly:

'Wall! where'll you go next?'

Rita and Nan hesitated; then Rita said:

'Do you suppose Miss Maria would like to see us? We met her niece just before she sailed for Europe. She asked us to call and give her aunts some messages, but if you think they are too much broken down by the fire and all—'

'Oh, no; it will do Maria good—it's no use cryin' over spilt milk, or burnt houses for that matter, and I guess you could look at Hannah too; she can't speak, I hear it said, but she lies right in the bed off of the livin'-room, and most everybody goes in to look at her.'

'The theatre is nowhere,' whispered Nan to Rita; 'but isn't it ghastly!'

Miss Maria sat in state in the front room at the Fifes'; her black dress, borrowed from a neighbour, was large for even her plump figure, and it had a tendency to make her look as if she had been ill for a long time and had grown thin; her face was pale with the recent excitement, and wore the air of one who was waiting; she sat quite erect in the rocking-chair, with her plump hands folded on her lap; there was an appealing look in her eyes—she missed Hannah; there was no one to give her a pattern for thought or act. Neighbours passed in and out, and there was something so passive in Maria's look that they talked of her freely as *she* as if she were not there.

There was plenty of sympathy for her, but it was swept out of sight by the tide of curiosity and detail,—how the house had caught fire; who had seen it first; how Hannah slept so heavily she could not be roused for a long time; how it happened that the well was so low; how the pump-handle broke; how the men tried to save something, but how little had been got out! and then, 'how bad Hannah looks,' and how old Simeon Bissell lived ten years after his stroke, and Hannah was younger than he, and the Keyses were a long-lived family.

They passed in and out of Hannah's room, Lucinda Fife asking each newcomer to 'just step in and look at Hannah!'

Borne along by their sympathy and curiosity, Rita and Nan went in and looked on poor Hannah, stiff and uncompromising as of old, lying in her unwonted bed. She eyed them with her impenetrable grey gaze, and it was evident that the mystery of the Little Room would never be revealed by her, even if one could be bold enough to storm that granite citadel. They talked with Maria. She heard the messages from her niece in gentle silence.

Rita took her passive hand and tried to tell her how they sympathized with her in her troubles, and to explain how it was they had happened to come at this time, but it evidently did not get below the surface of Maria's consciousness. She seemed most taken with Nan, however, and to like to have her near her. Just before they left her, Rita ventured to ask if any of their gilt-edged china was saved.

'No, I guess not,' said Maria.

163

'Did they save the blue-chintz sofa?' impetuously asked Nan.

'No, I didn't hear as they did.'

'You *did* have a gilt-edged china set, didn't you?' said Nan.

'And a blue sofa?' persuaded Rita.

'I don't seem to remember anything much,' said Maria, with an appealing glance towards the room where Hannah lay. It would be barbarity to press her further just then.

Rita and Nan went away—not to the Adirondacks, however, but to spend a few days with Jane Peebles, who gladly acceded to their petition to be boarded there for a time.

'Miss Peebles, where is that man Hiram who always lived at the Keys'?' asked Rita, as Jane helped them to apple-sauce and ginger-bread at supper.

'Hiram? I guess he's pretty well tuckered out, what with the fire and Hannah's stroke; he come over here this mornin' and wanted a piece of my huckleberry pie; he said he couldn't seem to relish any other food; he always did set a great store by my pie; it wan't any better than what Hannah made, so fer as I could see, but he always 'lotted on havin' the corner-piece when he brought me eggs from the farm.'

Miss Jane's secret was not so hard to discover as was the secret of the Little Room.

'I would like to talk with Hiram,' said Nan.

'Oh, Hiram he'll talk till doomsday, once set him goin', and say pretty smart things too, for a man.'

'Hiram, can't you tell us something about the old house?' asked Nan the next morning, as Hiram rose from the kitchen table where he had been taking the solace of a corner-piece of Jane's huckleberry pie.

'That depends,' said Hiram, 'upon what you want to know. I s'pose I can tell as much as anybody.'

'What we really want to know,' said Rita, candidly, 'is whether there was a closet or a little room on the north side of the Keys house, between the front and the back rooms.'

Hiram rubbed his ear carefully and began in a judicial way:

'When Jonathan Keys first built that house, sometime way back in 1700, he planned to have—'

'Jane Peebles! Jane Peebles! you're wanted right off, up to the Fifes', and Hiram too; Hannah she's took worse, and Maria she's no more use than a babe unborn. I'm on my way up there now,' concluded the Widder Luke, as she hurried up the hill.

When Rita and Nan went to say goodbye to Maria, a few days

later, Maria clung to them. She had begun to like these new friends who had taken it upon themselves to try and do for her what Mrs. Grant would have done had she been there. She followed them to the door, and said, in a whisper:

'I asked Hannah, only the day before her last shock, whether she *did* have any gilt-edged china, and she sort of nodded. Then I asked her if we had a blue sofy, and she nodded again; but come to think it over by myself, I don't think it really meant anything, because you know Hannah couldn't do anything else but nod after she had that first stroke; she couldn't shake her head; but I thought I would tell you, you have been so kind and you seemed so interested.'

Out on the stone wall at the Corners Nan and Rita sat and laughed and cried; the tragedy and the comedy appealed to them, and not even when Nan said, as they walked down to Jane Peebles' house, 'All the same, *I saw the Little Room*,' and Rita said, '*I saw the china-closet*,' did they feel any bitterness.

'Goodbye,' said Hiram; 'I'm real glad you came, and I want you to tell Miss Grant, when you write to her, that Hiram—she'll remember Hiram fast enough—Hiram is going to marry Jane Peebles, and that Maria shan't never want for a home so long as Jane can make huckleberry pies.'

'Oh, we are so glad; and you will send us a piece of wedding-cake, won't you?'

'I shouldn't wonder,' said Hiram.

'Won't you please tell us what you started to that time when Miss Hannah was taken worse so suddenly? we do so want to know whether there was a room or a china-closet there on the north side.'

'I do remember now that I started in to tell you that; it wan't much anyhow, only when their Grandfather Keys built the house, he boasted that he intended to build the *entire* house of timber that hadn't a knot in it. He spent ten years a-gettin' the timber ready, and when it was done, he found that right in the front-room closet they had put a piece of board with a great knot in it. He was dreadful mad, but he kept it there all the same—on purpose, he said, to show folks it wan't no use to set out to do anythin' perfect in this world.'

'Then there was a china-closet—'

'Wall, yes, there certainly was a closet there.'

'Oh, Nan!' said Rita, as the cars moved away from where Hiram stood, 'he didn't say exactly what kind of a closet even then.'

'No; but we can write to Jane and ask her to answer our questions with just yes or no. When she is Mrs. Hiram (I wonder if he ever had a last name) she will get it out of him if we can only interest her.'

★★★★★★★★★★★★

'Jane,' said Hiram that evening, 'if you could manage to wash on Saturday, so as to have an off-day on Monday, I don'no but we might as well be married then as any other time. I should feel sort of easier in my mind if Maria came down to live with us before they think her room is better than her company up to the Fifes', if Hannah should die.'

'That's so, Hiram. I'll hurry round and fix things, and you better stop tonight and tell Maria that I'll be real glad to have her come and live with us; and Hiram, I've been thinking that if the men folks did save that blue-chintz sofy—'

'Wait a minute, Jane, I sort of want to tell you somethin'; 'taint anythin' I should want you to repeat, but it's somethin' that sort of troubles me some. You see, Miss Hannah she's always been good to me, and I shouldn't want to say anythin' to set folks a-talkin'; but Miss Hannah haint been exactly well for some weeks, and only the day before the fire she came to me and she says she thought 'twas about time she put that old trunk full of duds, the one she's always kept in her closet, out of the way, and she guessed she'd have me burn it up. I thought 'twas most a pity to destroy the trunk—it was a real good one, and hadn't never seen no travel to speak of—and so I said I'd take the things out and burn 'em; that seemed to trouble her, and she was real short with me.

'She said I was no better than all the other folks, that I was pryin' round to see what she kep' in it. I sort of soothed her, and then she said she'd been pestered most to death by folks always askin' her about some old blue chintz, and about a little room; and she guessed that if she could put that trunk out of sight, mebby folks would mind their own business and let her have some peace. So, when Maria was out to the garden for some stuff for dinner, Miss Hannah she got me to help her carry the trunk out of her room and put it in the hall-closet; it wan't no kind of a place to keep it, but I thought it was better to humour her a mite, seein' she was out of sorts.

'In the middle of the night,' continued Hiram, dropping his voice and looking round to see that nobody was coming up the walk, 'in the middle of the night I smelt smoke, and thought right off that the barn must be a-burnin', but I couldn't see no light; then I heard a sort of smothered noise, and I suspicioned right off what was the matter. I run to Maria's room and found her stumblin' round in the dark—her

166

room bein' full of smoke she was sort of confused—and there was a turrible glare out in the hall. We found Miss Hannah out there wringin' her hands and callin' out: "Oh, the trunk will be burnt up, the trunk will be burnt up!" We couldn't coax her to go away, and it did seem as she'd burn up in her tracks if I hadn't just took her and carried her out. By that time the house was all blazin', and, though the folks began to come, it wan't no use—it had to go. Hannah she was all dressed, and I don't believe she had been to bed.'

'You don't think she *set* the house afire, Hiram?'

'No, not a-meanin' to; but what I think is that she felt lonesome without that trunk, and so she went down to the hall-closet when she thought we was asleep, and either she dropped her candle or else the things that hung in the closet caught fire, and she didn't see it till 'twas too late, and then she was so fearful that the trunk would burn she wouldn't go away.'

'What was in the trunk?'

Hiram shuffled from one foot to the other, then hesitated a little, and said:

'Jane, I've been comin' to see you a good many years, most ever since we was young, and yet we haint never exactly spoke of gittin' married till lately; but they ain't so slow down in the city, and I guess Hannah sort of expected to git married to that sea-captain down to Salem. Anyways, whatever she kept in that trunk it came from Salem, and I *guess* 'twas some stuff he gave her.'

'You don't say so, all these years!'

★★★★★★★★★★★★

In Paris, Mrs. Grant, with her husband, sat over the breakfast coffee in their little parlour in the Hotel St. Romain. The window opened on the balcony overhanging the Rue St. Roch. From the narrow street below floated the cry, '*Les moules, les moules?*' mingled with the clap, clap of the horses' hoofs on the asphalt below. The *concierge* sang as he swept the sidewalk before the door, and the newsboys cried, with their plaintive intonation, '*Le Figaro, Le Figaro! Le P'tit Journal!*'

'Roger,' said Mrs. Grant, 'I had such a curious dream last night. I suppose I must have been asleep, but I seemed to be awake, when suddenly I saw Aunt Hannah standing at the foot of my bed, just between the two posts. She stood quite still, and her eyes were fixed on me with her peculiar expression of reserve, but also as if she had an intense desire to speak. I was just going to cry out, "Why, Aunt Hannah, is that you?" when suddenly I felt very passive, and as if a change was going

167

on. The curtains of my bed moved back slowly, and I was again in that mysterious little room. I seemed to see either myself or my mother, I could not tell which it was, as a little girl, lying on the sofa; it was that same blue-chintz sofa I told you about; everything in the room was exactly as I remember seeing it when I was a child, even to the shell and the book on the shelf.

'I can't express to you how it was that I saw the little girl lying there; it was as if my mind was compelled by some other mind to see the little girl and the little room; and all the time I did not know whether it was my mother or myself as a child that I was looking at, and I could feel all the time my Aunt Hannah's grey eyes, though I could not see her while the vision of the little room lasted.

'It was some minutes before the scene began to fade, and it did so very gradually, just as it came: first, the roses and blue morning-glories on the paper began to waver and grow indistinct; then one object after another trembled and faded. It was exactly as if something outside of myself compelled me to see these things; and then, as the pressure of that other will was removed, the impression gradually disappeared.

'The last to go was the figure of the little girl, but she too faded; the bed-curtains seemed to evolve out of the walls of the room, and I was lying on my bed; but Aunt Hannah still stood between the foot-posts, with her eyes fixed on mine. Then came the impression that she could not speak, but that she wanted to convey some thought to me; and then these words came to me—not as if a voice spoke them, but as if they were being printed on my mind or consciousness:

'"Margaret, you must not worry any more about the Little Room, it has no connection with you or your mother, and it never had any: it all belongs to me. I am sorry that my secret ever troubled anyone else; I tried to keep it to myself, but sometimes it would get out. There'll never be any Little Room to trouble anybody else anymore."

'All the time I was hearing these words I felt Aunt Hannah's eyes; and then she began to move backward, slowly, and she seemed to vanish down a long, long distance, till I lost sight of her. The last thing I saw was her grey eyes fastened on my face. I awoke, and found myself sitting up, with my head bent forward, looking right between the foot-posts of the bed.'

'Your Aunt Hannah seems to be more fond of travelling than she used to be. Paris is further from Titusville than Brooklyn,' said Mr. Grant, lightly.

'Oh, don't, Roger, don't! I think Aunt Hannah must be dead.'

His Apparition

By W. D. Howells

1

The incident was of a dignity which the supernatural has by no means always had, and which has been more than ever lacking in it since the manifestations of professional spiritualism began to vulgarise it. Hewson appreciated this as soon as he realised that he had been confronted with an apparition. He had been very little agitated at the moment, and it was not till later, when the conflict between sense and reason concerning the fact itself arose, that he was aware of any perturbation. Even then, amidst the tumult of his whirling emotions he had a sort of central calm, in which he noted the particulars of the occurrence with distinctness and precision. He had always supposed that if anything of the sort happened to him, he would be greatly frightened, but he had not been at all frightened, so far as he could make out. His hair had not risen, or his cheek felt a chill; his heart had not lost or gained a beat in its pulsation; and his prime conclusion was that if the Mysteries had chosen him an agent in approaching the material world, they had not made a mistake.

This becomes grotesque in being put into words, but the words do not misrepresent, except by their inevitable excess, the mind in which Hewson rose, and flung open his shutters to let in the dawn upon the scene of the apparition, which he now perceived must have been, as it were, self-lighted. The robins were yelling from the trees and the sparrows bickering under them; catbirds were calling from the thickets of syringa, and in the nearest woods a hermit-thrush was ringing its crystal bells. The clear day was penetrating the east with the subtle light which precedes the sun, and a summer sweetness rose cool from the garden below, gray with dew.

In the solitude of the hour there was an intimation of privity to the event which had taken place, an implication of the unity of the natural and the supernatural, strangely different from that robust gayety of the plain day which later seemed to disown the affair, and leave the burden of proof altogether to the human witness. By this time Hewson had already set about to putting it in such phrases as should carry conviction to the hearer, and yet should convey to him no suspicion of the pride which Hewson felt in the incident as a sort of tribute to himself. He dramatised the scene at breakfast when he should describe it in plain, matter-of-fact terms, and hold everyone spellbound, as he or she leaned forward over the table to listen, while he related the fact with studied unconcern for his own part in it, but with a serious regard for the integrity of the fact itself, which he had no wish to exaggerate as to its immediate meaning or remoter implications. It did not yet occur to him that it had none; they were simply to be matters of future observation in a second ordeal; for the first emotion which the incident imparted was the feeling that it would happen again, and in this return would interpret itself.

Hewson was so strongly persuaded of something of the kind, that after standing for an indefinite period at the window in his pyjamas, he got hardily back into bed, and waited for the repetition. He was agreeably aware of waiting without a tremor, and rather eagerly than otherwise; then he began to feel drowsy, and this at first flattered him, as a proof of his strange courage in circumstances which would have rendered sleep impossible to most men; but in another moment he started from it. If he slept everyone would say he had dreamt the whole thing; and he could never himself be quite sure that he had not.

He got up, and began to dress, thinking all the time, in a dim way, how very long it would be till breakfast, and wondering what he should do till then with his appetite and his apparition. It was now only a little after four o'clock of the June morning, and nobody would be down till after eight; most people at that very movable feast, which St. John had in the English fashion, did not show themselves before nine. It was impossible to get a book and read for five hours; he would be dropping with hunger if he walked so long. Yet he must not sleep; and he must do something to keep from sleeping.

He remembered a little interloping hotel, which had lately forced its way into precincts sacred to cottage life, and had impudently called itself the St. Johnswort Inn, after St. John's place, by a name which he prided himself on having poetically invented from his own and that of a prevalent wild flower. Upon the chance of getting an early cup of coffee at this hotel, Hewson finished dressing, and crept downstairs to let himself out of the house.

He not only found the door locked, as he had expected, but the key taken out; and after some misgiving he decided to lift one of the long library windows, from which he could get into the garden, closing the window after him, and so make his escape. No one was stirring outside the house any more than within; he knocked down a trellis by which a clematis was trying to climb over the window he emerged from, and found his way out of the grounds without alarming anyone. He was not so successful at the hotel, where a lank boy, sweeping the long *piazzas*, recognised one of the St. Johnswort guests in the figure approaching the steps, and apparently had his worst fears roused for Hewson's sanity when Hewson called to him and wondered if he could get a cup of coffee at that hour; he openly owned it was an unnatural hour, and he had a fine inward sense that it was supernatural.

The boy dropped his broom without a word, and vanished through the office door, reappearing after a blank interval to pick up his broom and say, "I guess so," as he began sweeping again. It was well, for one reason that he did not state his belief too confidently, Hewson thought; but after another interval of unknown length a rude, sad girl came to tell him his coffee was waiting for him. He followed her back into the still dishevelled dining room, and sat down at a long table to a cup of lukewarm drink that in colour and quality recalled terrible mornings of Atlantic travel when he haplessly rose and descended to the dining-saloon of the steamer, and had a marine version of British coffee brought him by an alien table-steward.

He remembered the pock-marked nose of one alien steward, and how he had questioned whether he should give the fellow six-pence or a shilling, seeing that apart from this tribute he should have to fee his own steward for the voyage; at the same time his fancy played with the question whether that uncouth, melancholy waitress had found a moment to wash her face before hurrying to fetch his coffee. He amused himself by contrasting her sloven dejection with the brisk neatness of the service at St. Johnswort; but through all he never lost the awe, the sense of responsibility which he bore to the vision vouchsafed him, doubtless for some reason and to some end that it behoved him to divine.

He found a yesterday's paper in the office of the hotel, and read it till he began to drowse over it, when he pulled himself up with a sharp jerk. He discovered that it was now six o'clock, and he thought if he could walk about for an hour he might return to St. Johnswort, and worry through the remaining hour till breakfast somehow. He was still framing in his thoughts some sort of statement concerning the apparition which he should make when the largest number of guests had got together at the table, with a fine question whether he should take them between the *cantaloupe* and the broiled chicken, or wait till they had come to the corn griddle-cakes, which St. John's cook served of a filigree perfection in homage to the good old American breakfast ideal. There would be more women, if he waited, and he should need the sympathy and countenance of women; his story would be wanting in something of its supreme effect without the electrical response of their keener nerves.

2

When Hewson came up to the cottage he was sensible of a certain agitation in the air, which was intensified to him by the sight of St. John, in his bare, bald head and the *négligé* of a flannel housecoat, inspecting, with the gardener and one of the grooms, the fallen trellis under the library window, which from time to time they looked up at, as they talked. Hewson made haste to join them, through the garden gate, and to say shamefacedly enough, "Oh, I'm afraid I'm responsible for that," and he told how he must have thrown down the trellis in getting out of the window.

"Oh!" said St. John, while the two men walked away with dissatisfied grins at being foiled of their sensation. "We thought it was burglars. I'm so glad it was only you." But in spite of his profession, St. John did not give Hewson any very lively proof of his enjoyment. "Deuced uncomfortable to have had one's guests murdered in their beds. Don't say anything about it, please, Hewson. The women would all fly the premises, if there'd been even a suspicion of burglars."

"Oh, no; I won't," Hewson willingly assented; but he perceived a disappointment in St. John's tone and manner, and he suspected him, however unjustly, of having meant to give himself importance with his guests by the rumour of a burglary in the house.

He was a man quite capable of that, Hewson believed, and failing it, capable of pretending that he wanted the matter hushed up in the interest of others.

In any case he saw that it was not to St. John primarily, or secondarily to St. John's guests, that he could celebrate the fact of his apparition. In the presence of St. John's potential vulgarity, he keenly felt

172

his own, and he recoiled from what he had imagined doing. He even realised that he would have been working St. John an injury by betraying his house to his guests as the scene of a supernatural incident.

Nobody believes in ghosts, but there is not one in a thousand of us who would not be uncomfortable in a haunted house, or a house so reputed. If Hewson told what he had seen, he would not only scatter St. John's house-party to the four winds, but he would cast such a blight upon St. Johnswort that it would never sell for a tenth of its cost.

3

From that instant Hewson renounced his purpose, and he remained true to this renunciation in spite of the behaviour of St. John, which might well have tempted him to a revenge in kind. No one seemed to have slept late that morning; several of the ladies complained that they had not slept a wink the whole night, and two or three of the men owned to having waked early and not been able to hit it off again in a morning nap, though it appeared that they were adepts in that sort of thing. The hour of their vigils corresponded so nearly with that of Hewson's apparition that he wondered if a mystical influence from it had not penetrated the whole house.

The adventitious facts were of such a nature that he controlled with the greater difficulty the wish to explode upon an audience so aptly prepared for it the prodigious incident which he was keeping in reserve; but he did not yield even when St. John carefully led up to the point through the sensation of his guests, by recounting the evidences of the supposed visit of a burglar, and then made his effect by suddenly turning upon Hewson, and saying with his broad guffaw: "And here you have the burglar in person. He has owned his crime to me, and I've let him off the penalty on condition that he tells you all about it."

The humour was not too rank for the horsey people whom St. John had mainly about him, but some of the women said, "Poor Mr. Hewson!" when the host, failing Hewson's confession, went on to betray that he had risen at that unearthly hour to go down to the St. Johnswort Inn for a cup of its famous coffee. The coffee turned out to be the greatest kind of joke; one of the men asked Hewson if he could say on his honour that it was really any better than St. John's coffee there before them, and another professed to be in a secret more recondite than had yet been divined: it was that long grim girl, who served it; she had lured Hewson from his rest at five o'clock in the morning; and this humourist proposed a Welsh rarebit some night at the inn, where they could all see for themselves why Hewson broke out of the house and smashed a trellis before sunrise.

Hewson sat silent, not even attempting a defensive sally. In fact, it was only his surface mind which was employed with what was going on; as before, his deeper thought was again absorbed with his great experience. He could not, if his conscience had otherwise suffered him, have spoken of it in that company, and the laughter died away from his silence as if it had been his offence. He was not offended, but he was ashamed, and not ashamed so much for St. John as for himself, that he could have ever imagined acquiring merit in such company by exploiting an experience which should have been sacred to him. How could he have been so shabby? He was justly punished in the humiliating contrast between being the butt of these poor wits, and the hero of an incident which, whatever its real quality was, had an august character of mystery. He had recognised this from the first instant; he had perceived that the occurrence was for him, and for him alone, until he had reasoned some probable meaning into it or from it; and yet he had been willing, he saw it, he owned it! to win the applause of that crowd as a man who had just seen a ghost.

He thought of them as that crowd, but after all, they were good-natured people, and when they fancied that he was somehow vexed with the turn the talk had taken, they began to speak of other things; St. John himself led the way, and when he got Hewson alone after breakfast, he made him a sort of amend. "I didn't mean to annoy you, old fellow," he said, "with my story about the burglary."

"Oh, that's all right," Hewson brisked up in response, as he took the cigar St. John offered him. "I'm afraid I must have seemed rather stupid. I had got to thinking about something else, and I couldn't pull myself away from it. I wasn't annoyed at all."

Whether St. John thought this sufficient gratitude for his reparation did not appear. As Hewson did not offer to break the silence in which they went on smoking, his host made a pretext, toward the end of their cigars, after bearing the burden of the conversation apparently as long as he could, of being reminded of something by the group of women descending into the garden from the terraced walk beyond it and then slowly, with little pauses, trailing their summer draperies among the flower-beds and bushes toward the house.

"Oh, by-the-way," he said, "I should like to introduce you to Miss Hernshaw; she came last night with Mrs. Rock: that tall girl, there, lagging behind a little. She's an original."

"I noticed her at breakfast," Hewson answered, now first aware of having been struck with the strange beauty and strange behaviour of the slim girl, who drooped in her chair, with her little head fallen forward, and played with her bread, ignoring her food otherwise, while she listened with a bored air to the talk which made Hewson its prey. She had an effect of being both shy and indifferent, in this retrospect; and when St. John put up the window, and led the way out to the women in the garden, and presented Hewson, she had still this effect. She did not smile or speak in acknowledgement of Hewson's bow; she merely looked at him with a sort of swift intensity, and then, when one of the women said, "We were coming to view the scene of your burglarious exploit, Mr. Hewson. Was that the very window?" the girl looked impatiently away.

"The very window," Hewson owned. "You wouldn't know it. St. John has had the trellis put up and the spot fresh turfed," and he detached the interlocutory widow in the direction of their bachelor host, as she perhaps intended he should, and dropped back to the side of Miss Hernshaw.

She was almost spiritually slender. In common with all of us, he had heard that shape of girl called willowy, but he made up his mind that sweet-briery would be the word for Miss Hernshaw, in whose face a virginal youth suggested the tender innocence and surprise of the flower, while the droop of her figure, at once delicate and self-reliant, arrested the fancy with a sense of the pendulous thorny spray. She looked not above sixteen in age, but as she was obviously out, in the society sense of the word, this must have been a moral effect; and Hewson was casting about in his mind for some appropriate form of thought and language to make talk in when she abruptly addressed him.

"I don't see," she said, with her face still away, "why people make fun of those poor girls who have to work in that sort of public way."

Hewson silently picked his steps back through the intervening events to the drolling at breakfast, and with some misgiving took his stand in the declaration, "You mean the waitress at the inn?"

"Yes!" cried the girl, with a gentle indignation, which was so dear to the young man that he would have given anything to believe that it veiled a measure of sympathy for himself as well as for the waitress. "We went in there last night when we arrived, for some pins—Mrs. Rock had had her dress stepped on, getting out of the car—and that girl brought them. I never saw such a sad face. And she was very nice;

she had no more manners than a cow."

Miss Hernshaw added the last sentence as if it followed, and in his poor masculine pride of sequence Hewson wanted to ask if that were why she was so nice; but he obeyed a better instinct in saying, "Yes, there's a whole tragedy in it. I wonder if it's potential or actual." He somehow felt safe in being so metaphysical.

"Does it make any difference?" Miss Hernshaw demanded, whirling her face round, and fixing him with eyes of beautiful fierceness. "Tragedy is tragedy, whether you have lived it or not, isn't it? And sometimes it's all the more tragical if you have it still to live: you've got it before you! I don't see how anyone can look at that girl's face and laugh at her. I should never forgive anyone who did."

"Then I'm glad I didn't do any of the laughing," said Hewson, willing to relieve himself from the strain of this high mood, and yet anxious not to fall too far below it. "Perhaps I should, though, if I hadn't been the victim of it in some degree."

"It was the vulgarest thing I ever heard!" said the girl.

Hewson looked at her, but she had averted her face again. He had a longing to tell her of his apparition which quelled every other interest in him, and, as it were, blurred his whole consciousness. She would understand, with her childlike truth, and with her unconventionality she would not find it strange that he should speak to her of such a thing for no apparent reason or no immediate cause. He walked silent at her side, revolving his longing in his thought, and hating the circumstance which forbade him to speak at once. He did not know how long he was lost in this, when he was suddenly recalled to fearful question of the fact by her saying, with another flash of her face toward him, "You *have* lost sleep Mr. Hewson!" and she whipped forward, and joined the other women, who were following the lead of St. John and the widow.

Mrs. Rock, to whom Hewson had been presented at the same time as to Miss Hernshaw, looked vaguely back at him over her shoulder, but made no attempt to include him in her group, and he thought, for no reason, that she was kept from doing so on account of Miss Hernshaw. He thought he could be no more mistaken in this than in the resentment of Miss Hernshaw, which he was aware of meriting, however unintentionally. Later, after lunch, he made sure of this fact when Mrs. Rock got him into a corner, and cosily began, "I always feel like explaining Rosalie a little," and then her vague, friendly eye wandered toward Miss Hernshaw across the room, and stopped, as if waiting for the girl to look away. But Miss Hernshaw did not look away, and that afternoon, Hewson's week being up, he left St. Johnswort before dinner.

<h2 style="text-align:center">4</h2>

The time came, before the following winter, when Hewson was tempted beyond his strength, and told the story of his apparition. He told it more than once, and kept himself with increasing difficulty from lying about it. He always wished to add something, to amplify the fact, to heighten the mystery of the circumstances, to divine the occult significance of the incident. In itself the incident, when stated, was rather bare and insufficient; but he held himself rigidly to the actual details, and he felt that in this at least he was offering the powers which had vouchsafed him the experience a species of atonement for breaking faith with them. It seemed like breaking faith with Miss Hernshaw, too, though this impression would have been harder to reason than the other.

Both impressions began to wear off after the first tellings of the story; the wound that Hewson gave his sensibility in the very first cicatrised before the second, and at the fourth or fifth it had quite calloused over; so that he did not mind anything so much as what always seemed to him the inadequate effect of his experience with his hearers. Some listened carelessly; some nervously; some incredulously, as if he were trying to put up a job on them; some compassionately, as if he were not quite right, and ought to be looked after. There was a consensus of opinion, among those who offered any sort of comment, that he ought to give it to the Psychical Research, and at the bottom of Hewson's heart, there was a dread that the spiritualists would somehow get hold of him. This remained to stay him, when the shame of breaking faith with Miss Hernshaw and with Mystery no longer restrained him from exploiting the fact.

He was aware of lying in wait for opportunities of telling it, and he swore himself to tell it only upon direct provocation, or when the occasion seemed imperatively to demand it. He commonly brought it out to match some experience of another; but he could never deny a friendly appeal when he sat with some good fellows over their five-o'clock cocktails at the club, and one of them would say in behalf of a newcomer, "Hewson, tell Wilkins that odd thing that happened to you up country, in the summer." In complying he tried to save his self-respect by affecting a contemptuous indifference in the matter, and beginning reluctantly and pooh-poohingly. He had pangs afterwards as he walked home to dress for dinner, but his self-reproach was less afflicting as time passed. His suffering from it was never so great as from the slight passed upon his apparition, when Wilkins or what other it might be, would meet the suggestion that he should tell him about it, with the hurried interposition, "Yes, I have heard that; good story."

This would make Hewson think that he was beginning to tell his story too often, and that perhaps the friend who suggested his doing so, was playing upon his forgetfulness. He wondered if he were really something of a bore with it, and whether men were shying off from him at the club on account of it. He fancied that might be the reason why the circle at the five-o'clock cocktails gradually diminished as the winter passed. He continued to join it till the chance offered of squarely refusing to tell Wilkins, or whoever, about the odd thing that had happened to him up country in the summer. Then he felt that he had in a manner retrieved himself, and could retire from the five-o'clock cocktails with honour.

That it was a veridical phantom which had appeared to him he did not in his inmost at all doubt, though in his superficial consciousness he questioned it, not indeed so disrespectfully as he pooh-poohed it to others, but still questioned it. This he thought somehow his due as a man of intelligence who ought not to suffer himself to fall into superstition even upon evidence granted to few. Superficially, however, as well as interiorly, he was aware of always expecting its repetition; and now, six months after the occurrence this expectation was as vivid with him as it was the first moment after the vision had vanished, while his tongue was yet in act to stay it with speech. He would not have been surprised at any time in walking into his room to find It there; or waking at night to confront It in the electric flash which he kindled by a touch of the button at his bedside.

Rather, he was surprised that nothing of the sort happened, to confirm him in his belief that he had been all but in touch with the other life, or to give him some hint, the slightest, the dimmest, why this vision had been shown him, and then instantly broken and withdrawn. In that inmost of his where he recognised its validity, he could not deny that it had a meaning, and that it had been sent him for some good reason special to himself; though at the times when he had prefaced his story of it with terms of slighting scepticism, he had professed neither to know nor to care why the thing had happened. He always said that he had never been particularly interested in the supernatural, and then was ashamed of a lie that was false to universal human experience; but he could truthfully add that he had never in his life felt less like seeing a ghost than that morning. It was not full day, but it was perfectly light, and there the thing was, as palpable to vision as any of the men that moment confronting him with cocktails in their hands.

Asked if he did not think he had dreamed it, he answered scornfully that he did not think, he *knew*, he had not dreamed it; he did not value the experience, it was and had always been perfectly meaningless, but he would stake his life upon its reality. Asked if it had not perhaps been the final office of a nightcap, he disdained to answer at all, though he did not openly object to the laugh which the suggestion raised.

Secretly, within his inmost, Hewson felt justly punished by the laughter. He had been unworthy of his apparition in lightly exposing it to such a chance; he had fallen below the dignity of his experience. He might never hope to fathom its meaning while he lived; but he grieved for the wrong he had done it, as if at the instant of the apparition he had offered that majestic, silent figure some grotesque indignity: thrown a pillow at it, or hailed it in tones of mocking offence. He was profoundly and exquisitely ashamed even before he ceased to tell the story for his listeners' idle amusement. When he stopped doing so, and snubbed solicitation with the curt answer that everybody had heard that story, he was retrospectively ashamed; and mixed with the expectation of seeing the vision again was the formless wish to offer it some sort of reparation, of apology.

He longed to prove himself not wholly unworthy of the advance that had been made him from the other world upon grounds which he had done his worst to prove untenable. He could not imagine what the grounds were, though he had to admit their probable existence; such an event might have no obvious or present significance, but it had not happened for nothing; it could not have happened for nothing. Hewson might not have been in what he thought any stressful need of ghostly comfort or reassurance in matters of faith. He was not inordinately agnostic, or in the way of becoming so. He was simply an average sceptical American, who denied no more than he affirmed, and who really concerned himself so little about his soul, though he tried to keep his conscience decently clean, that he had not lately asked whether other people had such a thing or not.

He had not lost friends, and he was so much alone in this world that it seemed improbable the fate of any uncle or cousin, in the absence of more immediate kindred, should be mystically forecast to him. He was perfectly well at the time of the apparition, and it could not have been the figment of a disordered digestion, as the lusty hunger which willingly appeased itself with the coffee of the St. Johnswort Inn sufficiently testified. Yet, in spite of all this, an occurrence so out of the course of events must have had some message for him, and it must have been his fault that he could not divine it. A sense of culpability grew upon him with the sense of his ignominy in cheapening it by making it subservient to what he knew was, in the last analysis, a wretched vanity. At least he could refuse himself that miserable gratification hereafter, and he got back some measure of self-respect in forbidding himself the pleasure he might have taken in being noted for a strange experience he could never be got to speak of.

5

The implication of any such study as this is that the subject of it is continuously if not exclusively occupied with the matter which is supposed to make him interesting. But of course, it was not so with Hewson, who perhaps did not think of his apparition once in a fortnight, or oftener, say, than he thought of the odd girl with whom for no reason, except contemporaneity in his acquaintance, he associated with it. If he never thought of the apparition without subconsciously expecting its return, he equally expected when he thought of Miss Hernshaw that the chances of society would bring them together again, and it was with no more surprise than if the vision had intimated its second approach that he one night found her name in the minute envelope which the footman presented him at a house where he was going to dine, and realised that he was appointed to take her out.

It was a house where he rather liked to go, for in that New York of his where so few houses had any distinctive character, this one had a temperament of its own in so far that you might expect to meet people of temperament there, if anywhere. They were indeed held in a social solution where many other people of no temperament at all floated largely and loosely about, but they were there, all the same, and it was worth coming on the chance of meeting them, though the indiscriminate hospitality of the hostess might let the evening pass without promoting the chance.

Now, however, she had unwittingly put into Hewson's keeping, for two hours at least, the very temperament that had kept his fancy for the last half-year and more. He fairly laughed at sight of the name on the little card, and hurried into the drawing-room, where the first thing after greeting his hostess, he caught the wandering look and vague smile of Mrs. Rock. The look and the smile became personal to him, and she welcomed him with a curious resumption of the confidential terms in which they had seemed to part that afternoon at St. Johnswort. He thought that she was going to begin talking to him where she had left off, about Rosalie, as she had called her, and he was disappointed in the commonplaces that actually ensued. At the end of these, however, she did say: "Miss Hernshaw is here with me. Have you seen her?"

"Oh, yes," Hewson returned, for he had caught sight of the girl in a distant group, on his way up to Mrs. Rock, but in view of the affluent opportunity before him had richly forborne trying even to make her bow to him, though he believed she had seen him. "I am to have the happiness of going out with her."

"Oh, indeed," said Mrs. Rock, "that is nice," and then the people began assorting themselves, and the man who was appointed to take Mrs. Rock out, came and bowed Hewson away.

He hastened to that corner of the room where Miss Hernshaw was waiting, and if he had been suddenly confronted with his apparition, he could not have experienced a deeper and stranger satisfaction than he felt as the girl lifted up her innocent fierce face upon him.

It brought back that whole day at St. Johnswort, of which she, with his vision, formed the supreme interest and equally the mystery; and it went warmly to his heart to have her peremptorily abolish all banalities by saying, "I was wondering if they were going to give me you, as soon as you came in."

She put her slim hand on his arm as she spoke, and he thought she must have felt him quiver at her touch. "Then you were not afraid they were going to give you me?" he bantered.

"No," she said, "I wanted to talk with you. I wanted you to tell me what Mrs. Rock said about me!"

"Just now? She said you were here."

"No, I mean that day at St. Johnswort."

Hewson laughed out for pleasure in her frankness, and then he felt a gathering up of his coat-sleeve under her nervous fingers, as if (such a thing being imaginable) she were going unwittingly to pinch him for his teasing. "She said she wanted to explain you a little."

"And then what!"

"And then nothing. She seemed to catch your eye, and she stopped."

The fingers relaxed their hold upon that gathering up of his coat-sleeve. "I won't *be* explained, and I have told her so. If I choose to act myself, and show out my real thoughts and feelings, how is it any worse than if I acted somebody else!"

"I should think it was very much better," said Hewson, inwardly warned to keep his face straight.

6

They had time for no more talk between the drawing-room and the dinner table, and when Miss Hernshaw's chair had been pushed in behind her, and she sat down, she turned instantly to the man on her right and began speaking to him, and left Hewson to make conversation with anyone he liked or could.

He did not get on very well, not because there were not enough amusing people beside him and over against him, but because he was all the time trying to eavesdrop what was saying between Miss Hernshaw and the man on her right. It seemed to be absolute trivialities they were talking; so far as Hewson made out, they got no deeper than the new play which was then commanding the public favour apparently for the reason that it was altogether surface, with no measure upwards or downwards. Upon this surface the comment of the man on Miss Hernshaw's right wandered indefatigably.

Hewson could not imagine of her sincerity a deliberate purpose of letting the poor fellow show all the shallowness that was in him, and of amusing itself with his satisfaction in turning his empty mind inside out for her inspection. She seemed, if not genuinely interested, to be paying him an unaffected attention; but when the lady across the table addressed a word to him, Miss Hernshaw, as if she had been watching for some such chance, instantly turned to Hewson.

"What do you think of 'Ghosts'?" she asked, with imperative suddenness.

"Ghosts?" he echoed.

"Or perhaps you didn't go?" she suggested, and he perceived that she meant Ibsen's tragedy. But he did not answer at once. He had had a shock, and for a timeless space he had been back in his room at St. Johnswort, with that weird figure seated at his table. It seemed to vanish again when he gave a second glance, as it had vanished before, and he drew a long sigh, and looked a little haggardly at Miss Hernshaw. "Ah, I see you did! Wasn't it tremendous? I think the girl who did Regina was simply awful, don't you?"

182

"I don't know," said Hewson, still so trammelled in his own involuntary associations with the word as not fully to realise the strangeness of discussing "Ghosts" with a young lady. But he pulled himself together, and nimbly making his reflection that the latitude of the stage gave room for the meeting of cultivated intelligences in regions otherwise tabooed, if they were of opposite sexes, he responded in kind. "I think that the greatest miracle of the play—and to me it was altogether miraculous"—

"Oh, I'm glad to hear you say that!" cried the girl. "It was the greatest experience of my life. I can't bear to have people undervalue it. I want to hit them. But go on!"

Hewson went on as gravely as he could in view of her potential violence: he pictured Miss Hernshaw beating down the inadequate witnesses of "Ghosts" with her fan, which lay in her lap, with her cobwebby handkerchief, drawn through its ring, and her long limp gloves looking curiously like her pretty young arms in their slenderness. "I was merely going to say that the most prodigious effect of the play was among the actors—I won't venture on the spectators—"

"No, don't! It isn't speakable."

"It's astonishing the effect a play of Ibsen's has with the actors. They can't play false. It turns the merest theatrical sticks into men and women, and it does it through the perfect honesty of the dramatist. He deals so squarely with himself that they have to deal squarely with themselves. They have to be, and not just *seem*."

Miss Hernshaw sighed deeply. "I'm glad you think that," she said, and Hewson felt very glad too that he thought that.

"Why?" he asked.

"Why? Because that is what I always want to do; and it's what I always shall do, I don't care what they say."

"But I don't know whether I understand exactly."

"Deal squarely with everybody. Say what I really feel. Then they say what they really feel."

There was an obscure resentment unworthily struggling at the bottom of Hewson's heart for her long neglect of him in behalf of the man on her left. "Yes," he said, "if they are capable of really feeling anything."

"What do you mean? Everybody really feels."

"Well, then, thinking anything."

She drew herself up a little with an air of question. "I believe everybody really thinks, too, and it's your duty to let them find out what they're thinking, by truly saying what you think."

"Then *she* isn't dealing quite honestly with him," said Hewson, with a malicious smile.

The man at Miss Hernshaw's left was still talking about the play, and he was at that moment getting off a piece of pure parrotry about it to the lady across the table: just what everybody had been saying about it from the first.

"No, I should think she was not," said the girl, gravely. She looked hurt, as if she had been unfairly forced to the logic of her postulate, and Hewson was not altogether pleased with himself; but at least he had had his revenge in making her realise the man's vacuity.

He tried to get her back to talk about "Ghosts," again, but she answered with indifference, and just then he was arrested by something a man was saying near the head of the table.

7

It was rather a large dinner, but not so large that a striking phrase, launched in a momentary lull, could not fuse all the wandering attentions in a sole regard. The man who spoke was the psychologist Wanhope, and he was saying with a melancholy that mocked itself a little in his smile: "I shouldn't be particular about seeing a ghost myself. I have seen plenty of men who had seen men who had seen ghosts; but I never yet saw a man who had seen a ghost. If I had it would go a long way to persuade me of ghosts."

Hewson felt his heart thump in his throat. There was a pause, and it was as if all eyes but the eyes of the psychologist turned upon him; these rested upon the ice which the servant had just then silently slipped under them. Hewson had no reason to think that any of the people present were acquainted with his experience, but he thought it safest to take them upon the supposition that they had, and after he had said to the psychologist, "Will you allow me to present him to you?" he added, "I'm afraid everyone else knows him too well already."

"You!" said his *vis-à-vis*, arching her eyebrows; and others up and down the table, looked round or over at Hewson where he sat midway of it with Miss Hernshaw drooping beside him. She alone seemed indifferent to his pretension; she seemed even insensible of it, as she broke off little corners of her ice with her fork.

The psychologist fixed his eyes on him with scientific challenge as well as scientific interest. "Do you mean that *you* have seen a ghost?"

"Yes—ghost. Generically—provisionally. We always consider them

184

ghosts, don't we, till they prove themselves something else? I once saw an apparition."

Several people who were near-sighted or far-placed put on their eye-glasses, to make out whether Hewson were serious; a lady who had a handsome forearm put up a lorgnette and inspected him through it; she had the air of questioning his taste, and the subtle aura of her censure penetrated to him, though she preserved a face of rigid impassivity. He returned her stare defiantly, though he was aware of not reaching her through the lenses as effectively as she reached him. Most of those who prepared themselves to listen seemed to be putting him on trial, and they apparently justified themselves in this from the cross-questioning method the psychologist necessarily took in his wish to clarify the situation.

"How long ago was it?" he asked, coldly.

"Last summer."

"Was it after dark?"

"Very much after. It was at daybreak."

"Oh! You were alone?"

"Quite."

"You made sure you were not dreaming?"

"I made sure of that, instantly. I was not awakened by the apparition. I was already fully awake."

"Had your mind been running on anything of the kind?"

"Nothing could have been farther from it. I was thinking what a very long while it would be till breakfast." This was not true as to the order of the fact; but Hewson could not keep himself from saying it, and it made a laugh and created a diversion in his favour.

"How long did it seem to last?"

"The vision? That was very curious. The whole affair was quite achronic, as I may say. The figure was there and it was not there."

"It vanished suddenly?"

"I can't say it vanished at all. It ought still to be there. Have you ever returned to a place where you had always been wrong as to the points of the compass, and found yourself right up to a certain moment as you approached, and then without any apparent change, found yourself perfectly wrong again? The figure was not there, and it was there, and then it was not there."

"I think I see what you mean," said the psychologist, warily. "The evanescence was subjective."

"Altogether. But so was the apparescence."

"Ah!" said Wanhope. "You hadn't any headache?"

"Not the least."

"Ah!" The psychologist desisted with the effect of letting the defence take the witness.

A general dissatisfaction diffused itself, and Hewson felt it; but he disdained to do anything to appease it. He remained silent for that appreciable time which elapsed before his host said, almost compassionately, "Won't you tell us all about it, Mr. Hewson."

The guests, all but Miss Hernshaw, seemed to return to their impartial frame, with a leaning in Hewson's favour, such as the courtroom feels when the accused is about to testify in his own behalf; the listeners cannot help wishing him well, though they may have their own opinions of his guilt.

"Why, there *isn't* any 'all-about-it,'" said Hewson. "The whole thing has been stated as to the circumstances and conditions." He could see the baffled greed in the eyes of those who were hungering for a morsel of the marvellous, and he made it as meagre as he could. He had now no temptation to exaggerate the simple fact, and he hurried it out in the fewest possible words.

8

The general disappointment was evident in the moment of waiting which followed upon his almost contemptuous ending. His audience some of them took their cue from his own ironical manner, and joked; others looked as if they had been trifled with. The psychologist said, "Curious." He did not go back to his position that belief in ghosts should follow from seeing a man who had seen one; he seemed rather annoyed by the encounter. The talk took another turn and distributed itself again between contiguous persons for the brief time that elapsed before the women were to leave the men to their coffee and cigars.

When their hostess rose, Hewson offered his arm to Miss Hernshaw. She had not spoken to him since he had told the story of his apparition. Now she said in an undertone so impassioned that every vibration from her voice shook his heart, "If I were you, I would never tell that story again!" and she pressed his arm with unconscious intensity, while she looked away from him.

"You don't believe it happened?" he returned. "It did."

"Of course, it happened! Why shouldn't I believe that? But that's the very reason why I wouldn't have told it. If it happened, it was something sacred—awful! Oh, I don't see how you could bear to speak of it at a dinner, when people were all torpid with—"

She stopped breathlessly, with a break in her voice that sounded just short of a sob.

"Well, I'm sufficiently ashamed of doing it, and not for the first time," he said, in sullen discontent with himself. "And I've been properly punished. You can't think how sick it makes me to realise what a detestable sensation I was seeking."

She did not heed what he was saying. "Was it that morning at St. Johnswort when you got up so early, and went for a cup of coffee at the inn?"

"Yes."

"I thought so! I could follow every instant of it; I could see just how it was. If such a thing had happened to me, I would have died before I spoke of it at such a time as this. Oh, *why* do you suppose it happened to you?" the girl grieved.

"Me, of all men?" said Hewson, with a self-contemptuous smile.

"I thought you were different," she said absently; then abruptly: "What are you standing here talking to me so long for? You must go back! All the men have gone back," and Hewson perceived that they had arrived in the drawing-room, and were conspicuously parleying in the face of a dozen interested women witnesses.

In the dining-room he took his way toward a vacant place at the table near his host, who was saying behind his cigar to another old fellow: "I used to know her mother; she was rather original too; but nothing to this girl. I don't envy Mrs. Rock her job."

"I don't know what the pay of a chaperon is, but I suppose Hernshaw can make it worth her while, if he's like the rest out there," said the other old fellow. "I imagine he's somewhere in his millions."

The host held up one of his fingers. "Is that all? I thought more. Mines?"

"Cattle. Ah, Mr. Hewson," said the host, turning to welcome him to the chair on his other side. "Have a cigar. That was a strong story you gave us. It had a good fault, though. It was too short."

9

Hewson had begun now to feel a keen, persistent, painful sympathy for the apparition itself as for someone whose confidence had been abused; and this feeling was none the less, but all the more, poignant because it was he himself who was guilty towards it. He pitied it in a sort as if it had been the victim of a wrong more shocking perhaps for the want of taste in it than for any real turpitude. This was a quality of the event not without a strange consolation. In arraying him on the side of the apparition, it antagonised him with what he had done, and enabled him to renounce and disown it.

From the night of that dinner, Hewson did not again tell the story of his apparition, though the opportunities to do so now sought him as constantly as he had formerly sought them. They offered him a fresh temptation through the different perversions of the fact that had got commonly abroad, but he resisted this temptation, and let the perversions, sometimes annoyingly, sometimes amusingly, but always more and more wildly, wide of the reality, take their course. In his reticence he had the sense of atoning not only to the apparition but to Miss Hernshaw too.

Before he met her again, Miss Hernshaw had been carried off to Europe by Mrs. Rock, perhaps with the purpose of trying the veteran duplicities of that continent in breaking down the insurgent sincerity of her ward. Hewson heard that she was not to be gone a great while; it was well into the winter when they started, and he understood that they were merely going to Rome for the end of the season, and were then going to work northward, and after June in London were coming home. He did not fail to see her again before she left for any want of wishing, but he did not happen to meet her at other houses, and at the house of Mrs. Rock, if she had one, he had not been asked to call, or invited to any function. In thinking the point over it occurred to Hewson that this was so because he was not wanted there, and not wanted by Miss Hernshaw herself; for it had been in his brief experience of her that she let people know what she wanted, and that with Mrs. Rock, whose character seemed to answer to her name but poorly, she had ways of getting what she wanted.

If Miss Hernshaw had wished to meet him again, he could not doubt that she would have asked him, or at the least had him asked to come and see her, and not have left it to the social fortuities to bring them together. Towards the end of the term which rumour had fixed to her stay abroad Hewson's folly was embittered to him in a way that he had never expected in his deepest shame and darkest foreboding. But evil, like good, does not cease till it has fulfilled itself in every possible consequence. It seeing even more active and persistent. Good seems to satisfy itself sometimes in the direct effect, but evil winds sinuously in and out, and reaches round and over and under its wretched author, and strikes him in every tender and fatal place, with an ingenuity in finding the places out that seems truly of hell.

Hewson thought he had paid the principal of his debt in full through the hurt to his vanity in failing to gain any sort of consequence from his apparition, but the interest of his debt had accumulated, and the sorest pinch was in paying the interest. His penalty took the form that was most of all distasteful to him: the form of publicity in the Sunday edition of a newspaper. A young lady attached to the staff of this journal had got hold of his story, and had made her reporter's story of it, which she imaginatively cast in the shape of an interview with Hewson. But worse than this, and really beyond the vagary of the wildest nightmare, she gave St. Johnswort as the scene of the apparition, with all the circumstances of the supposed burglary, while tastefully disguising Hewson's identity in the figure of A Well-Known Society-man.

When Hewson read this Story (and it seemed to him that no means of bringing it to his notice at the club, and on the street, and by mail was left unemployed), he had two thoughts: one was of St. John, and one was of Miss Hernshaw. In all his exploitations of his experience he had carefully, he thought religiously, concealed the scene, except that one only time when Miss Hernshaw suddenly got it out of him by that demand of hers, "Was it that morning at St. Johnswort when you got up so early and went for a cup of coffee at the inn?" He had confided so absolutely in her that his admission had not troubled him at the time, and it had not troubled him since, till now when he found the fact given this hideous publicity, and knew that it could have become known only through her: through her who had seemed to make herself the protectress of his apparition and to guard it with indignation even against his own slight!

He could not tell himself what to think of her, and in this disability he had at least the sad comfort of literally thinking nothing of her; but he could not keep his thoughts away from St. John. It appeared to him that he thought and lived nothing else till his dread concreted itself in the letter which came from St. John as soon as that fatal newspaper could reach him, and his demand for an explanation could come back to Hewson. He wrote from St. Johnswort, where he had already gone for the season, and he assumed, as no doubt he had a right to do, that the whole thing was a fake, and that if Hewson was hesitating about denying it for fear of giving it further prominence, or out of contempt for it, he wished that he would not hesitate. There were reasons, which would suggest themselves to Hewson, why the thing, if merely and entirely a fake, should be very annoying, and he thought that it would be best to make the denial immediate and imperative. To this end he advised Hewson's sending the newspaper people a lawyer's letter; with the ulterior trouble which this would intimate they would move in the matter with a quickened conscience.

Apparently, St. John was very much in earnest, and Hewson would eagerly have lied out of it, he felt in sudden depravity, from a just regard for St. John's right to privacy in his own premises, but no lying, not the boldest, not the most ingenious, could now avail. Scores of people could witness that they had heard Hewson tell the story at first hand; at second hand hundreds could still more confidently affirm its truth. But if he admitted the truth of the fact and denied merely that it had happened at St. Johnswort, he would have Miss Hernshaw to deal with and what could he hope from truth so relentless as hers? She was of a moral make so awful that if he ventured to deny it without appeal for her support (which was impossible), she was quite capable of denying his denial.

He did the only thing he could. He wrote to St. John declaring that the newspaper story, though utterly false in its pretensions to be an interview with him, was true in its essentials. The thing *had* really happened, he *had* seen an apparition, and he had seen it at St. Johnswort that morning when St. John supposed his house to have been invaded by burglars. He vainly turned over a thousand deprecatory expressions in his mind, with which to soften the blow but he let his letter go without including one.

10

A week of silence passed, and then one night, St. John himself appeared at Hewson's apartment. Hewson almost knew that it was his ring at the door, and in the tremulous note of his voice asking the man if he were at home, he recognised the great blubbery fellow's most plaintive mood.

"Well, Hewson," he whimpered, without staying for any form of greeting when they stood face to face, "this has been a terrible business for me. You can't imagine how it's broken me up in every direction."

"I—I'm afraid I can, St. John," Hewson began, but St. John cut him off.

"Oh, no, you can't. Look here!" He showed a handful of letters. "All from people who had promised to stay with me, taking it back, since that infernal interview of yours, or from people who hadn't answered before, saying they can't come. Of course, they make all sorts of civil excuses. I shouldn't know what to do with these people if any of them came. There isn't a servant left on the place, except the gardener who lives in his own house, and the groom who sleeps in the stable. For the last three days I've had to take my meals at that infernal inn where you got your coffee."

"Is it so bad as that?" Hewson gasped.

"Yes, it is. It's so bad that sometimes I can't realise it. Do you actually mean to tell me, Hewson that you saw a ghost in my house?"

"I never said a ghost. I said an apparition. I don't know what it was. It may have been an optical delusion. I call it an apparition, because that's the shortest way out. You know I'm not a spiritualist."

"Yes, that's the devil of it," said St. John. "That's the very thing that makes people believe it *is* a ghost. There isn't one of them that don't say to himself and the other fellows that if a cool, clear-headed chap like you saw something queer, it *must* have been a ghost; and so they go on knocking my house down in price till I don't believe it would fetch fifteen hundred under the hammer tomorrow. It's simply ruin to me."

"Ruin?" Hewson echoed.

"Yes, ruin," St. John repeated. "Before this thing came out, I refused twenty-five thousand for the place, because I knew I could get twenty-eight thousand. Now I couldn't get twenty-eight hundred. Couldn't you understand that the reputation of being haunted simply plays the devil with a piece of property?"

"Yes; yes, I did understand that, and for that very reason I was always careful—"

"Careful! To tell people that you had seen a ghost in my house?"

"No! *Not* to tell them where I had seen a ghost. I never—"

"How did it get out then?"

"I," Hewson began, and then he stood with his mouth open, unable to close it for the articulation of the next word, which he at last huskily whispered forth, "can't tell you."

"Can't tell me?" wailed St. John. "Well, I call that pretty rough!"

"It is rough," Hewson admitted; "and Heaven knows that I would make it smooth if I could. I never once—except once only—mentioned your place in connection with the matter. I was scrupulously careful not to do so, for I did imagine something like what has happened. I would do anything—anything—in reparation. But I can't even tell you how the name of your place got out in the connection, though certainly you have a right to ask and to know. The circumstances were—peculiar. The person— was one that I wouldn't have dreamt was capable of repeating it. It was as if I had said the words over to myself."

"Well, I can't understand all that," said St. John, with rueful sulkiness, from which he brisked up to ask, as if by a sudden inspiration, "If it was only to one person, why couldn't you deny it, and throw the onus on the other fellow?" He looked up at Hewson, standing nerveless before him, from where he lay mournfully wallowing in an easy-chair, as if now for the first time, there might be a gleam of hope for them both in some such notion.

Hewson slowly shook his head. "It wouldn't work. The person— isn't that kind of person."

"Why, but see here," St. John urged. "There must be something in the fellow that you can appeal to. If you went and told him how it was playing the very deuce with me pecuniarily, he would see the necessity of letting you deny it, and taking the consequences, if he was anything of a man at all."

"He isn't anything of a man at all," said Hewson, in mechanical and melancholy parody.

"Then in Heaven's name what is he?" demanded St. John, savagely.

"A woman."

"Oh!" St. John fell back in his chair. But he pulled himself up again with a sudden renewal of hope. "Why, see here! If she's the right kind of woman, she'll enjoy denying the story, and putting the people in the wrong that have circulated it!"

Hewson shook his head in rejection of the general principle, while, as to the particular instance, he could only say: "She isn't that kind. She's the kind that would rather die herself, and let everybody else die, than be party to any sort of deception."

"She must be a queer woman," St. John bewailed himself, looking at the point of his cigar, and discovering to his surprise that it was out. He did not attempt to light it. "Of course, I can't ask you *who* she is; but why shouldn't I see her, and try what *I* can do with her? I'm the one that's the principal sufferer in this matter," he added, perhaps seeing refusal in Hewson's troubled eye.

"Because—for one reason—she's in London."

"Oh Lord!" St. John lamented.

"But if she were here in New York, I couldn't allow it," he continued. "It was in confidence between us."

"She doesn't seem to have thought so," said St. John, with sarcasm which Hewson could not resent.

"There's only one thing for me to do," said Hewson, who had been thinking the point over, and saw no other way out for him as a gentleman, or even merely as a just man. He was not rich, and in the face of the mounting accumulations of other men he had grown comparatively poor, without actually losing money, since he had begun to lead the life which had long been his ideal. After carefully ascertaining at the time in question that he had sufficient income from inherited means to live without his profession, he had closed his law-office without shutting many clients out, and had contributed himself to the formation of a leisure class, which he conceived was regrettably lacking in our conditions. He had taste, he had reading, he had a pretty knowledge of the world from travel, he had observed manners, and it seemed to him that he might not immodestly pretend to supply, as far as one man went, a well-recognised want.

Hitherto he had been able to live up to his ideal with, sufficient satisfaction, and in proposing to himself never to marry, but to grow old gradually and gracefully as a bachelor of adequate income, he saw no difficulties in his way for the future, until this affair of the apparition. If now he incurred the chances of an open change in his way of living—the end was simply a question of very little time. He must not only declass, he must depatriate himself, for he would not have the means of living even much more economically than he now lived in New York, if he did what a sense of honour, of just responsibility urged him to do with regard to St. John.

He would have been glad of any interposition of Providence that would have availed him against his obvious duty. He would have liked to recall the words saying that there was only one thing for him to do, but he could not recall them and he was forced to go on. "Will you sell me your place?" he said to St. John, colourlessly.

"Sell you my place? What do you mean?"

"Simply that if you will, I shall be glad to buy it at your own valuation."

"Oh, look here, now, Hewson! I can't let you do this," St. John began, trying to feel a magnanimity which proved impossible to him. "What do you want with my place? You couldn't get anybody to live there with you."

"I couldn't afford to live there in any case," said Hewson; "but I am entirely willing to risk the purchase."

Was it possible that Hewson knew something of the neighbour-hood or its future, which encouraged him to take the chances of the property appreciating in value? This thought passed through St. John's mind, and he was not the man to let himself be overreached in a deal. "The place ought to be worth thirty thousand," he said, for a bluff.

It was a relief for Hewson to feel ashamed of St. John instead of himself, for a moment. "Very well, I'll give you thirty thousand."

St. John examined himself for a responsive generosity. The most he could say was, "You're doing this because of what I'd said."

"What does it matter? I make you a *bona fide* offer. I will give you thirty thousand dollars for St. Johnswort," said Hewson, haughtily. "I ask you to sell me that place. I cannot see that it will ever be any good to me, but I can assure you that it would be a far worse burden for me to carry round the sense of having injured you, however unwill-ingly—God knows I never meant you harm!—than to shoulder the chance of your place remaining worthless on my hands."

St. John caught at the hope which the form of words suggested. "If anything can bring it up, it will be the fact that you have bought it. Such a thing would give the lie to that ridiculous story, as nothing else could. Everyone will see that a house can't be very badly haunted, if the man that the ghost appeared to is willing to buy it."

"Perhaps," said Hewson sadly.

"No perhaps about it," St. John retorted, all the more cheerfully because he would have been glad before this incident to take twen-ty thousand for his place. "It's just on the borders of Lenox, and it's bound to come up when this blows over." He talked on for a time in an encouraging strain, while Hewson, standing with his back against the mantel, looked absently down upon him. St. John was inwardly struggling through all to say that Hewson might have the property for twenty-eight thousand, but he could not. Possibly he made himself believe that he was letting it go a great bargain at thirty; at any rate he ended by saying, "Well, it's yours—if you really mean it."

"I mean it," said Hewson.

St. John floundered up out of his chair with seal-like struggles. "Do you want the furniture?" he panted.

"The furniture? Yes, why not?" said Hewson. He did not seem to know what he was saying, or to care.

"I will put that in for a mere nominal consideration—the rugs alone are worth the money—say a thousand more."

Hewson's man came in with a note. "The messenger is waiting, sir," he said.

Hewson was aware of wondering that he had not heard any ring. "Will you excuse me?" he said, toward St. John.

"By all means," said St. John.

Hewson opened the note, and read it with an expression which can only be described as a radiant frown. He sat down at his desk, and wrote an answer to the note, and gave it to his man, who was still waiting. Then he said to St. John, "What did you say the rugs were worth?"

"A thousand."

"I'll take them. And what do you want for the rest of the furniture?"

Clearly, he had not understood that the furniture, rugs, and all, had been offered to him for a thousand dollars. But what was a man in St. John's place to do? As it was, he was turning himself out of house and home for Hewson, and that was sacrifice enough. He hesitated, sighed deeply, and then said, "Well, I will throw all that in for a couple of thousand more."

"All right," said Hewson, "I will give it. Have the papers made out and I will have the money ready at once."

"Oh, there's no hurry about that, my dear fellow," said St. John, handsomely.

11

Hewson's note was from Mrs. Rock, asking him to breakfast with her at the Walholland the next morning. She said that they were just off the steamer, which had got in late, and they had started so suddenly from London that she had not had time to write and have her apartment opened. She came to business in the last sentence where she said that Miss Hernshaw joined her in kind remembrances, and wished her to say that he must not fail them, or if he could not come to breakfast, to let them know at what hour during the day he would be kind enough to call; it was very important they should see him at the earliest possible moment.

Hewson instantly decided that this summons was related to the affair of his apparition, without imagining how or why, and when Miss Hernshaw met him, and almost before she could say that Mrs. Rock would be down in a moment, began with it, he made no feint of having come for anything else.

As he entered the door of Mrs. Rock's parlour, where the breakfast table was laid, the girl came swiftly toward him, with the air of having turned from watching for him at the window. "Well, what do you think of me?" she demanded as soon as she had got over Mrs. Rock's excuses for having her receive him.

He had of course to repeat, "What do I think of you?" but he knew perfectly what she meant.

She disdained to help him pretend that he did not know. "It was I who told that horrible woman about your experience at St. John-swort. I didn't dream that she was an interviewer, but that doesn't excuse me, and I am willing to take any punishment for my—I don't know what to call it—mischief."

She was so intensely ready, so magnificently prepared for the stake, if that should be her sentence, that Hewson could not help laughing. "Why there isn't any punishment severe enough for a crime like that," he began, but she would not allow him to trifle with the matter.

"Oh, I didn't think you would be so uncandid! The instant I read that interview I made Mrs. Rock get ready to come. And we started the first steamer. It seemed to me that I could not eat or sleep, till I had seen you and told you what I had done and taken the consequences. And now do you think it right to turn it off as a joke?"

"I don't wish to make a joke of it," said Hewson, gravely, in compliance with her mood. "But I don't understand, quite, how you could have got the story over there in time for you—"

"It was cabled to their London edition—that's what it said in the paper; and by this time, they must have it in Australia," said Miss Hernshaw, with unrelieved severity.

"Oh!" said Hewson, giving himself time to realise that he was the psychical hero of two hemispheres. "Well," he resumed "what do you expect me to say?"

"I don't know what I expect. I expected you to say something without my prompting you. You know that it was outrageous for me to talk about your apparition without your leave, and to be the means of its getting into the newspapers."

"I'm not sure you were the means. I have told the story a hundred times, myself."

"But that doesn't excuse me. You knew the kind of people to tell it to, and I didn't."

"Oh, I am afraid I was willing to tell it to all kinds of people—to any kind that would listen."

"You are trying to evade me, Mr. Hewson," she said, with a severity

196

he found charming. "I didn't expect that of you."

The appeal was not lost upon Hewson. "What do you want me to say?"

"I want you," said Miss Hernshaw, with an effect of giving him another trial, "to say—to acknowledge that you were terribly annoyed by that interview."

"If you will excuse me from attaching the slightest blame to you for it, I will acknowledge that I was annoyed."

Miss Hernshaw drew a deep breath as of relief. "I will arrange about the blame," she said loftily. "And now I wish to tell you how I never supposed that girl was an interviewer. We were all together at an artist's house in Rome, and after dinner, we got to telling ghost-stories, the way people do, around the fire, and I told mine—yours I mean. And before we broke up, this girl came to me—it was while we were putting on our wraps—and introduced herself, and said how much she had been impressed by my story—of course, I mean your story—and she said she supposed it was made up. I said I should not dream of making up a thing of that kind, and that it was every word true, and I had heard the person it happened to tell it himself. I don't know! I was vain of having heard it, so, at first hand."

"I can understand," said Hewson, sadly.

"And then I told her who the person was, and where it happened—and about the burglary. You can't imagine how silly people get when they begin going in that direction."

"I am afraid I can," said Hewson.

"She seemed very grateful somehow; I couldn't see why, but I didn't ask; and then I didn't think about it again till I saw it in that awful newspaper. She sent it to me herself; she was such a simpleton; she thought I would actually like to see it. She must have written it down, and sent it to the paper, and they printed it when they got ready to; she needed the money, I suppose. Then I began to wonder what you would say, when you remembered how I blamed you for telling the same story—only not half so bad—at that dinner."

"I always felt you were quite right," said Hewson. "I have always thanked you in my own mind for being so frank with me."

"Well, and what do you think now, when you know that I was ten times as bad as you—ten times as foolish and vulgar!"

"I haven't had time to formulate my ideas yet," Hewson urged.

"You know perfectly well that you despise me. Can you say that I had any right to give your name?"

"It must have got out sooner or later. I never asked anyone not to mention my name when I told the story—"

"I see that you think I took a liberty, and I did. But that's nothing. That isn't the point. How I do keep beating about the bush! Mrs. Rock says it was a great deal worse to tell where it happened, for that would give the place the reputation of being haunted and nobody could ever live there afterwards, for they couldn't keep servants, even if they didn't have the creeps themselves, and it would ruin the property."

Hewson had not been able, when she touched upon this point, to elude the keen eye with which she read his silent thought.

"Is that true?" she demanded.

"Oh, no; oh, no," he began, but he could not frame in plausible terms the lies he would have uttered. He only succeeded in saying, "Those things soon blow over."

"Then how," she said, sternly, "does it happen that in every town and village, almost, there are houses that you can hardly hire anybody to live in, because people say they are haunted? No, Mr. Hewson, it's very kind of you, and I appreciate it, but you can't make me believe that it will ever blow over, about St. Johnswort. Have you heard from Mr. St. John since?"

"Yes," Hewson was obliged to own.

"And was he very much troubled about it? I should think he was a man that would be, from the way he behaved about the burglary. Was he?" she persisted, seeing that Hewson hesitated.

"Yes, I must say he was."

There was a sound of walking to and fro in the adjoining room, a quick shutting as of trunk-lids, a noise as of a skirt shaken out, and steps advanced to the door. Miss Hernshaw ran to it and turned the key in the lock. "Not yet, Mrs. Rock," she called to the unseen presence within, and she explained to Hewson, as she faced him again, "She promised that I should have it all out with you myself, and now I'm not going to have her in here, interrupting. Well, did he write to you?"

"Yes, he wrote to me. He wanted me to deny the story."

"And did you?"

"Of course not!" said Hewson, with a note of indignation. "It was true. Besides it wouldn't have been of any use."

"No, it would have been wicked and it would have been useless. And then what did he say?"

198

"Nothing."

"Nothing? And you have never heard another word from him?"

"Yes, he came to see me last night."

"Here in New York? Is he here yet?"

"I suppose so."

"Where?"

"I believe at the Overpark."

Miss Hernshaw caught her breath, as if she were going to speak, but she did not say anything.

"Why do you insist upon all this, Miss Hernshaw?" he entreated. "It can do you no good to follow the matter up!"

"Do you think I want to do myself *good?*" she returned. "I want to do myself *harm!* What did he say when he came to see you?"

"Well, you can imagine," said Hewson, not able to keep out of his tone the lingering disgust he felt for St. John.

"He complained?"

"He all but shed tears," said Hewson, recalled to a humorous sense of St. John's behaviour. "I felt sorry for him; though," he added, darkly, "I can't say that I do now."

Miss Hernshaw didn't seek to fathom the mystery of his closing words. "Had he been actually inconvenienced by that thing in the paper?"

"Yes—somewhat."

"How much?"

"Oh," Hewson groaned. "If you must know—"

"I must! The worst!"

"It had fairly turned him out of house and home. His servants had all left him, and he had been reduced to taking his meals at the inn. He showed me a handful of letters from people whom he had asked to visit him, withdrawing their acceptances, or making excuses for not accepting."

"Ah!" said Miss Hernshaw, with a deep, inward breath, as if this now were indeed something like the punishment she had expected. "And will it—did he think—did he say anything about the pecuniary effect—the—whether it would hurt the property?"

"He seemed to think it would," answered Hewson, reluctantly, and he added, unfortunately for his generous purpose, "I really can't enter upon that part."

She arched her eyebrows in grieved surprise. "But that is the very part that I want you to enter upon Mr. Hewson. You *must* tell me, now! Did he say that it had injured the property very much?"

"He did, but—"

"But what?"

"I think St. John is a man to put the worst face on that matter."

"You are saying that to keep me from feeling badly. But I ought to feel badly—I *wish* to feel badly. I suppose he said that it wasn't worth anything now."

"Something of that sort," Hewson helplessly admitted.

"Very well, then, I will buy it for whatever he chooses to ask!" With the precipitation which characterised all her actions, Miss Hernshaw rose from the chair in which she had been provisionally sitting, pushed an electric button in the wall, swirled away to the other side of the room, unlocked the door behind which those sounds had subsided, and flinging it open, said, "You can come out, Mrs. Rock; I've rung for breakfast."

Mrs. Rock came smoothly forth, with her vague eyes wandering over every other object in the room, till they rested upon Hewson, directly before her. Then she gave him her hand, and asked, with a smile, as if taking him into the joke. "Well, has Rosalie had it out with you?"

"I have had it out with him, Mrs. Rock," Miss Hernshaw answered, "and I will tell you all about it later. Now I want my breakfast."

12

Hewson ate the meal before him, and it was a very good one, as from time to time he noted, in a daze which was as strange a confusion of the two consciousnesses as he had ever experienced. Whatever the convention was between Miss Hernshaw and Mrs. Rock with regard to the matter in hand, or lately in hand, it dropped, after a few uninterested inquiries from Mrs. Rock, who was satisfied, or seemed so, to know that Miss Hernshaw had got at the worst. She led the talk to other things, like the comparative comforts and discomforts of the line to Genoa and the line to Liverpool; and Hewson met her upon these polite topics with an apparent fulness of interest that would have deceived a much more attentive listener.

All the time he was arguing with Miss Hernshaw in his nether consciousness, pleading with her to keep her away from the fact that he had himself bought St. Johnswort, until he could frame some fitting form in which to tell her that he had bought it. With his outward eyes, he saw her drooping on the opposite side of the table, and in spite of her declaration that she wanted her breakfast, making nothing of it, after the preliminary melon, while to his inward vision she was passionately refusing, by every charming perversity, to be tempted away from the subject.

As the Cunard boats always get in on Saturday, this morrow of their arrival was naturally Sunday; and after a while, Hewson fancied symptoms of going to church in Mrs. Rock. She could not have become more vague than she ordinarily was, but her wanderings were of a kind of devotional character. She spoke of the American church in Rome, and asked Hewson if he knew the rector. Then, when he said he was afraid he was keeping her from going to church, she said she did not know whether Rosalie intended going. At the same time, she rose from the table, and Hewson found that he should not be allowed to sit down again, unless by violence. He had to go away, and he went, as little at ease in his mind as he very well could be.

He was no sooner out of the house than he felt the necessity of returning. He did not know how or when Miss Hernshaw would write to St. John, but that she would do so, he did not at all doubt, and then, when the truth came out, what would she think of him? He did not think her a very wise person; she seemed to him rather a wild and whirling person in her ideals of conduct, an unbridled and undisciplined person; and yet he was aware of profoundly and tenderly respecting her as a creature of the most inexpugnable innocence and final goodness. He could not bear to have her feel that he had trifled with her. There had not been many meetings between them, but each meeting had been of such event that it had advanced their acquaintance far beyond the point that it could have reached through weeks of ordinary association.

From the first there had been that sort of intimacy which exists between spirits which encounter in the region of absolute sincerity. She had never used the least of those arts which women use in concealing the candour of their natures from men unworthy of it; she had not only practiced her rule of instant and constant veracity, but had avowed it, and as it were, invited his judgment of it. Hitherto, he had met her half-way at least, but now he was in the coil of a disingenuousness which must more and more trammel him from her, unless he found some way to declare the fact to her.

This ought to have been an easy matter, but it was not easy; upon reflection it grew rather more difficult. Hewson did not see how he could avow the fact, which he wished to avow, without intolerable awkwardness; without the effect of boasting, without putting upon her a burden which he had no right to put. To be sure, she had got herself in for it all by her divine imprudence, but she had owned her error in that as promptly as if it had been the blame of someone else. Still Hewson doubted whether her magnanimity was large enough to go round in the case of a man who tried to let his magnanimity come upon her with any sort of dramatic surprise. This was what he must seem to be doing if he now left her to learn from another how he had kept St. John from loss by himself assuming the chance of depreciation in his property. But if he went and told her that he had done it, how much better for him would that be?

He took a long, unhappy walk up into the Park, and then he walked back to the Walholland. By this time, he thought Mrs. Rock and Miss Hernshaw must have been to church, but he had not the courage to send up his name to them. He waited about in the region of the dining-room, in the senseless hope that it would be better for him to surprise them on their way to luncheon, and trust to some chance for introducing his confession, than to seek a direct interview with Miss Hernshaw. But they did not come to luncheon, and then Hewson had the clerk send up his card. Word came back that the ladies would see him, and he followed the messenger to Mrs. Rock's apartment, where if he was surprised, he was not disappointed to be received by Miss Hernshaw alone.

"Mrs. Rock is lying down," she explained, "but I thought that it might be something important, and you would not mind seeing me."

"Not at all," said Hewson, with what seemed to him afterwards superfluous politeness, and then they both waited until he could formulate his business, Miss Hernshaw drooping forward, and looking down in a way that he had found was most characteristic of her. "It *is* something important—at least it is important to me. Miss Hernshaw, may I ask whether you have done anything—it seems a very unwarrantable question—about St. Johnswort?"

"About buying it?"

"Yes. It will be useless to make any offer for it."

"Why will it be useless to do that?"

"Because—because I have bought it myself."

"You have bought it?"

"Yes; when he came to me last night, and made those representations—Well, in short, I have bought the place."

"To save him from losing money by that—story?"

"Well—yes. I ought to have told you the fact this morning, as soon as you said you would buy the place. I know that you like people to be perfectly truthful. But—I couldn't—without seeming to—brag."

"I understand," said Miss Hernshaw.

"I took the risk of your writing to St. John; but then I realised that if he answered and told you what I ought to have told you myself, it would make it worse, and I came back."

"I don't know whether it would have made it worse; but you have come too late," said Miss Hernshaw. "I've just written to Mr. St. John."

They were both silent for what Hewson thought a long time. At the end of it, he asked, "Did you—you must excuse me—refer to me at all?"

"No, certainly not. Why should I?"

"I don't know. I don't know that it would have mattered." He was silent again, with bowed head; when he looked up he saw tears in the girl's eyes.

"I suppose you know where this leaves me?" she said gently.

"I can't pretend that I don't," answered Hewson. "What can I do?"

"You can sell me the place for what it cost you."

"Oh, no, I can't do that," said Hewson.

"Why do you say that? It isn't as if I were poor; but even then, you wouldn't have the right to refuse me if I insisted. It was my fault that it ever came out about St. Johnswort. It might have come out about you, but the harm to Mr. St. John—I did that, and why should you take it upon yourself?"

"Because I was really to blame from the beginning to the end. If it had not been for my pitiful wish to shine as the confidant of mystery, nothing would have been known of the affair. Even when you asked me that night if it had not happened at St. Johnswort, I know now that I had a wretched triumph in saying that it had, and I was so full of this that I did not think to caution you against repeating what I had owned."

"Yes," said the girl, with her unsparing honesty, "if you had given me any hint, I would not have told for the world. Of course, I did not think—a girl wouldn't—of the effect it would have on the property."

"No, you wouldn't think of that," said Hewson. Though he agreed with her, he would have preferred that she should continue to blame herself; but he took himself severely in hand again. "So, you see, the fault was altogether mine, and if there is to be any penalty it ought to fall upon me."

"Yes," said Miss Hernshaw, "and if there has been a fault there ought to be a penalty, don't you think? It would have been no penalty for me to buy St. Johnswort. My father wouldn't have minded it." She blushed suddenly, and added, "I don't mean that—You may be so rich that—I think I had better stop."

"No, no!" said Hewson, amused, and glad of the relief. "Go on. I will tell you anything you wish to know."

"I don't wish, to know anything," said Miss Hernshaw, haughtily.

Her words seemed to put an end to an interview for which there was no longer any excuse.

Hewson rose. "Goodbye," he said, and he was rather surprised at her putting out her hand, but he took it gratefully. "Will you make my *adieux* to Mrs. Rock? And excuse my coming a second time to trouble you!"

"I don't see how you could have helped coming," said Miss Hernshaw, "when you thought I might write to Mr. St. John at once."

Whether this implied excuse or greater blame, Hewson had to go away with it as her final response, and he went away certainly in as great discomfort as he had come. He did not feel quite well used; it seemed to him that hard measure had been dealt him on all sides, but especially by Miss Hernshaw. After her futile effort at reparation to St. John she had apparently withdrawn from all responsibility in the matter. He did not know when he was to see her again, if ever, and he did not know what he was to wait for, if anything.

Still he had the sense of waiting for something, or for someone, and he went home to wait. There he perceived that it was for St. John, who did not keep him waiting long. His nervous ring roused Hewson half an hour after his return, and St. John came in with a look in his greedy eyes which Hewson rightly interpreted at the first glance.

"See here, Hewson," St. John said, with his habitual lack of manners. "I don't want to get you in for this thing at St. Johnswort. I know why you offered to buy the place, and though of course you are the original cause of the trouble, I don't feel that it's quite fair to let you shoulder the consequences altogether."

"Have I been complaining?" Hewson asked, dryly.

"No, and that's just it. You've behaved like a little man through it all, and I don't like to take advantage of you. If you want to rue your bargain, I'll call it off. I've had some fresh light on the matter, and I believe I can let you off without loss to myself. So that if it's me you're considering—"

"What's your fresh light?" asked Hewson.

"Well," said St. John, and he swallowed rather hard, as if it were a pill, "the fact is, I've had another offer for the place."

"A better one?"

"Well, I don't know that I can say that it is," answered St. John, saving his conscience in the form of the words.

Hewson knew that he was lying, and he had no mercy on him. "Then I believe I'll stick to my bargain. You say that the other party hasn't bettered my offer, and so I needn't withdraw on your account. I'm not bound to withdraw for any other reason."

"No, of course not." St. John rubbed his chin, as if hesitating to eat his words, however unpalatable; but in the end he seemed not to find it possible. "Well," he said, disgustedly, as he floundered up to take his leave, "I thought I ought to come and give you the chance."

"It's very nice of you," said Hewson, with a smile that made itself a derisive grin in spite of him, and a laugh of triumph when the door had closed upon St. John.

13

After the first flush of Hewson's triumph had passed he began to enjoy it less, and by-and-by he did not enjoy it at all. He had done right not only in keeping St. John from plundering Miss Hernshaw, but in standing firm and taking the punishment which ought to fall upon him and not on her. But the sense of having done right sufficed him no more than the sense of having got the better of St. John. What was lacking to him? In the casuistry of the moment, which was perhaps rather emotional than rational, it appeared to Hewson that he had again a duty toward Miss Hernshaw, and that his feeling of dissatisfaction was the first effect of its non-fulfilment. But it was clearly impossible that he should go again to see her, and tell her what had passed between him and St. John, and it was clearly impossible that he should write and tell her what it was quite as clearly her right to know from him.

If he went to her, or wrote to her, he felt himself in danger of wanting to shine in the affair, as her protector against the rapacity of St. John, and as the man of superior quality who had outwitted a greedy fellow. The fear that she might not admire his splendour in either sort caused him to fall somewhat nervelessly back upon Providence; but if the moral government of the universe finally favoured him it was not by traversing any of its own laws. By the time he had determined to achieve both the impossibilities which formed his dilemma—had decided to write to Miss Hernshaw and call upon her, and leave his letter in the event of failing to find her—his problem was as far solved as it might be, by the arrival of a note from Miss Hernshaw herself, hoping that he would come to see her on business of pressing importance.

She received him without any pretence of Mrs. Rock's intermediary presence, and put before him a letter which she had received, before writing him, from St. John, and which she could not answer without first submitting it to him. It was a sufficiently straightforward expression of his regret that he could not accept her very generous offer for St. Johnswort because the place was already sold. He had the taste to forbear any allusion to the motives which (she told Hewson) she had said prompted her offer; but then he became very darkling and sinuous in a suggestion that if Miss Hernshaw wished to have her offer known as hers to the purchaser of St. Johnswort he would be happy to notify him of it.

"You see," she eagerly commented to Hewson, "he does not give your name; but I know who it is, though I did not know when I made him my offer. I must answer his letter now, and what shall I say? Shall I tell him I know who it is? I should like to; I hate all concealments! Will it do any harm to tell him I know?"

Hewson reflected. "I don't see how it can. I was trying to come to you, when I got your note, to say that St. John had been to see me, and offered to release me from my offer, because, as I thought, you had made him a better one. He's amusingly rapacious, St. John is."

"And what did you—I beg your pardon!"

"Oh, not at all. I said I would stand to my offer."

She repressed, apparently, some form of protest, and presently asked, "And what shall I say?"

"Oh, if you like, that you have learned who the purchaser of St. Johnswort is, and that you know he will not give way."

"Well!" she said, with a quick sigh, as of disappointment. After an indefinite pause, she asked, "Shall you be going to St. Johnswort?"

"Why, I don't know," Hewson answered. "I had thought of going to Europe. But, yes, I think I shall go to St. Johnswort, first, at any rate. One can't simply turn one's back on a piece of real estate in that way," he said, recognising a fact that would doubtless have presented itself in due order for his consideration. "My one notion was to forget it as quickly as possible."

"I should not think you would want to do that," said the girl, seriously.

"No, one oughtn't to neglect an investment."

"I don't mean that. But if such a thing had happened to me, there, I should want to go again and again."

"You mean the apparition? Did I tell you how I had always had the expectation that I should see it again, and perhaps understand it? But when I had behaved so shabbily about it, I began to feel that it would not come again."

"If I were in your place," said the girl, "I should never give up; I should spend my whole life trying to find out what it meant."

"Ah!" he sighed. "I wish you could put yourself in my place."

"I wish I could," she returned, intensely.

They looked into each other's faces.

"Miss Hernshaw," he demanded, solemnly, "do you really like people to say what they think?"

"Of course, I do!"

"Then I wish you would come to St. Johnswort with me!"

"Would that do?" she asked. "If Mrs. Rock—"

He saw how far she was from taking his meaning, but he pushed on. "I don't want Mrs. Rock. I want you—you alone. Don't you understand me? I love you. I—of course it's ridiculous! We've only met three or four times in our lives, but I knew this as well the first moment as I do now. I knew it when you came walking across the garden that morning, and I haven't known it any better since, and I couldn't in a thousand years. But of course—"

"Sit down," she said, wafting herself into a chair, and he obeyed her. "I should have to tell my father," she began.

"Why, certainly," and he sprang to his feet again.

She commanded him to his chair with an imperative gesture. "I have got to find out what I think, first, myself. If I were sure that I loved you—but I don't know. I believe you are good. I believed that when they were all joking you there at breakfast, and you took it so nicely; I have *always* believed that you were good."

She seemed to be appealing to him for confirmation, but he could not very well say that she was right, and he kept silent. "I didn't like your telling that story at the dinner, and I said so; and then I went and did the same thing, or worse; so that I have nothing to say about that. And I think you have behaved very nobly to Mr. St. John." As if at some sign of protest in Hewson, she insisted, "Yes, I do! But all this doesn't prove that I love you." Again, she seemed to appeal to him, and this time he thought he might answer her appeal.

"I couldn't prove that *I* love *you*, but I feel sure of it."

"And do you believe that we ought to take our feelings for a guide?"

"That's what people do," he ventured, with the glimmer of a smile in his eyes, which she was fixing so earnestly with her own.

"I am not satisfied that it is the right way," she answered. "If there is really such a thing as love there ought to be some way of finding it out besides our feelings. Don't you think it's a thing we ought to talk sensibly about?"

"Of all things in the world; though it isn't the custom."

Miss Hernshaw was silent for a moment. Then she said, "I believe I should like a little time."

"Oh, I didn't expect you to answer me at once,—I"

"But if you are going to Europe?"

"I needn't go to Europe at all. I can go to St. Johnswort, and wait for your answer there."

"It might be a good while," she urged. "I should want to tell my father that I was thinking about it, and he would want to see you before he approved."

"Why, of course!"

"Not," she added, "that it would make any difference, if I was sure of it myself. He has always said that he would not try to control me in such a matter, and I think he would like you. I do like you very much myself, Mr. Hewson, but I don't think it would be right to say I loved you unless I could prove it."

Hewson was tempted to say that she could prove it by marrying him, but he had not the heart to mock a scruple which he felt to be sacred. What he did say was: "Then I will wait till you can prove it. Do you wish me not to see you again, before you have made up your mind?"

"I don't know. I can't see what harm there would be in our meeting."

"No, I can't, either," said Hewson, as she seemed to refer the point to him. "Should you mind my coming again, say, this evening?"

"Tonight?" She reflected a moment. "Yes, come tonight."

When he came after dinner, Hewson was sensible from the perfect unconsciousness of Mrs. Rock's manner that Miss Hernshaw had been telling her. Her habit of a wandering eye, contributed to the effect she wished to produce, if this were the effect, and her success was such that it might easily have deceived herself. But when Mrs. Rock, in a supreme exercise of her unconsciousness, left him with the girl for a brief interval before it was time for him to go, Miss Hernshaw said, "Mrs. Rock knows about it, and she says that the best way for me to find out will be to try whether I can live without you."

"Was that Mrs. Rock's idea?" asked Hewson, as gravely as he could.

"No, it was mine; I suggested it to her; but she approves of it. Don't you like it?"

"Yes. I hope I shan't die while you are trying to live without me. Shall you be very long?" She frowned, and he hastened to say, "I do like your idea; it's the best way, and I thank you for giving me a chance."

"We are going out to my father's ranch in Colorado, at once," she explained. "We shall start tomorrow morning."

"Oh! May I come to see you off?"

"No, I would rather begin at once."

"May I write to you?"

"I will write to you—when I've decided."

She gave him her hand, but she would not allow him to keep it for more than farewell, and then she made him stay till Mrs. Rock came back, and take leave of her too; he had frankly forgotten Mrs. Rock, who bade him *adieu* with averted eyes, and many civilities about seeing him again. She could hardly have been said to be seeing him then.

14

The difficulties of domestication at St. Johnswort had not been misrepresented by the late proprietor, Hewson found, when he went to take possession of his estate. He thought it right in engaging servants to say openly that the place had the reputation of being haunted, and if he had not thought it right he would have thought it expedient, for he knew that if he had concealed the fact it would have been discovered to them within twenty-four hours of their arrival. His declaration was sufficient at once with most, who recoiled from his service as if he had himself been a ghost; with one or two sceptics who seemed willing to take the risks (probably in a guilty consciousness of records that would have kept them out of other employ) his confession that he had himself seen the spectre which haunted St. Johnswort, was equally effective.

He prevailed at last against the fact and his own testimony with a Japanese, who could not be made to understand the objection to the place, and who willingly went with Hewson as his valet and general house-workman. With the wife of the gardener coming in to cook for them during the long daylight, he got on in as much comfort as he could have expected, and by night he suffered no sort of disturbance from the apparition. He had expected to be annoyed by believers in spiritualism, and other psychical inquirers, but it sufficed with them to learn from him that he had come to regard his experience, of which he had no more question now than ever, as purely subjective.

It seemed to Hewson, in the six weeks' time which he spent at St. Johnswort, waiting to hear from Rosalie (he had come already to think of her as Rosalie), that all his life was subjective, it passed so like a dream. He had some outward cares as to the place; he kept a horse in the stable, where St. John had kept half a dozen, and he had the gardener look after that as well as the shrubs and vegetables; but all went on in a suspensive and provisional sort.

In the meantime, Rosalie's charm grew upon him; everything that she had said or looked, was hourly and daily sweeter and dearer; her truth was intoxicating, beyond the lures of other women, in which the quality of deceit had once fascinated him.

Now, so late in his youthful life, he realised that there was no beauty but that of truth, and he pledged himself a thousand times that if she should say she could not live without him he would henceforward live for truth alone, and not for the truth merely as it was in her, but as it was in everything.

In those day's he learned to know himself, as he never had before, and to put off a certain shell of worldliness that had grown upon him. In his remoteness from it, New York became very distasteful to him; he thought with reluctance of going back to it; his club, which had been his home, now appeared a joyless exile; the life of a leisure class, which he had made his ideal, looked pitifully mean and little in the retrospect; he wondered how he could have valued the things that he had once thought worthy.

He did not know what he should replace it all with, but Rosalie would know, in the event of not being able to live without him. In that event there was hardly any use of which he could not be capable. In any other event—he surprised himself by realising that in any other event—still the universe had somehow more meaning than it once had. Somehow, he felt himself an emancipated man.

He began many letters to Rosalie, and some he finished and some not, but he sent none; and when her letter came at last, he was glad that he had waited for it in implicit trust of its coming, though he believed she would have forgiven him if he had not had the patience. The letter was quite what he could have imagined of her. She said that she had put herself thoroughly to the test, and she could not live without him. But if he had found out that he could live without her, then she should know that she had been to blame, and would take her punishment. Apparently in her philosophy, which now seemed to him so divine, without punishment there must be perdition; it was the penalty that redeemed; that was the token of forgiveness.

Hewson hurried out to Colorado, where he found Hernshaw a stout, silent, impersonal man, whose notion of the paternal office seemed to be a ready acquiescence in a daughter's choice of a husband; he appeared to think this could be best expressed to Hewson in a good cigar. He perceptibly enjoyed the business details of the affair, but he enjoyed despatching them in the least possible time and the fewest words, and then he settled down to the pleasure of a superficial passivity. Hewson could not make out that he regarded his daughter as at all an unusual girl, and from this he argued that her mother must have been a very unusual woman. His only reason for doubting that Rosalie must have got all her originality from her mother was something that fell from Hernshaw when they were near the end of their cigars. He said irrelevantly to their talk at that point, "I suppose you know Rosalie believes in that ghost of yours?"

"Was it a ghost?—I've never been sure, myself," said Hewson.

"How do you explain it?" asked his prospective father-in-law.

"I don't explain it. I have always left it just as it was. I know that it was a real experience."

"I think I should have left it so, too," said Hernshaw. "That always gives it a chance to explain itself. If such a thing had happened to me, I should give it all the time it wanted."

"Well, I haven't hurried it," Hewson suggested.

"What I mean," and Hernshaw stepped to the edge of the porch and threw the butt of his cigar into the darkness, where it described a glimmering arc, "is that if anything came to me that would help shore up my professed faith in what most of us want to believe in, I would take the common-law view of it. I would believe it was innocent till it proved itself guilty. I wouldn't try to make it out a fraud myself."

"I'm afraid that's what I've really done," said Hewson. "But before people I've put up a bluff of despising it."

"Oh, yes, I understand that," said Hernshaw. "A man thinks that if he can have an experience like that, he must be something out of the common, and if he can despise it—"

"You've hit my case exactly," said Hewson, and the two men laughed.

15

After his marriage, which took place without needless delay, Hewson returned with his wife to spend their honeymoon at St. John-swort. The honeymoon prolonged itself during an entire year, and in this time, they contrived so far to live down its reputation of being a haunted house that they were able to conduct their *ménage* on the ordinary terms. They themselves never wished to lose the sense of something supernatural in the place, and were never quite able to accept the actual conditions as final. That is to say, Rosalie was not, for she had taken Hewson's apparition under her peculiar care, and defended it against even his question. She had a feeling (it was scarcely a conviction) that if he believed more strenuously in the validity of his apparition as an authorised messenger from the unseen world it would yet come again and declare its errand.

She could not accept the theory that if such a thing actually happened it could happen for nothing at all, or that the reason of its occurrence could be indefinitely postponed. She was impatient of that, as often as he urged the possibility, and she wished him to use a seriousness of mind in speaking of his apparition which should form some sort of atonement to it for his past levity, though since she had taken his apparition into her keeping he had scarcely hazarded any suggestion concerning it; in fact it had become so much her apparition that he had a fantastic reluctance from meddling with it.

"You are always requiring a great occasion for it," he said, at last. "What greater event could it have foreshadowed or foreshown, than that which actually came to pass?"

"I don't understand you, Arthur," she said, letting her hand creep into his, where it trembled provisionally as they sat together in the twilight.

"Why, that was the day I first saw you."

"Now, you are laughing!" she said, pulling her hand away.

"Indeed, I'm not! I couldn't imagine anything more important than the union of our lives. And if that was what the apparition meant to portend it could not have intimated it by a more noble and impressive behaviour. Simply to be there, and then to be gone, and leave the rest to us! It was majestic, it was—delicate!"

"Yes, it was. But it was too much, for it was out of proportion. A mere earthly love-affair—"

"Is it merely for earth?"

"Oh, husband, I hope you don't think so! I wanted you to say you didn't. And if you don't think so, yes, I'll believe it came for that!"

"You may be sure I don't think so."

"Then I know it will come again."

My Ghost of a Chance

By Madeline Yale Wynne

Truly, a most fitting place for the Starvation Act,' said the Author, as he laid a fresh supply of stationery on the table, 'and a whole week to do it in, unless the story pans out well, which of course it won't; I don't suppose there's a ghost of a chance of that.'

'Here I am!'

'Oh, there you are! yes, to be sure, so you are. And how do you do? I hope you will excuse my saying it, but aren't you an uncommonly small ghost?'

'Yes, I am slim; but I've seen smaller chances, and you know I am all the one you have got.'

'Why, yes, as William has it, "A poor thing, but mine own." Allow me to help you up on the table; there, how is that? Do you think you could sit on that cuff-box and rest your feet on the pen-wiper? I am afraid the table is rather bare and cold, and you don't look very well. Is that comfortable?'

'Oh, very, thank you;—and now you may begin.'

'Yes, in a minute. I want to ask you first if you really are my only chance?'

'Yes, absolutely your only one,' said the small figure sitting on the box, with his hands resting on his knees. He was a clever-looking little ghost, eight or nine inches high, clean shaven, with his hair brushed back to hide an evidently increasing tendency to baldness—he was not in his first youth. He was plainly but neatly dressed, though his clothes looked a little shiny at the seams. His face was careworn and anxious in its expression, but attractive, and his manners were unobjectionable.

'So, you are my only chance, are you? May I ask where you came from?'

215

'Oh, I am sent here from the "Bureau of Chances"; we have to go just wherever we are sent, you know; we haven't any choice in the matter.'

'Yes, of course, that stands to reason; I can readily understand no ghost of the slightest financial instinct would have chosen me to come to; I am all the more obliged for any chance at all, on any terms. It is very encouraging to have you sit there; I like it. I think I will try and do some work.'

'Yes, I would,' said the little Ghost, with alacrity.

The Author leaned back, and, clasping his hands behind his head, he fixed his eyes on the little Ghost, and began:

'It is to be a story, you know—a romance. *She* is to be the central figure—a splendid red-haired creature, with great instincts, primeval, untrained, capacious; she is to *devour* the world; she can't wait for experience; she hungers and thirsts for sensations; she is to *boom* through the story—no lagging, no questioning; see?'

'Yes,' nodded the little Ghost.

'And then,' continued the Author, 'she is to meet the hero; he is to be Tradition, Culture, Development, Conservatism; and there will be, so to speak, no one else in the world except these two forces, and the battle royal will be between these two.'

'Yes,' nodded the little Ghost.

'I think I will write that out before I go any further with the plot.'

'I would,' said the little Ghost.

'Well, here goes,' said the Author, drawing himself up to the table.

He wrote for some hours; his pen moved ceaselessly over the pages, and from time to time he laid a sheet at the feet of the little Ghost. The clock struck twelve, the clock struck one; the Author's hair fell lankly over his pale face; on and on went his pen. At two, he looked up and saw the little Ghost sitting, all alert, on the cuff-box, with his blue eyes wide open; he gave a bright little smile in answer to the Author's glance.

'Why bless me! I had clean forgotten you! aren't you tired?' said the Author.

'Not in the least; I feel quite fresh.'

'Upon my word, you look it; I believe you are going to be a tough little chap, and will see me through. And now where will you sleep?'

'Why, here, anywhere—I am not particular.'

'Aren't you hungry? you haven't had anything to eat since you came. By the way, what do you eat?'

'Oh, I'm all right, don't bother about me; I live very well on hope, and we are supposed to supply that ourselves.'

'That's extremely lucky for you; I haven't had a scrap of hope for a month, and I'm afraid you'd starve if you depended on me.'

'Thank you, that's all right—good night.'

The Author slept heavily, all dressed as he was when he threw himself down on the bed. The little Ghost took off his necktie and his little boots, and, folding his coat carefully for a pillow, he too slept, after adjusting the pen-wiper for a coverlid. At six o'clock the little Ghost got up and rambled about the table for a while. He regulated the loose sheets of manuscript and counted the pages. He looked quite well in the morning light, and his step had the assurance and measured quality that comes only to the prosperous. He carried his left hand carelessly in his pocket, with his elbow slightly raised, after the manner of the man of the world.

He began to be restless towards seven o'clock, and at half-past seven he took his breakfast, very sparingly, off of his stock of hope, evidently considering the possibility of a longer stay than he had an-ticipated when he first got up. At eight o'clock, his face was full of anxiety, and he had dropped his nonchalant air and had taken his hand out of his pocket. At nine, his head was bent, and he paced to and fro from the inkstand to the dictionary, with his hands clasped behind him. He looked old and feeble. At ten, he had a slight fainting turn and had to sit down on the cuff-box. His forehead was damp and he shivered; he was evidently deeply disturbed, and he was a pitiful little object to look at.

Then the Author awoke, and, sitting up, called out: 'Why, great heavens! what is the matter, are you ill?'

'Thank you, I do feel a little off this morning.'

'Morning, is it? Why, I feel as if I had just dropped off; you haven't been drinking my ink, have you? You are all blue around the gills?'

The little Ghost was offended, but he did not answer except by a reproachful look.

'Oh, don't play the lachrymose role; I'll be up in no time, and you must remember I wrote a pile last night; just hear me read some of it. Why, did I do all this? It reads better than I thought.'

'Yes, it reads very well—*very well indeed*. I think I will go out and take a stroll, and lunch at the club, and not write any more till to-night; I do my best work at night.'

As the Author said this, he looked right at the Ghost; there was a feeling in the room that somebody was justifying himself, but the little Ghost said nothing. Then the Author made himself a cup of coffee and freshened himself up, all the time not looking at the little Ghost. Then he took his cane, and, going out, he nodded carelessly, and said:

'Goodbye, old boy; I will be back in good time, don't worry.'

All the way down the street the Author kept hearing the words: 'I am all the chance you've got—I am all the chance you've got—I am all the chance you've got.'

'Hang it all,' said he, 'I might as well go back and grind; it will please the little chap, and it don't matter to anyone else. I don't suppose he is much of a critic—he'll never know how bad the stuff is that I wrote last night.'

So back he went. When the door opened, he was shocked to see his little Ghost of a chance apparently on the verge of dissolution. He lay across the dictionary, where he had evidently thrown himself in despair; his arm hung down over the edge of the book, and he was limp and almost like a lifeless thing. He smiled a wan but forgiving smile on the Author and then wearily composed himself, as if for death. The Author bent his head over the little Ghost to see if he was still breathing. The Ghost was alive, and he heard him whisper:

'*Write, write, write!*'

Seizing his pen, the Author dashed ahead, hardly knowing what words came; he knew that write he must to save his dear little Ghost of a chance—his only little chance. By the time he had written one chapter the Ghost was up and strutting around the table like a little king, but the poor Author was in the depths of despair; he knew that every word he was writing was trash; that nobody, even the most philanthropic of editors, would ever take his story, and that starve he must. Still, the little Ghost improved; he grew stout, he grew rosy, he even seemed to be getting a fresh accession of yellow hair to cover his bald spot. At last, the Author spoke:

'Little *fiend*,' said he, 'you fatten on my despair; you are nourished on my misery; the vagaries of my tired brain are wine and bread to your morbid taste. Why should I drain my brain to feed you, you *pigmy* of chance! you respectable little *vampire*! you masquerader in the form of "my chance," "my only chance!" Away with you, vanish, wither, be gone! I will burn my words, even though you perish with the flame. I will not be saved by such a chance, if the price of my life be this unworthy work!'

And the Author thrust his manuscript into the fire. He turned, thinking to see the Ghost wither and die before him; but instead of that there was the queer little contradictory fellow dancing on the table. He danced, he capered, he looked fairly fat; in truth he began to puff with his exertions, and then he shouted out:

'O you authors! O you strange creatures! You think you can kill me by burning your manuscript; why, you are feeding me, you are pampering me, and you yourself are improving in spite of yourself. Your chance is great, your chance is sure, you will *write* now; you will be a success!'

And sure enough the next day the story was done. The Author went out with it, knowing it to be good; it was a go. The Author's hand rested lightly in his trousers' pocket, and he walked with the assurance of a prosperous man. As he came back, he said to himself:

'Now, I am going to say to that little Ghost chap: "Here, half of this gold is yours, half is mine; remain with me, and we will be partners, share and share alike."'

But when he went into the room, the fat little Ghost had gone back to the 'Bureau of Chances,' to be sent out again along with all the other little Ghost Chances. I recognised him the other day sleeping in the pigeonhole of the desk of a friend of mine.

ALSO FROM LEONAUR
AVAILABLE IN SOFTCOVER OR HARDCOVER WITH DUST JACKET

MR MUKERJI'S GHOSTS *by S. Mukerji*—Supernatural tales from the British Raj period by India's Ghost story collector.

KIPLINGS GHOSTS *by Rudyard Kipling*—Twelve stories of Ghosts, Hauntings, Curses, Werewolves & Magic.

THE COLLECTED SUPERNATURAL AND WEIRD FICTION OF WASHINGTON IRVING: VOLUME 1 *by Washington Irving*—Including one novel 'A History of New York', and nine short stories of the Strange and Unusual.

THE COLLECTED SUPERNATURAL AND WEIRD FICTION OF WASHINGTON IRVING: VOLUME 2 *by Washington Irving*—Including three novelettes 'The Legend of the Sleepy Hollow', 'Dolph Heyliger', 'The Adventure of the Black Fisherman' and thirty-two short stories of the Strange and Unusual.

THE COLLECTED SUPERNATURAL AND WEIRD FICTION OF JOHN KENDRICK BANGS: VOLUME 1 *by John Kendrick Bangs*—Including one novel 'Toppleton's Client or A Spirit in Exile', and ten short stories of the Strange and Unusual.

THE COLLECTED SUPERNATURAL AND WEIRD FICTION OF JOHN KENDRICK BANGS: VOLUME 2 *by John Kendrick Bangs*—Including four novellas 'A House-Boat on the Styx', 'The Pursuit of the House-Boat', 'The Enchanted Typewriter' and 'Mr. Munchausen' of the Strange and Unusual.

THE COLLECTED SUPERNATURAL AND WEIRD FICTION OF JOHN KENDRICK BANGS: VOLUME 3 *by John Kendrick Bangs*—Including twor novellas 'Olympian Nights', 'Roger Camerden: A Strange Story', and ten short stories of the Strange and Unusual.

THE COLLECTED SUPERNATURAL AND WEIRD FICTION OF MARY SHELLEY: VOLUME 1 *by Mary Shelley*—Including one novel 'Frankenstein or the Modern Prometheus', and fourteen short stories of the Strange and Unusual.

THE COLLECTED SUPERNATURAL AND WEIRD FICTION OF MARY SHELLEY: VOLUME 2 *by Mary Shelley*—Including one novel 'The Last Man', and three short stories of the Strange and Unusual.

THE COLLECTED SUPERNATURAL AND WEIRD FICTION OF AMELIA B. EDWARDS *by Amelia B. Edwards*—Contains two novelettes 'Monsieur Maurice', and 'The Discovery of the Treasure Isles', one ballad 'A Legend of Boisguilbert'and seventeen short stories to cill the blood.

ALSO FROM LEONAUR

AVAILABLE IN SOFTCOVER OR HARDCOVER WITH DUST JACKET

THE COMPLETE FOUR JUST MEN: VOLUME 2 *by Edgar Wallace*—*The Law of the Four Just Men & The Three Just Men*—disillusioned with a world where the wicked and the abusers of power perpetually go unpunished, the Just Men set about to rectify matters according to their own standards, and retribution is dispensed on swift and deadly wings.

THE COMPLETE RAFFLES: 1 *by E. W. Hornung*—*The Amateur Cracksman & The Black Mask*—By turns urbane gentleman about town and accomplished cricketer, life is just too ordinary for Raffles and that sets him on a series of adventures that have long been treasured as a real antidote to the 'white knights' who are the usual heroes of the crime fiction of this period.

THE COMPLETE RAFFLES: 2 *by E. W. Hornung*—*A Thief in the Night & Mr Justice Raffles*—By turns urbane gentleman about town and accomplished cricketer, life is just too ordinary for Raffles and that sets him on a series of adventures that have long been treasured as a real antidote to the 'white knights' who are the usual heroes of the crime fiction of this period.

THE COLLECTED SUPERNATURAL AND WEIRD FICTION OF WILKIE COLLINS: VOLUME 1 *by Wilkie Collins*—Contains one novel 'The Haunted Hotel', one novella 'Mad Monkton', three novelettes 'Mr Percy and the Prophet', 'The Biter Bit' and 'The Dead Alive' and eight short stories to chill the blood.

THE COLLECTED SUPERNATURAL AND WEIRD FICTION OF WILKIE COLLINS: VOLUME 2 *by Wilkie Collins*—Contains one novel 'The Two Destinies', three novellas 'The Frozen deep', 'Sister Rose' and 'The Yellow Mask' and two short stories to chill the blood.

THE COLLECTED SUPERNATURAL AND WEIRD FICTION OF WILKIE COLLINS: VOLUME 3 *by Wilkie Collins*—Contains one novel 'Dead Secret,' two novelettes 'Mrs Zant and the Ghost' and 'The Nun's Story of Gabriel's Marriage' and five short stories to chill the blood.

FUNNY BONES *selected by Dorothy Scarborough*—An Anthology of Humorous Ghost Stories.

MONTEZUMA'S CASTLE AND OTHER WEIRD TALES *by Charles B. Cory*—Cory has written a superb collection of eighteen ghostly and weird stories to chill and thrill the avid enthusiast of supernatural fiction.

SUPERNATURAL BUCHAN *by John Buchan*—Stories of Ancient Spirits, Uncanny Places & Strange Creatures.

LEONAUR

ALSO FROM LEONAUR
AVAILABLE IN SOFTCOVER OR HARDCOVER WITH DUST JACKET

THE COLLECTED SCIENCE FICTION AND FANTASY OF STANLEY G. WEINBAUM 1—INTERPLANETARY ODYSSEYS *by Stanley G. Weinbaum*—Classic Tales of Interplanetary Adventure Including: A Martian Odyssey, its Sequel Valley of Dreams, the Complete 'Ham' Hammond Stories and Others.

THE COLLECTED SCIENCE FICTION AND FANTASY OF STANLEY G. WEINBAUM 2—OTHER EARTHS *by Stanley G. Weinbaum*—Classic Futuristic Tales Including: *Dawn of Flame* & its Sequel The Black Flame, plus The Revolution of 1960 & Others.

THE COLLECTED SCIENCE FICTION AND FANTASY OF STANLEY G. WEINBAUM 3—STRANGE GENIUS *by Stanley G. Weinbaum*—Classic Tales of the Human Mind at Work Including the Complete Novel The New Adam, the 'van Manderpootz' Stories and Others.

THE COLLECTED SCIENCE FICTION AND FANTASY OF STANLEY G. WEINBAUM 4—THE BLACK HEART *by Stanley G. Weinbaum*—Classic Strange Tales Including: the Complete Novel The Dark Other, Plus Proteus Island and Others.

THE COLLECTED SCIENCE FICTION & FANTASY OF JACK LONDON 1—BEFORE ADAM & OTHER STORIES *by Jack London*—included in this Volume Before Adam The Scarlet Plague A Relic of the Pliocene When the World Was Young The Red One Planchette A Thousand Deaths Goliah A Curious Fragment The Rejuvenation of Major Rathbone.

THE COLLECTED SCIENCE FICTION & FANTASY OF JACK LONDON 2—THE IRON HEEL & OTHER STORIES *by Jack London*—included in this Volume The Iron Heel The Enemy of All the World The Shadow and the Flash The Strength of the Strong The Unparalleled Invasion The Dream of Debs.

THE COLLECTED SCIENCE FICTION & FANTASY OF JACK LONDON 3—THE STAR ROVER & OTHER STORIES *by Jack London*—included in this Volume The Star Rover The Minions of Midas The Eternity of Forms The Man With the Gash.